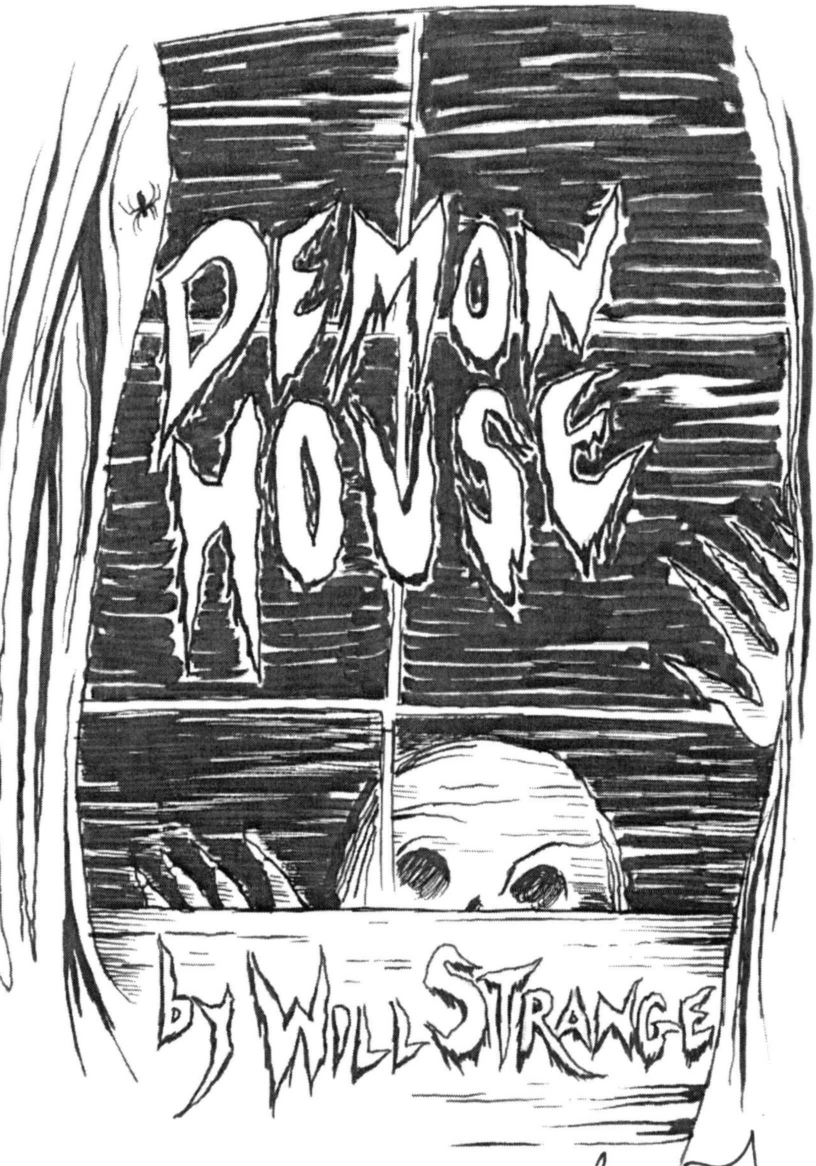

for Lee
from Will Strange

Copyright © 2015 by Will Strange.

ISBN: Softcover   978-1-5035-8192-0
         eBook   978-1-5035-8191-3

All rights reserved. No part of this book may be reproduced or transmitted in any form or by any means, electronic or mechanical, including photocopying, recording, or by any information storage and retrieval system, without permission in writing from the copyright owner.

This is a work of fiction. Names, characters, places and incidents either are the product of the author's imagination or are used fictitiously, and any resemblance to any actual persons, living or dead, events, or locales is entirely coincidental.

Any people depicted in stock imagery provided by Thinkstock are models, and such images are being used for illustrative purposes only.
Certain stock imagery © Thinkstock.

Print information available on the last page.

Rev. date: 07/13/2015

To order additional copies of this book, contact:
Xlibris
1-888-795-4274
www.Xlibris.com
Orders@Xlibris.com
718932

Contents

ACKNOWLEDGMENTS 9

PROLOGUE: STRANGE STORIES 11

PART I: RETURN TO THE MONSTER 15

PART II: RUNNING AWAY 33

PART III: AFTON, GEORGIA, JUNE 1993 55

PART IV: THE HOUSE ON WITCHER STREET 69

PART V: THE MOST HAUNTED TOWN 107

PART VI: DESCENT 163

PART VII: FACING THE MONSTER 197

EPILOGUE: WAKING AND WRITHING 217

Except that the monster never dies. Werewolf, vampire, ghoul, unnameable creature from the wastes. The monster never dies
--Stephen King
Cujo

ACKNOWLEDGMENTS

MANY THANKS TO many people. But especially: Mark Larsen for the mouth in the stairs. Dr. Nadia Behizadeh who told me the house should be green. Kevin Peart, co creator of *Chiller House*. The ladies of 320 Brooks Avenue for putting up with me. Edmund Royster, Matt Laoisa and Joshua Shaffrick for taking such an interest in Afton's haunted goings on. J. D. Vann for introducing me to H. P. Lovecraft. Dad for sharing stories of the real Afton. Mom for believing.

PROLOGUE

STRANGE STORIES

I have heard, as everybody else has, of a spirit's haunting a house; but I have had my own personal experience of a house's haunting a spirit.
--Wilkie Collins

HEY-- HEY KID, turn off your walkman. Get off your skateboard and come here a second, will ya? Yeah, I recognize you, too-- from the plane. We sat next to each other. Remember? Yup, it's you. We keep running into each other, don't we? I thought, at first, it was a coincidence, but not anymore.

Do you like strange stories?

Would you like to hear mine?

I used not to like strange things; but that's not the case anymore.

Do you have a few minutes?

What's that? No, it won't take long.

You'll want to hear this. Trust me.

It's sort of a romance, to be honest. No, not like Jane Austen. It's about a guy-- me, Kevin Yoo. Hi. A morbidly obsessed, down on his luck fella who moves to a small town in the middle of nowhere and falls in love-- with a house. Yes, a house. He develops a dark obsession with it, really. And the house, well, it falls in love with him, too. Then the house, see, it has no intention of letting him go, so it tries to kill him-- over and over again. To eat him alive, you might say. Literally. Pretty gruesome, huh? So you see, this is a different kind of romance altogether. One with buckets of blood pouring out of the walls and severed heads turning up in unexpected places and things that go bump in the night.

But that's not all. There's more. And worse. An Old God lurking in the darkness beneath the house. Endless labyrinthine passages carved out by the dead. Red litten caverns where unspeakable rites are acted out-- gruesome sacrifices made with offerings of blood and flesh all in an attempt to raise a necromancer. A gateway to the land of the dead. An attempt to bring about the end of the world-- all that kind of stuff.

Now I have your attention, right? Would you still like to hear it? Think you can handle it after what I've just told you? Okay, great. But you've been warned.

Well, let's see... Where to begin.

I know.

We'll start in medias res, as the Romans say-- you know, to get the action going.

It seems like it was all such a long time ago-- a lifetime ago, which, in reality, I guess it was.

Because, you see, this story starts the day before I died.

PART I

RETURN TO THE MONSTER

Once inside, one would go endlessly along its twisting paths without ever finding the exit... There was no possible way to escape. In whatever way they ran, they might be running straight to the monster.
--Edith Hamilton
Mythology

"THE HOUSE, IT got her."
That's all I can say.

Over and over again.

I keep muttering it to myself. I can't stop.

I've got a crazy, shaky feeling like I haven't eaten in days. Maybe I haven't.

"Where'd you find him, Jerry?"

Sheriff Sadler is kneeling in front of me, looking back over his shoulder at Deputy Hansford who is standing a few steps back, thick arms folded over his barrel chest.

I have a vague recollection of having seen him before once or twice since I came to this town.

I glance down, see a pair of hands resting in my lap, filthy, mud covered, knuckles scraped and bleeding. They belong to something that just crawled out of a grave. Sight of them startles me. I jerk back. The hands leap up at me.

Oh God, they're my hands.

I let them fall back into my lap. No less relieved knowing they're mine.

"Over off Witcher Street," says deputy Hansford. "He was just wandering down the road, barefoot."

"Did he say anything?"

"Only what he's been saying."

The house. It got her.

"Kid, where's your shoes?"

For the first time, I realize I'm barefoot. My feet are caked with dried mud. I have no idea what happened to my shoes.

I'm shaking so bad that when the sheriff fills a plastic cup with water from the water cooler and tries handing it to me I can't even hold it. He reaches up to steady my hand, helps me hold the cup and tilt it so I can take a drink. Even so, most of the water spills down my chin and onto my bloody, shredded shirt.

"Looks like you got clawed by a lion," Sheriff Sadler says, meaning the ragged tears in my shirt, the numerous scrapes and cuts on my face and arms.

"The house. She did it."

My thoughts are murky like the water at the bottom of a lake. I can only remember nightmare flashes. The putrescent eyeless horror peering in through my bedroom window, staring at me with black sockets. The wormy mass in the unlit upstairs hall that sucked my arm in up to the elbow. The halls and doors and stairs that shifted and changed, subtly, so subtly I couldn't ever place my finger on just what it was that was different from before. I also remember--

The heart.

The hideous heart. Beating-- pounding like thunder in the darkness beneath that monster house.

The forest of veins spreading out through the blackness, thickening as they went, pulsing with sick life, splitting the rock, delving down, down, down...

God, how far down does it go?

The House.

It is just the beginning. The wart on the surface. The tip of an iceberg.

The bulk of the horror lies undisturbed in the darkness underneath. Waiting to manifest itself-- to break out of the sewer holes all over Afton in the form of gore dripping squid tentacles.

The house is finite. It has walls, a roof, floors, can be measured more or less, despite its trickery.

But that gorey web of pulsing veins in the darkness underneath spreads and spreads...

Thoughts of that bloody skein fills me with revulsion and I shudder almost convulsively, put one filthy hand to my mouth, smell the dank earth beneath my nails as my fingertips touch my lips.

The earth I'm smelling came out of that darkness. I jerk my hand away quickly, feel tempted to spit on the floor.

"The heart? Son, what are you talking about?"

I must have been babbling out loud, because Sheriff Sadler is giving me a funny look, squinting at me, trying to make sense of what I'm saying, like he's talking to a crazy person.

A sudden clear picture of the heart flashes in my mind and my stomach rolls. It feels like I'm going to be sick. I lurch forward, but nothing comes out. I've already thrown up all there is to throw up. Nothing else is coming out. I'm shivering bad again, leaning forward, hugging myself for reassurance, sobbing a little, I realize.

"He's in shock, Jim," Hansford says.

"Yeah," the Sheriff agrees. "Edith, go call Dr. Crickshaw, get him over here right away."

"Yes, chief," says a woman standing nearby and she hurries across the room to the phone at her desk.

The wave of nausea passes. A few moments more and I can raise my head again without the world swimming out of focus.

Sheriff Sadler has his hand on my shoulder, bracing me, keeping me from falling out of my chair. I look around now, take in my surroundings. I'm sitting beside a water cooler. The sun is shining in brightly through the glass door.

God, it's beautiful.

The sun.

Especially after the darkness.

Across the room, the woman, Edith, is on the phone. I can hear her speaking in hushed tones to the doctor, I guess.

"Yes, Jim asked if you could come over right away. Like I say, I don't think it can wait. No, he seems pretty bad off."

"More water?" the Sheriff asks me.

I shake my head, answer weakly, "Please."

My throat feels coarse as sandpaper. My voice is hoarse, raspy like I've been screaming a lot lately.

Which I have.

The heart.

Oh God.

He fills another cup, hands it to me. I can handle this one on my on. I gulp down the water greedily. I've never been so thirsty in my entire life. I see the tension go out of Sheriff Sadler's shoulders, like taut rope slackening all of a sudden, falling from the ceiling, coiling in a heap, a conjurer's trick dismissed. He knows he's not going to lose me. I'm not going to go catatonic or start foaming at the mouth and babbling unstoppably like a lunatic. He gives me a little relieved smile.

"That's better. I'm Jim Sadler," he says with a sigh.

I nod. I know.

"You've had a bad scare, looks like. Do you remember your name, son?"

Yes, I know my name. It just takes a moment and a massive amount of effort to move my lips and form the words.

"K-- Kevin--" A pause, a deep breath and then I can get the full name out. "Kevin Yoo."

The name sounds alien to me. That name belonged to a person I used to know, a dim lit stranger, a half remembered dream. A lifeless silhouette. It was the name of the person who went into the house on Witcher Street three months ago. Even as I say it, hear the name in my own ears, traveling what seems like miles of ear canal to reach my brain, I don't know if the name still applies to me anymore.

Sheriff Sadler gives me another encouraging smile.

"That's a start. More water?"

Still shaky, but feeling more confident now, encouraged by his support, the familiar surroundings of a normal and unpossessed building, the warm sun on my face and scratched arms, I say, "No thank you."

"Do you know where you are?"

"Yes. Afton, Georgia."

"The day?"

That's a puzzler. I don't know. I've been lost in that house so long, I can't remember.

"The month and year, at least?"

That one, I can handle.

"August... 1993."

He nods.

"Jim," Edith says from behind her desk. "Dr. Crickshaw, well, he said-- um, there was no way in hell he would come over here. But not to worry; I called Dr. Simmons over in Clay County. He's on his way. Might be a minute."

"Thanks Eddy."

"Why the hell won't Crickshaw come?" Hansford asks.

"Don't know, Jerry. He didn't say."

Sheriff Sadler turns back to me. "You worked for Dr. Crickshaw, didn't you Kevin? Did something happen between you two?"

I'm trying hard to remember. But honest to God, the fog just hasn't cleared that much, yet. I give up. Shrug.

"You hungry? Want a sandwich or anything? I've got egg salad in the fridge or Jerry can run down and pick up something for you at Birdie's."

I shake my head violently. I can't eat now. Not yet. Not after what I've seen.

Maybe I'll never eat again.

Maybe I'll never sleep again, either.

"So kid, what in the hell happened to you?" deputy Hansford asks.

I'm not a kid-- not by a long shot. I'm thirty three. But I have a youngish look. Asian genes, I guess. It always used to bother me that people thought I was younger than I was. But he doesn't mean any harm. So I let it pass. People thinking I'm still a kid is the least of my worries right now.

How to say it? How to explain?

They'll think I'm insane.

Am I?

No.

I know what I saw. What happened-- the terror I've experienced these past weeks-- it's real. I lived it. I survived.

I open my mouth and let the words come out, the only words that will come.
"The house. It got her."

Sheriff Sadler and Deputy Hansford glance at each other. The troubled look in Sheriff Sadler's eyes passes quickly, but not before I catch it.

We're sharing something. A feeling of mutual unease, a feeling that crawls and squirms like worms in the stomach.

In that moment I realize.

He's heard this before.

Deputy Hansford doesn't believe me. I can tell by his face, the smirk tugging at the right corner of his mouth, just waiting for the right excuse to be a smartass. But Sheriff Sadler-- he knows something. Has seen something. That momentary wince of unease and long suppressed pain gave it all away. Sheriff Sadler clears his throat.

"What house are you talking about, son?"

It's not so much a question, I can tell. More like a formality. He knows the answer already, even if he doesn't want to hear it.

"The one-- on Witcher Street."

There are other houses on that street, of course. And yet, there's really just the one.

One house.

IT.

I can tell at a glance that he knows. For a second, the hairline fractures of vulnerability show on his face. Then he straightens up, gives me a stern look. "Kevin, I'm a pretty easy going guy, anybody in Afton will tell you that, but if this is some kind of joke--"

"It's not a joke!"

My voice is louder than I intend.

"Okay, okay," he says.

"You know the house."

Sheriff Sadler sighs. "Yes, I do."

And Hansford agrees. "Everybody knows that damn house."

There's a sense of weird relief in Sheriff Sadler's secret knowing. He is tied to it somehow. I don't know exactly how, but those bloody threads are stretching out thin and invisible from all the way across town, from deep in that basement beneath the house on Witcher Street and they've slithered inside Jim Sadler's shirt, burrowed down into the flesh of his chest and pierced his heart. He might not know the full extent of the horror that I've been through, but he knows something. Something from a long time ago.

"That house has given lots of people in Afton trouble through the years," Sheriff Sadler says.

"I read the book," I manage. "The one by Stanley Shaftrick. You know it?"

"Yup, I know it," says Sheriff Sadler, but he doesn't sound glad that he does.

"Demon House," says deputy Hansford. His tone says it all.

Here we go again.

"A young woman went missing thirty years ago in that house," I say.

"Yup," says Sheriff Sadler. "I know that too."

"And Shaftrick, he wrote a book about the disappearance."

Sheriff Sadler is quick to correct me. "He wrote *a* book-- loosely based on the disappearance that occurred in that house in the summer of 1963." He has had to make this correction many times over the years, I can tell-- to tourists, thrillseekers. He says it flat from rote memory, emotionless like an automaton. "Shaftrick was an opportunist. A schlock meister. He heard about what had happened here-- and he saw a way to make a little money off of it. So he cobbled together what little he knew about the case-- which wasn't much, by the way," he adds emphasis on that point. "And what he didn't know he made up, threw a few ghosts and goblins into the mix, bleeding walls, screams in the night, pigs climbing on the ceiling, that sort of thing-- and churned out a sensationalist piece of garbage. He got rich on other people's suffering-- that poor girl's family for one-- I know. I remember. I was there.

"And the good people of Afton? Well, they got stuck with Demon House." He says the last part, the title of the book, with a touch of bitterness like the words taste bad in his mouth.

"That's what I thought, too," I tell him. "I came-- not believing in that sort of thing at all."

"Yup, we get plenty of gawkers. Every year. Vandals. Kids starting fires on Halloween. Crank calls-- 'Help, Demon House got my friend, my mother, my cousin', that sort of thing."

"I would probably have thought it was funny once too, I guess."

"But it's not funny now?" he asks me.

"No, not anymore."

"Can you talk about it?"

I nod, swallow.

Silence.

What are they waiting for?

I realize they're waiting for me to start talking.

I take a moment to get my thoughts together, take a shaky breath and begin.

"I moved in there three months ago, at the beginning of the summer."

That's the only sentence I get out before deputy Hansford interrupts with a snort.

"Jesus, I knew it. A damn prankster."

Sheriff Sadler gives me a disgruntled look, points a finger in my face. "Son, I warned you, if this is a joke, it ain't funny."

"What? I moved in there three months ago. Do you want to hear this or not?"

"Bullshit," says Hansford, shaking his head. He's scowling down at me, face reddening, fed up suddenly. He was maybe ready to give my story a chance but not now.

Why? What's so unbelievable in what I've just said.

"No one's lived in that house for thirty years. Not since the disappearance. Not since the summer of sixty three."

"What?"

I heard what he said, but it doesn't make sense, like he's telling me up is down and down is up. There's a sudden danger things might start spinning again. Maybe-- maybe I'm still in the demon haunted house, lying asleep in that drafty upstairs bedroom with that eyeless thing crouched down out on the roof, looking in at me, prying at the window with its chicken bone fingers, trying to get in. Things are about to turn terrifying-- walls crumbling, corpses rising, the sheriff's flesh melting off his face.

I give it a second, expecting the worst, expecting the world around me to toilet flush down into a sewerific nightmare. But nothing happens. The sheriff is still the sheriff, flesh clad and there are no corpses. I'm awake.

That might be even worse.

"It's abandoned, kid, boarded up," Hansford says to me. "Condemned. Not fit to live in. Certifiably uninhabitable."

They see the confusion on my face. I feel a little dizzy. My stomach has turned leaden all of a sudden.

"No-- I lived there. For three months. I was there. In that house."

Sheriff Sadler's stern look has softened to one of near pity. He just shakes his head.

I feel a sense of panic spring up in my gut, let loose like a bunch of terror stricken mice darting out of holes in the ground, scattering in all directions, shitting little pez sized mouse pellets as they flee.

"Take me there."

Sheriff Sadler raises both his hands in a preemptive kid calming gesture. "Son--"

"Take me there," I say, stiffening in the chair. I'm starting to breath heavy. Now the panic stricken mice running loose inside me have eyes tinged red with anger.

"Calm down, son; you've had a shock, that much is clear. Getting upset is only going to make it worse."

"You have to take me," I say again. "I can prove it. I've lived there all summer. I-- "

I look helplessly from Sheriff Sadler to deputy Hansford and back again.

"I can prove it-- if you'll just take me over there. Let me show you. Please."

I need to see it too, I guess. What they've said has started to pick at my already unbalanced brain. Little weeds of self doubt are already springing up like dandelions through the cracks, spreading their seeds of confusion in turn.

They have to know. I have to show them.

I can't stop that crazy person pleading tone from creeping into my voice.

Deputy Hansford gives a shrug-- a *what-the-hell* gesture.

Sheriff Sadler looks me in the eyes for a few seconds. I'm shaky, but I hold his gaze.

The clock on the wall ticks away the seconds. It's right over my head, but it sounds echoey and a million miles away. A dream sound.

I'm not crazy.

That's what I want him to read in my eyes.

But those dandelions have spread all over the inside my skull, a whole dark field full of them, fuzzy heads swaying in a cold cranial breeze. I look away.

Am I sure anymore?

Every second that passes makes everything that happened in that house feel more and more like a bad dream. They're so hard to remember when you wake, even though they're so blood drippingly vivid at the time. Now that I'm out and away from the house, I feel free of Its spell. It's power-- It's hold over me is fading.

No.

That's what It-- the House-- wants me to think-- so It can go on spreading those veins in the dark in all directions, fathomless and without end, snaring the whole damn town. I must face the house on Witcher Street once more.

Sheriff Sadler takes a deep breath, blows it out, runs his fingers through his hair, mulls it over a second, chin resting in his hand. He's looking off somewhere far away in his mind, I can tell, chasing a memory from a long time ago. Maybe he's looking for that woman who went missing all those summers back.

Maybe he's got those dandelions in his head, too.

When he looks at me again, it's with the ghost of old hurt is his eyes, old wounds being opened up. A trickle of fresh blood rising to the surface. Three decades late. I can see it.

"Alright," he says. "Let's go."

Before we leave, he makes me take a shower. I don't want to. I just want to go back to the house and get it over with. But I am admittedly a bit of a mess, shredded, mud spattered and bleeding. When I see myself in the locker room mirror it's a shock. My hands were bad. My face is worse.

Not just the dirt and dried blood. But I'm looking gaunt. Hollow eyes. Crazy looking eyes.

Weird.

That's not the reflection I saw in the mirrors at the house on Witcher Street.

That's not what the house wanted me to see, I guess.

Sheriff Sadler gives me a pair of spare sweats and a tee shirt from the locker room to wear. And we're off.

"What am I supposed to tell Dr. Simmons?" Edith asks. "He canceled all his afternoon appointments for you."

"Tell him we'll be back," Sheriff Sadler says over his shoulder. "Give him the egg salad if he wants it."

"But Jim--" Edith protests, there is something so comforting-- so reassuring in her small town worries and daylight concerns.

Neither of us waits long enough to hear what she is going to say.

On the car ride over my heart is pounding. I'm running my thumb knuckle back and forth over my lower lip. Over and over. I don't even realize I'm doing it.

"You okay?" Sheriff Sadler asks, glancing over.

I stop picking at my lip, straighten up, say, "Yeah, yeah, I'm fine."

I'm not, of course.

What if he's right?

What if we get there and the house is boarded up, abandoned, in ruins, just like he says?

What then?

Does it mean I'm crazy.

Or--

Does it mean the house has a power?

A power to twist reality in this town.

"Slow down. Take a breath."

The day is bright and warm. I close my eyes, lean my head back, try to breathe-- to calm down knowing that in a few minutes it will all be over. In a few minutes I'll know the truth, whatever it turns out to be. How I handle that truth will be another thing entirely.

Who knew you could feel so sick on such a beautiful summer day.

I'm going back-- back to the monster. I thought I had escaped. Maybe there is no escape. Any path I choose, it all leads back to Her.

The car slows eventually. It feels like an eternity. The engine dies. I can hear Sheriff Sadler breathing. He shifts in his seat. He's looking at me. I can tell, even with my eyes closed.

"Want to get out and have a look?"

I open my eyes, making sure I'm looking at him and not out the window.

There's a steel girder of a knot in my stomach but I tell him, "Yes, lets have a look."

But I don't move. I don't look. My bravery is a bluff, anxiety betrays itself through the tremor in my voice.

"Take your time. I'll be outside."

Sheriff Sadler gets out, closes his door, walks around to the front of the car.

I sit, eyes fastened on the floorboard like there's a fascinating, Pompeiian mosaic beneath my feet instead of the cracked, grey rubber mat with its petrified wad of pink chewing gum. I can't stay in the passenger seat forever.

I have to face--

It.

I open the door, keeping my head down, watching my feet very carefully as I step out, as if this is always the way I get out of cars. I close the door behind me.

I raise my head slowly and look up.

It's just as I remember.

The twisted wrought iron fence laced with variegated threads of ivy. The old oaks reaching out their long arms overhead, casting sleepy shadows. A breeze stirs the air. Golden sunlight flits like shoals of minnows through the rustling leaves. Somewhere down the street, a world away, I hear a couple of children shouting to each other. The slightest hint of autumn is alive on the air.

I raise my eyes to the house.

The sight of it sends me staggering back, victim of a supernatural sucker punch. I reach back to brace myself against the patrol car. Sheriff Sadler is hurrying around to help me, to catch me before I fall.

"I gotcha. Let's sit down here on the curb. There you go. Easy does it."

It's just like he said.

I guess I knew it would be, but that doesn't make facing the monster any easier.

The ruin of three decades has buried the house in decay. Thirty years of wind and rain, sun and snow have turned it into a rickety corpse of cracked grey wood, rusted iron and moss covered stone. The porch sags hangdog all around the front of the house, broken down to the ground in most places with splinters of gingerbread jutting out beneath. Shutters hang askew like butcher blades tilted at helter skelter angles. Pollock like spatters of bird shit, baked to perfection by the summer sun, adorn the walls of the house, hanging like stalactites from the warped eaves. The glass has been busted out of nearly every window leaving jagged black gaps, eye sockets of a skull, wormholes into dark wonders.

"Fit for the Addams' Family, huh?" says Sheriff Sadler and he gives me a humorless smile. "A real Halloween classic."

A mesmerizing horror-- the house on Witcher Street.

I can almost hear a dark calliope playing inside my head.

And somehow, even though I see it-- that stark, vine entombed ruin jutting up into the clear August sky, I'm not convinced-- not by a long shot. It's a trick, got to be-- an illusion contrived by the house.

I know it.

Beyond all knowing.

I've seen what She can do.

The breeze picks up, rustles the leaves and carries with it the faintest scent of promised autumn and also the ghost of a laugh-- like a sigh, soft and sensual.

Sheriff Sadler is looking at the house, eyes squinted against the sun, pondering, thinking long ago thoughts.

We both see the house, of course, its naked desolation. But the whisper of the laugh is heard only by me.

I stand up, start towards the house.

Sheriff Sadler, leaning back against the hood of the car, stands up, follows behind. "Careful, son, there could be anything in those weeds. Rusted nails, broken glass, snakes for sure. Did you hear me?"

I do and I don't. I start, at first, on a straight line up the chipped tooth brick path towards the front steps. I'm moving slow-motion-dream-fast. And I know I should trip and fall, under normal circumstances, bust my kneecaps into a thousand agonizing splinters, but it-- the house--

She won't let me.

She wants me back.

It's the sheriff, a few steps behind, who gives a curse as he stumbles on a tilted brick-- one I was sure had been lying flat and at peace a moment before. It's not so unreasonable, really. I've seen the house do worse to people.

Far worse.

I leap off the crazy angle path, push through the golden, waist high weeds, heedless of rusty nails and snakes. I veer right, head around at a madman's disjointed pace towards the side of the house, clap boards warped and bulging as if bloated with years of blood gorging. I reach the storm cellar doors.

That's where I lost her.

The basement.

My heart is pounding with enough force to crack my ribs, send them exploding in splinters through my chest.

I don't know what I expect to find-- some supernatural, world ending terror-- too abominable to grasp-- a gaping, sharp-toothed maw, a set of rotten stairs leading down into a bloody charybdic whirlpool, fleshless corpses thrashing in the muddy darkness below.

... the black and pulsing heart, perhaps?

...or the spider?

No.

The doors are shut, withered, cracked and warped. Rust encrusted chains lie heavily across the splintery wood like twin fat worms slain in the sun.

I reach down, clench the chains in my hands and pull back. They're heavier than I imagined and the strain sends a sharp pain down my back, but I can't let them go.

I owe it to her-- my friend.

Holly.

Suddenly, I am Saint George.

The House-- a scabrous dragon.

I yank on the chains again and again until the sweat stands out in glittery beads on my forehead. The chains won't come loose and I am flooded with sudden anger.

The house. It got her.

Give her back! Give her back! What have you done with her?

I don't realize that I'm kicking and shouting until I feel Sheriff Sadler pulling me away.

I drop the chains and they clatter down, dead, lifeless, irresistant in that late summer sun.

Some battles cannot be won by force, sheer might or will.

Some battles, I suppose, one is destined to lose.

A hard learned lesson. I'm feeling it now, head drooped, noodle arms hanging limp at my sides.

Sheriff Sadler, tentative arm draped around my shoulders, leads me back around to the front steps. He helps me sit down on the porch. It cracks under our combined weight, letting out a long pent up groan. I think for a second it might cave in beneath us. But it holds. For a long time he doesn't say anything, just lets me sit there in abstracted silence and stare off into space. I trace a swirl in the dirt with my finger, mindlessly.

A looping fingerprint pattern, a downward spiraling labyrinth.

At last he says, "Well, you want to talk about it?"

Coming from anyone else, I might have taken the question as patronizing. But there's secret truth in his tone. He wants to know. Needs to know. And me? I need to let it go. I hope to God he's ready to hear it. Hope he can brace himself against the tidal wave of horror about to break all around him, the torrents of terror I'm about to unleash from my mouth like Noah's flood.

Because it's not just the house. One haunted house is easy enough to deal with, I guess. But I know things. The whole town's dark and twisted secrets. Afton is drenched in blood.

I know about the Old Ones.

I know about Unglit.

I know about their plan.

It's all coming back now. The fog is thinning. I almost wish it wouldn't.

"Yes, I'll tell you," I say. "But not here."

"Don't blame you. Come on," he says and points. "There's a space there across the street where we can talk."

The House on Witcher Street broods alone at the rise of a jagged hill. Solitary. Without neighbors. The next house on either side is a long, vacant lot away. Easily a football field of weeds surrounds the house on all sides.

Across the street is a run down little park with a couple of stone picnic tables-- not that anyone wants to have a picnic in the shadow of that house, not even on the best of days.

Sheriff Sadler and I sit at one of the graffiti stained tables, he on one side, me on the other. I look back at the house for a few minutes, gathering my thoughts.

I look Her over-- from one black window to the next, from the caved in roof, shedding its shingles like splintery tears, to the highest turret leaning dangerously in the glare of the sun, its pointed gable jousting with every passing cloud. An unhealthy yearning for destruction, for submission to the thing that nearly killed me, stirs deep down inside me, kicks clawed rat feet fitfully in its sleep and wakes with a start. It scratches at my guts, trying to scrape its way out of my abdomen and pull me back tethered by strands of my own shredded entrails-- back across the weed infested yard, down the crickety-crazy brick path-- back to the house.

I fight the urge.

But I wonder if the same veins, spat out from the darkness under the house, that have embedded themselves like barbs in Sheriff Sadler's heart have done the same in mine now. I rub my hands together trying to wipe away the rust stains left by the chains. When I finish they're still red.

Even in my loathing for it-- my disgust for the house on Witcher Street, I yearn for it.

My head feels suddenly heavy, weeks of weariness taking their toll, pouring down over my shoulders, dripping down like sludge, a spirit killing tar drowning the last glimmer of my own self awareness.

Give in. Give in. Come back to me, my love. My door will open for you alone. For you my windows will shine. All will be as it was. As it should be.

My heart-- what you mistook for a horror, beats only for you. Can you hear it still? Come back.

The house has bound me with the lure of its phantasmagoric beauty, snagged my flesh with sharp thorned temptations, luring me with the promise of dark, forbidden enchantments within. Even with the afternoon sun revealing every detail of its revolting ruin and decay, I am drawn.

The House.

Still hideously beautiful-- even after everything it has done to me-- after everything it still wants to do to me.

God, how can it be?

Even after it tried to devour me.

It casts a spell.

Even still.

"Why don't you tell me what happened, son."

I look away from the *Demon House*. It takes a little effort. I can still change my mind. Why not? He doesn't need to know. I don't need to tell him. I can just laugh it off, tell him I was having a few rough days-- a nervous breakdown, even. And when he's gone away, I can go back.

I can go back and be within the house.

Complete. One. At peace.

Just me and *IT*. Safe in the darkness of its ouroboric embrace.

It will take me back. It's not too late, not yet. I can be free within the sacred ring of the tail devouring serpent. The world beyond is meaningless. It's the darkness within--that's the truth and fulfillment of all-- the only truth worth knowing.

Sheriff Sadler is sitting with his hands clasped on the stone tabletop, waiting.

I shake off the desire to send him away. I will tell him, if that's what he wants. It might kill me-- probably will in some way I can't yet see, but I'll tell him all the same.

"Yes."

"You can tell me everything. I'll listen."

I know that he will.

"Yes, I will tell you everything. You won't believe it."

"Don't judge too quick."

I feel like he needs to hear it as much as I need to tell it.

God, I'm so weary.

Jim Sadler, lines like crevices beneath his eyes, looks pretty weary, too, all of a sudden-- tired out from years of chasing ghosts. Can I give both of us a little peace?

I hope to God I can.

The truth, they say, will set you free. It can probably also kill you.

In that moment of silence I feel the kiss of a hopeful breeze on my cheek and with eyelids flitting on the cusp of exhaustion, I catch a glimpse of sunlight glinting on the waters of Lake Afton down the curve of the road, sparkling like diamonds. For a second I'm lost in the play of scintillating sunlight, a shimmering illusion of freedom and ethereal escape.

I force my eyes open and I'm back in the shadow of the house, weighed down, crushed by the boulder of horrific nightmare reality which I must now lay at another man's feet.

One deep breath before the dive into dark inner waters. Deceptively still waters, but perilous. Tentacled horrors lurking, blind eyed, hungry, just below the surface. Ready to snatch, grab and devour-- to chew to pieces any deceptions about escape.

The House, I know, It had me well before I had ever heard of Afton.

The revelation is a relief. I can do it now. I can dive open hearted back into the mouth of that house on Witcher Street.

In my mind, I walk to the edge. I stand shaking on the brink. I look down into what was.

There is no going back.
I leap into the air.
The dark waters rush up to greet me.
To welcome me home.
To drown me in a mercy of horror and blood and creeping nighttime terrors.

Three months earlier...

PART II

RUNNING AWAY

Unexpressed emotions will never die. They are buried alive and will come forth later in uglier ways.
--Sigmund Freud

IT ALL STARTS with Mrs. Lebowitz. She is the first.

Though I guess it has been in my mind for a long time.

It is innocent enough to begin with. My heart is in the right place. I have good intentions.

It's just when they bring her in with her white, cotton puff cloud of hair drenched in syrupy, bright blood...

Wait, let me back up.

I am a nurse in the emergency room at a hospital in Seattle. I work nights. I see a lot of troubling things. Tonight, the payphone behind me is ringing off the hook, an audible reflection of my rattled nerves. I'm about to answer it-- to scream at whoever is on the line, *'Would you please knock it the fuck off!'* when they wheel her in-- Mrs. Lebowitz.

I think I'm just getting overwhelmed. But I can't admit it, even to myself. Can't admit that the pressure of these long, death riddled nights are starting to weigh me down, threatening to crush me.

Let's see-- where was I? Oh, yeah, Mrs. Lebowitz (I find out her name later) with her cotton puff of white hair drenched in blood. It looks like she has been whacked on the top of her head with an ax. I hurry after the gurney, leave the phone ringing angrily behind me in the hall.

I sit with her a long time that night, at her bedside, holding her feeble, veiny hand.

She is delirious, keeps looking at me with blue eyes that won't focus. At one point she tries to sit up, says she has to get ready for church, she will be late. They are going to bury her poor mother today. Do I know where her shoes are?

It is mindless talk, of course. She is remembering something from sixty years earlier. She is out of her head-- an ax to the skull will do that, I guess. But she is so gentle and she smiles at me and calls me *'sweet boy,'* which I find endearing.

"You know, I've always liked reading about China. Did you know that?"

"No ma'am, I didn't."

"Well, I do." She pats my hand. "I think it's a marvelous place."

She must think I'm Chinese. I don't bother telling her I'm Korean.

"Thank you," I say.

She smiles weakly at me. She looks so pale-- thin and white like a piece of notebook paper crinkled up under the covers. My heart goes out to her. This is someone's mother, grandmother, sister, wife.

"Will you stay with me until I find my shoes? Joe will be here any minute to pick me up."

"I'll stay."

She's not going to make it. I can tell. There's a certain intuition you develop on a job like this. You know, at a glance, the ones who are goners.

That's when she sits up suddenly.

Joe's here, I think.

"You watch out for that spider, do you hear me? You stay away from those Old Ones."

More head trauma induced nonsense.

She turns, leans over the side of the safety rail on the bed and retches violently. Her bloody vomit splatters all over my shoes. I don't jerk back in terror or disgust. I just go on holding her hand. When she's finished, I help lay her back, make sure she's comfortably propped up against her pillows.

She's muttering something, but I can't understand what she's saying. All I catch is something about making sure the horse is tied up and an admonition for Joe to wipe his boots off before coming in.

I watch her sleep for a few minutes, vomit soaking into my shoes.

Her chest rises and falls, light as a feather. She takes one dainty breath after another as if air is a rare commodity. Her lungs as small as envelopes.

"Kevin... Kevin!"

I turn around, didn't even hear Allison, the shift supervisor, calling my name.

"Hmmm?"

"You've got throw up on your shoes."

Behind her, Tim, a candy striper, laughs.

"Did you hear me? You need to go get cleaned up."

"What about Joe?" I ask confusedly, looking back at Mrs. Lebowitz.

Allison's brow wrinkles, puzzled by my remark. "She'll be fine, Kevin. You can come back and see her when you get your shoes changed."

"I'll be right back," I tell Mrs. Lebowitz.

I start to get up. Tim laughs again, says, "It's not like she's going anywhere."

Allison turns to him, hands on her hips, gives him a stern look, says, "Get a mop."

"Aw, shit," says Tim, no longer smiling.

After I change my shoes, I go back to check on her and find the curtained off area empty, her bed gone. Tim is the only one there, pushing the mop, swishing pinkish sudsy water across the tiles. He stops, thrusts the mop in the bucket, swirls it around.

"Did they move her to ICU?"

"Nope." Tim doesn't look up from mopping.

I didn't think they had, really.

At the end of my shift, Allison comes up, gives me a pat on the back.

"Nice shoes," she says, trying to get me to smile. When I don't, she looks concerned.

"You okay?"

"Uh-huh."

She knows I'm not telling the truth.

It really shouldn't bother me this much. I see people die all the time. Every night almost-- in the most painful ways sometimes.

The image stays with me all week. Sweet Mrs. Lebowitz with her bloody head. I can't concentrate on my work.

A few days later I do something I've never done before.

I check the local obituaries, find out about Mrs. Lebowitz's funeral arrangements and I go to the wake.

I'm not sure why I go. Maybe it is a relief. I give my condolences to the family. I even ask who Joe was. I explain how in her delirium she asked for him.

No one knows who Joe is.

Maybe it was a long ago lover, seventy summers gone. A secret she took to the grave.

I guess I'll never know, either.

I lean over, a little too close, I guess, trying to get a look at how the mortician managed to stitch up and cover her gaping head wound. I can't find any sign of that red crevasse. How in the hell did he do it? I glance up, get a puzzled look from a nearby mourner. I straighten up, adjust my tie, stammer a few words.

"She-- she looks so lovely, so at peace."

No one ever mentions anything about her head wound, how it happened. No one, in all the little conversations I have that day with her family members, ever says anything like, "Oh, it was such a terrible fall," or "I told them that loose ceiling tile should have been fixed."

Nothing.

Not knowing might drive me crazy, but I can't ask. Can I?

I come close, trying to figure a way to insert the question into the conversation, but I just can't do it.

It must provide me with some sort of relief-- going to the wake, seeing the body, waxy and reposed after the struggle with death is over. There's a sense of morbid peace in it, I guess.

That's how I get hooked. I think it is a way to deal with the stress of the job.

A few days after Mrs. Lebowitz's wake, Allison gives me a hug, says, "That was really sweet, Kevin. That woman's niece stopped by earlier to say how kind it was that you came by to pay your respects."

"Oh, it was nothing," I say awkwardly, caught off guard a little. "I just-- I just, um-- "

"I know. Sometimes you just need to."

"Yeah."

I'm blushing guiltily. I don't know why I feel so embarrassed. I did a good thing. Right?

But I know, can tell, already, where this is heading.

I am on the lookout after that for anyone who I can sit with, spend a few minutes bonding with, knowing that they're going to die and that afterwards, I will get to attend the wake, see the waxworks looking body lying in its casket, arms draped over its chest. The people I sit with-- the goners, I call them, think I'm there to comfort them-- which I am, sorta. But I'm also thinking, guiltily, I know you're gonna die and when you do I'm gonna put on my brown corduroy coat and go to your wake, exchange a few awkward sympathies with your loved ones and leave feeling high as a kite.

I know it's fucked up. But I can't help it.

It's at these wakes that you hear about someone, hear their life all summed up nice and neat. I can't help wondering what people will say at my funeral, how they'll summarize my life.

Yeah, Kevin Yoo... he was, well, he was really boring. A death obsessed, jittery shut in.

I can't get enough. I'm like a druggie-- addicted to death. The emergency roomers aren't enough. I start checking the local obits, going to complete stranger's wakes, pretending I knew the person, acting as a representative of the hospital.

It's after attending the sixteenth funeral that I realize I may have a problem. I admit it.

I am obsessed with death.

I try to keep my morbid little hobby a close guarded secret.

But Allison finds out.

She pulls me aside one night near the end of my shift.

"Kevin, I got a call today from a Mr. Ayerdi."

She pauses, waiting to see how I react. I think I clench my jaw. Honestly, I can't say I know who Mr. Ayerdi is, but he's connected somehow to my new obsession, that much I'm sure of.

"He just called to thank me for sending a representative from the hospital to his wife's funeral."

"Oh."

"Kevin, I know it was you. How long have you been doing this?"

No answer.

"A lot." It's not a question.

I look at my feet.

"Kevin, this isn't healthy."

"I'm just trying to-- to-- "

What am I trying to do?

"I've seen this before, Kevin. You're too close. You're-- morbidly obsessed. You need to take a step back."

I decide to take some time off. Well, I didn't really have a choice. It's a medical leave of absence, but Allison tries to make it sound better for me by calling it a vacation. I am sitting in a coffee shop at a table by the window, the glass is streaked with rain. My boyfriend, James Sarisicki is sitting across from me with an uncomfortable expression on his face, the same one he gets when he has to say something unpleasant.

The look makes me feel tense.

We've been dating for two and a half years; it's the longest relationship I've ever had. The longest anyone has been willing to put up with me. Lately, he's been more distant. I feel like he's turning into a stranger. Evenings at the apartment have gotten more silent and uncomfortable. We don't talk much anymore. I wonder if he knows-- about the funerals, that I was placed on leave at work.

I take a sip of my coffee. It tastes unusually bitter. My stomach feels suddenly unsettled.

James sighs, runs his fingers through his strawberry blond hair. I used to love that gesture, that pouty look, his James Dean handsomeness. Not today. I feel like I'm in trouble.

"Kevin, I'll be blunt, because you deserve it. I'm not in love with you anymore."

He doesn't look at me when he says it, just stares hard at his hands cradling his coffee cup.

I feel like I have been sucker punched. He glances up, can tell I have been thrown for a loop.

"Kev, you had to know. Right?"

I can tell by the way he says it, he's hoping I don't think it's a real question. He hates long explanations.

Did I know?

I do and I don't. But I'm going for denial.

"I-- I don't understand. Everything has been going so good."

"Things haven't been right with us for a long time. I've been really unhappy."

"Why didn't you say something?"

"That's just it, you should have been able to see that I was unhappy."

I'm feeling a little crab snappy all of a sudden and I get snarky right off the bat.

"I'm not a psychic, James. You should have said something."

James is surprised and irritated by the remark. By being combative, I'm giving him more of a reason to break it off. Despite my goading, he remains calm, detached, professional. A real adult.

My antipathy rises.

"I've thought about it a lot," he says. "We're just too different. I like to get out, to do things, to embrace life. You like to stay in all cloistered like some kind of monk."

"I like to go out."

"Kevin, you go to the grocery store."

"That's... um, still out."

"Or... to all those funerals."

The knot in my stomach tightens. I'm embarrassed, feel my cheeks glowing. He knows my dirty little secret after all.

"Who told you?" I ask, my tone accusing, like he has no right to mention these things.

"Kevin, it doesn't matter who told me. People are concerned."

"I told Allison not to tell," I mutter. "She promised."

"Kevin, this obsession with death that you're cultivating-- it's unhealthy."

"I just go to support the families. They were all patients."

"And what about the rest of them, the ones you circled in red in the obituaries? Did you know them, too?"

"I can-- I can quit any time I want."

"Kev, you sound like an addict, you know that, right?"

"I'm not addicted."

James shakes his head, waves a hand, letting it go.

"You're having a nervous breakdown, Kevin. And you need professional help."

I bristle like a porcupine, immediately on the defensive.

Who is he to tell me I'm having a nervous breakdown? I'll decide when and if I'm having a nervous breakdown.

"I'm not having a-- I don't need to-- I'll quit going to the funerals. I can stop today. Right now. You want me to go out? Fine, we'll go out-- anywhere you want, anytime you want. Let's go."

I sound a little too gung ho. It's like a WWF challenge. Maybe subconsciously I want this to crash and burn.

Yeah, I guess that's it.

James can see through the blustering, he's got a look of pity in his eyes. He says with a sigh, "It's not just that."

"What else then? What else do I need to change? What else can I do for you, James, to make you happy, huh?" I'm shifting in my seat, squirming like I have ants in my pants, or like that over large cup of too strong coffee is doing its best on my colon. I know I sound desperate, accusatory, but when I speak, I can't stop those dual tones from twining together like twin serpents. Yes, I'm doing it on purpose, helping the situation to self destruct. Making sure I completely destroy any chance at salvaging my relationship. Why? Who knows. I'm imploding. I can feel it. I feel disgusted with myself, but it's too late.

And he's right, I'm teetering on the brink of a nervous breakdown.

It's working. James looks exasperated.

"We're just too different. All that antiquing stuff you do, old houses, old home tours, old home fixer upper t.v. shows, quite frankly, it's boring."

"You think I'm boring?"

"I didn't say that. I said, I think your hobbies are boring."

"It's the same thing."

Another *you-just-don't-get-it* sigh from James.

"We just haven't been honest with each other, that's all. It's time we started."

"I've always been honest with you."

"Fine, then I haven't been honest with you," he says, irritated now that I haven't just taken his word for it. "But I am now."

I am about to protest but he cuts me off.

"Don't make this harder than it has to be. It's over, Kev. I love you, I do. But I'm not *in love* with you. And I just can't live with you anymore."

"Is that supposed to make me feel better."

"It's not supposed to make you feel anything. It's just the truth."

"Who are you? What planet are you from?"

"Don't be so dramatic."

"Is there someone else? Is it Aaron? It's Aaron, isn't it?"

"This is not about Aaron. This is about you and me. And to be honest, it's really not even about me, either. It's about you, Kevin. You."

"God, it's Aaron."

We both look down at our coffees, watch the steam swirl and rise.

James knows I'm a lost cause.

For a moment, neither of us says anything. All I can hear is the rain coming down outside, usually so soothing, today feels suddenly very depressing. I close my eyes, reach up, rub my fingers in circles, massaging my temples. "I feel like my head's going to explode."

"That's another thing. You're always so morose-- Dr. Schwartz thinks it's unhealthy for me to be around such a depressive personality. Aaron agrees."

"Who's Dr. Schwartz?"

"My therapist."

"You're seeing a therapist?"

"Yes."

"Why didn't you tell me?"

"Well, to be honest Kev, it's really none of your business."

"It's none of my business that behind my back you've been telling people I'm a depressive personality."

"Actually, *he* defined you as depressive."

"I-- I don't know what to say."

"You don't have to say anything. It's over." There, he has said it. It's final. I can tell by the look on his face. He swallows, looks a little sad about what he has to say next. "I'm going out of town today. I'll be in New York for two weeks. I'd really like you out of the apartment by the time I get back. I'm sorry if this sounds harsh, but Dr. Schwartz says I need to be more firm."

"Well does Dr. Schwartz have any bright ideas about where the hell I'm supposed to go?"

James just shakes his head. "He warned me about this, told me not to let you draw me into a debate. So did Aaron. Goodbye, Kevin."

He gets up, gives my shoulder a gentle pat as he walks by, leaves me sitting alone.

I see him walk away down the street, his form made grey and indistinct in the drizzle.

I sit there a few minutes, listening to the rain beating down outside. I start feeling dizzy. I close my eyes again, take a deep breath, let it out slowly. All I can hear is my heart beating in my chest. Then I get up, leave my half finished coffee on the table and walk out into the rain.

"Hyuk, what are you going to do in Atlanta?" my mother asks.

Whenever I visit she always refers to me by my Korean name. We only speak Korean at home. I am a bit rusty and have a little trouble keeping up. Two glasses of red wine on an empty stomach isn't helping.

"I'll find a nursing job out there," I say defiantly in English.

My mother purses her lips. She knows I'm purposely refusing to speak Korean. I don't know why I'm being cruel to her. I don't want to hurt her, but I'm feeling sullen, combative. I don't care who I hurt. I'll just blame it on the wine.

My stepfather, sitting next to her, mutters something. The stroke he had three years ago has impaired his speech. The left side of his mouth is tugged down in a permanent frown. My mom leans close to him, listens, shakes her head. I know what she'll say before she says it.

"He says, if you're going to be a nurse, why not go ahead and be a doctor?"

I sigh, down the last swallow of wine, can feel it going straight to my head. My face feels flushed, the room-- unusually warm. "Not tonight, please."

My stepfather grumbles unhappily. To him, for any male, but especially his stepson, to be a nurse is just so atrociously unmanly. Over the years, whenever people have asked him what I do, he just tells them I'm in the medical profession and leaves it at that. He hopes they all assume I'm a doctor.

He's muttering again. My mother listens obediently, but does not repeat what he has said, even though he gestures with his good hand, making it clear that he wants me and everyone else at the table to hear what he has said.

I already know what he wants me to hear. Being a male nurse, it's humiliating to a military man like him and-- he never fails to add, to my dead father, too.

Mention of my real dad always causes my mother's face to tighten painfully. She does not want to repeat what he has said. Instead, my mother ignores his gesticulations and asks, "Where will you stay?"

"I'm staying with cousin Alan."

My step father makes a little grunting noise that sounds like a laugh and mutters something else.

My mother listens, nods again. This-- she will say aloud.

"He says your cousin Alan is a meathead."

My stepsister, Amy, gives a coquettish laugh, then looks slyly at me.

"So, I guess you'll be moving out from your *friend's* apartment?"

She is bating me as usual. She even makes rabbit ears when she says *'friend'*. Absurdly childish. She's in college, yet an eternal elementary schooler-- I guess we'll always have that in common. Amy is five years younger than me. She has been a bratty torment ever since my mother remarried. She is the kid sister from hell, spat right out of Satan's mouth. But she is smart and pretty and at the top of her class at the University of Seattle and this makes her daddy's little angel.

She glances at my step father for approval. He stares solemnly, but gives her a nearly imperceptible nod. He approves, of course. His thoughts are so obvious I can almost hear them.

We have to toughen this boy up.

My friend. The words irritate me more than they should. Amy, she really knows how to push my proverbial buttons. Always has. What's worse-- she knows it, too. I guess the wine is making me more irritable with her than usual. I realize I'm grinding my teeth. James, on those rare occasions when he is mentioned, is only ever referred to as my *friend*. Amy never fails to put the proper emphasis on the word.

My lifestyle is an aberration. I am Quasimodo-- minus the hunchback... and the bell ringing. But an unmentionable freak, nonetheless.

I try to speak. My mouth is sickeningly dry. My tongue sticks to the roof of my mouth.

"Yes, I'm moving out. James and I... broke up. Fuck."

I mutter the last part. I know I've told them I'm gay in some meek, chickenshit standoff a few years earlier, but still...

We're a ultra traditional Korean family, product of mass American missionary efforts-- 1950's style-- so these sorts of things, like brimstone inducing homosexuality, are not spoken of in polite conversation-- or in any conversation, for that matter.

"Hyuk, watch your language, says my mother.

"Well, it's about time, if you ask me," my sister says, playing the mature one, "I'm relieved you've decided to stop seeing your *friend*. It was causing us all so much stress and embarrassment."

I'm about to shout.

"This kimchi is wonderful," says Jin Woo, my sister's boyfriend. He says it awkwardly, and a little loud, trying to keep the peace. He has been at enough of our family dinners to know when to speak up. He always knows just the right thing to say. He really is trying. Usually I'm grateful to him. Tonight I'm just irritated. He looks at me, gives me a reassuring nod.

I respect Jin Woo and I relax a little. He's a bit awkward, but handsome as hell, so maybe that helps defuse things a bit.

"It's an old family recipe." My mother winks at him, glad for the change of subject, happy to talk about anything-- even kimchi, if it means avoiding mentioning my... perversion. They're all in denial.

Jin Woo tugs at his collar. His smile is way too big-- like a Korean Cheshire cat. "You said it was your great aunt's, right?"

"That's right, Jin Woo." Her voice sounds more relieved now. Things are getting back on track. The dinner is still salvageable if we shove in just a little more normal mealtime conversation. "How are things at the bank, young man?"

The return to forced normalcy is accompanied by an exponential increase in stiff and formal politeness.

"Good. Thank you. Very good, actually. I got a raise."

"Ah, we're so proud of you, Jin Woo. Isn't that right, Hyuk?"

She is being sincere, trying to include me in the conversation, but after Amy's bating, I'm on the offensive.

"Yes, Jin Woo, we're so proud," I say testily. I'm pouring myself more wine. I raise my glass in mock toast, slosh some of the wine onto the white table cloth. "Hip-hip-hooray for Jin Woo."

My sister looks disgusted at me like I've just flicked a booger at her, like she was not the aggressor to begin with.

"You're drunk."

I scowl at the table. "Maybe."

The red wine blotch spreads through the cloth like a bloodstain.

My stepfather shakes his head disappointed, but not surprised.

"Hyuk, don't be bitter," Amy says in a condescending, grown up kind of way as if she is worldly wise and I am a petulant child. She pats Jin Woo on the leg lovingly as if they are a married couple. "Jin Woo has his head on straight. You might take a lesson from him."

"Amy, don't," Jin says to her.

She frowns at her lap.

But my stepfather won't have anyone admonition his princess.

"Why can't you be more like Jin Woo," he says, his voice slurred by the stroke, but loud enough this time for me to hear without my mother translating.

Jin is a really good guy. He and I actually get along great together. Unfortunately, tonight, his natural, no guile goodness makes it worse, increases my irritability.

"Don't you have parents of your own, Jin Woo? Or have you already impressed the shit out of them-- killed 'em with your accolades?"

"Enough," says my mother, slapping her hand on the table.

It's an unfair dig. Jin's shoulders drop a little. He looks down at his plate.

I want to say I'm sorry, but I don't.

A few moments of silence pass.

"You were saying about the bank?" My mother says a little too hastily, trying hard to salvage a scrap of this last family meal together.

It's so ridiculously absurd, the fact that they're all still trying to keep up the charade of normalcy. But for them, anything is better than chaos, I guess. Maybe it's an Asian thing. I turn into a stone. My plate of untouched food jerks drunkenly back and forth. I just sit, arms crossed, as my mother and Jin Woo go on talking. I glance up once to see Amy glaring at me.

The rest of the stilted conversation revolves around the Korean perfection known as Jin Woo.

When they leave, Jin gives me a stiff hug, says, "I hope you find what you're looking for."

He is sincere and I feel guilty as hell for my snarky attitude towards him.

"Thank you."

He gives Amy a nod, wants her to say something nice-- to make sure we part on good terms.

"Call us when you get there," she says flatly. She smiles half heartedly, squeezes my arm. Maybe she's sorry, too.

I'm a little too dizzy, um, drunk, to leave. Once they're gone, I go to the kitchen for a glass of water. My mother has already set one on the table for me. I sit alone for a while, gulp down one glass of water, stumble to the faucet for another.

A few minutes later, my mother returns after putting my stepfather to bed. We sit at the kitchen table in silence. I can hear my stepfather snoring softly in the next room.

"I'm sorry," I mutter.

"Hush," she says.

She gets up, goes to a cabinet, rummages around, pulls out a box of traditional Korean cookies-- maejakgwa, my favorite.

"I was saving it for your trip, but I think you need it tonight."

She places the tissue lined box in front of me.

"Hey, you said you didn't have time to make any."

"I didn't want Amy to have any." She smiles and winks at me.

That makes me laugh a little.

My mother shrugs. "I'm sorry if that's dishonest. Go on-- eat."

She doesn't have to tell me twice. I stuff a cookie in my mouth. My mother smiles, reaches up, touches my cheek. She lays her other hand gently on top of mine.

"Cheer up, handsome boy. It's not that bad."

"It might be. I'm... I'm so lost. I'm afraid any minute I'm gonna round the corner, get gored to death by a-- what do ya call it-- Minotaur."

She nods solemnly, thinks it over, not getting the Minotaur reference, perhaps, but needing to provide some encouraging words. "You'll find your place, you'll see."

There's a lump in my throat all of a sudden. Stupid wine.

"Thank you," I say, speaking, for the first time that evening, in Korean.

She looks serious all of a sudden.

"Hyuk, your James called me. He told me about your going to-- all of these funerals."

The peaceful moment is spoiled. I feel angry again. I'm ready to yell about James, to tell her she should know better than to listen to stupid rumors, but she holds up her hand, says gently, "He was worried about you. He wanted to know what he could do to help."

My anger melts away like butter in a hot skillet. I feel another lump in my throat. I have trouble swallowing the cookie clump. James does care. He is worried about me. He was being sincere. He was even concerned enough to call my mother. Now, I'm never going to see him again. I feel like a jerk, like I'm going to cry. I have to look away.

"He asked me if I knew where all of this might have started," my mother says. "I think I do." She takes a deep breath. This is hard for her, too. "Is this about your father?"

At first I think she means my stepfather.

"No," I say adamantly.

"I mean appa, Hyuk."

Appa-- my real dad. A vague image of my father comes to mind. It's a summer day. We're in the garage putting together a plastic model car. I can almost smell the enamel paint, the nose hair burning super glue. We used to do that a lot together-- model making. I feel yet another bulging lump sliding up in my throat.

He died when I was eight years old. A brain tumor. I was traumatized, so upset I couldn't go to the funeral. I stormed into the garage and smashed all the models we made together. I screamed that I hated him for doing this-- for dying. I remember my mother trying to hold me, squeezing me against her breasts while I kicked and screamed.

Is that why I'm so obsessed with death and funerals? Am I making up for missing his? It seems so hokey and way too obvious. I start to feel a little panicky. I can't look too closely into this pandora's box of the past right now. There's too much pain. I shove another cookie in my mouth instead, swallow it down along with the lump in my throat.

"Your father loved you very much. You don't have to carry around any guilt-- about anything. You know that?"

About anything? Does she just mean missing my father's funeral or could she possibly mean me and James? The-- the way I am? Is it okay?

I'm afraid I will cry if I try to make any response. Instead I focus on eating another cookie. I chew and swallow mechanically.

I can still see the last model car dad and I made, clear as day in my mind. A black '64 thunderbird with red pinstripes. I remember how he smiled at me when it was finished and we put the car with its still wet paint on a shelf to dry. Then he picked me up and made *vroom vroom* noises as he spun me around in his arms.

On the flight from Seattle I try making conversation with the people sitting beside me. I always request a middle seat. Weird, right? But how else can you get to know people? When I'm not feeling so gloomy, I guess I can be a bit of a talker and I'm excited about the change. I need this. I need a change of scene. I need to get away from death.

I have been talking architecture, that's my passion.

Houses.

Victorian homes are my specialty. It used to drive James crazy. He thought it was boring as hell. Maybe he's right. But I don't care. I love it. Old homes. Wainscoting. Bay windows, Cornices. Entablatures. I could go on and on.

After researching it, I found out that middle-of-nowhere Afton, Georgia is known for some of the finest turn of the century homes in the southeast. An old home guidebook also said it was 'the most haunted town south of the Mason Dixon.'

That's cool, too.

But I don't believe in ghosts.

The place isn't far from Atlanta, so once I get settled in with cousin Alan, I'm going to take a well earned vacation. Might even settle down there. I'm so excited I have butterflies. I may be the only person who gets this giddy over old homes.

Well, the only person under ninety.

I've even been in touch with the president of the Afton Historical Society, a man named Buddy Haygood-- he also owns the Afton hardware, and he has agreed to meet me for lunch when I come up to Afton for a visit.

This is a big deal for me. The president of the Afton Historical Society is going to pick up me-- Kevin Yoo, at the airport. Wow. That might not excite many people.

But wow!

I guess James is right, sometimes I'm a goober.

I was sad about leaving Seattle, leaving my mother, leaving James. But once in the air, I'm feeling a hell of a lot more hopeful. My attitude miraculously improves with the jump in altitude. This is the new beginning I have so desperately needed. It's a huge change for me-- moving all the way across the country. I gave everything away-- all my books, most of my clothes. I threw out all the photos of me and James... well, except one-- of me and him cuddled up in a seat at the top of a ferris wheel. A friend of ours snapped the picture at the county fair. The furniture all belonged to James, anyway, so I didn't have to worry about that. I just packed a bookbag with the bare necessities and left everything else behind.

Nothing ever felt so good as getting rid of it all.

Clearing it out. Letting go.

This is a brand new start. I don't want to take any baggage from my old life with me.

This is the brand new Kevin Yoo.

I've been telling all this to the Japanese kid sitting on my right.

But he is asleep, skateboard propped up between his legs, a Spider-Man Pez dispenser clutched in one hand. The flight attendant didn't agree that the skateboard could be classified as a carry on, but she let him keep it if he promised to stow it under the seat during landing.

His head is lolled over to the right, mouth slack, half open with a little saliva glistening in one corner.

How long has he been asleep?

No telling.

More important, how long have I been talking to him while he's been conked out?

Oh well, I shift in my seat, turn to the lady on my left. She's looking out the window.

"Nice view," I say.

She glances at me, gives me an uncomfortable smile.

That's it-- the slim window of opportunity I need. She might be a good listener.

I start talking houses.

I don't get far.

"I don't mean to be rude, but would you please shut up."

Oh, I get it. She thinks I'm hitting on her.

"Look, I'm, not hitting on you because I'm, uh, you know--" I swallow hard. It's still hard for me to say the word *gay*-- being from a very traditional Korean family and all. It makes me feel fidgety and awkward, short of breath like I might hyperventilate. James always said I was a bit of a closet case. I take a deep breath. Who gives a damn what James thinks?

I didn't pack guilt on this trip, I tell myself. No, sir.

"I'm not uh, well, you know… So there's no situation, see?"

"Let me tell you the *situation*," she says acridly. "That poor Japanese boy," she goes on, "committed suicide somewhere over Phoenix because he realized you were never going to stop talking."

I glance at the kid. He's deep sleep breathing.

"He's just asleep."

She looks irritated.

"You don't do so well with sarcasm, do you?"

"Is that sarcasm?"

"God, I feel sorry for your therapist."

Someone chuckles from the seat in front of me, a man turns, peeks over the top of his seat, says, "Ouch."

"Oh, I don't have a therapist," I tell her.

The woman growls in frustration, turns back to the window.

Oh well, no skin off my back. Not gonna bring me down with their negativity. No sir. Not me. Not Kevin Yoo. This is the new me. Happy go lucky, unconcerned.

"I'm going to see houses," I say matter-of-factly. "It's gonna be great."

I settle back, a smile on my face.

I doze off.

I dream I'm in a dark cave, clawing my way through the mud, panting, desperate, trying to save my life-- and my soul. The walls around me are red, dripping with blood, spider webbed with gorey, pulsing veins. In the darkness I hear a thudding-- like a giant heart, beating somewhere behind me.

Wah-woom. Wah-woom. Wah-woom.

It's coming closer, slithering up behind me. The heart-- it wants to suck me in, absorb me, dissolve me like acid, even my bones. I thrash and claw frantically, trying to make my way up to the small square of dim light. A doorway to salvation. My last shred of hope. It's up ahead. Not far, really, but in my life ending terror it may as well be a million miles off. But I can't get away. I can't reach the light. A thick, drippy vein has lassoed me around the ankle and it's pulling me back to my doom. I slip slide back down against my will into the nasty darkness. I twist around in time to see the monstrous heart throbbing over me. And beyond it a hideous eight legged horror-- a giant, fire-eyed spider with red thorny hairs poking out all over its body. My feet touch the pulsing mass of veins at the heart's quivering base...

The scruff of the plane's tires touching down on the runway jars me awake. I jerk forward, clutching my chest, feeling my own heart pounding inside my ribcage.
wah-woom, wah-woom, wah-woom...
The woman and the Japanese kid are both looking at me.
I'm dripping with sweat. Did I scream?
The Japanese kid is staring hard at me, giving me a knowing look-- almost a smile? He has the Spider-Man Pez dispenser in his hand. He flips back Spidey's head and pops a Pez, crunches one, then two before stuffing the dispenser back in his pocket. Slowly, he hitches his thumbs together, makes a creepy crawly motion with his fingers like a spider.
How does he know?

Cousin Alan picks me up at the airport. He pulls up at the sidewalk in his bright red sportster, *Journey* blaring from the radio, rag top down. He blows the horn way more than necessary, waves wildly, shouts my name.
"Kev-- Kev meister! What's up, little man?"
He hops out of the car and I see he's wearing a tank top that says *'Chick magnet.'* He has biceps that bulge like tree trunks and an oriental dragon tattoo on his left arm. He wears thick, nerdy glasses, but Alan is no nerd. His shirt, as much as I hate to admit it-- is correct. There's an expression about getting more ass than a toilet seat and I'm pretty sure that saying was invented for Alan.
It wasn't always that way. When we were little kids, he was fat. They used to call him *doughboy*. Maybe that's why he works out so hard now. He's determined to be the Korean Hercules, flawless in body if not in mind.
"What's up cuz!" he shouts, giving me a bear hug that threatens to splinter my ribs.
"Where's all your shit?"
"This is it," I say.
He holds me at arm's length, shakes his head, big, goofy grin spreading across his face. "Welcome to Atlanta, bro!"
With one arm around me, he half drags me to the car.

I stay with Alan for a month. He's a good guy, he really is. A little messy, maybe-- *month-expired-milk-in-the-fridge* kind of guy. But he is probably the best natured guy you'll ever meet. He'll do anything for you, give you the shirt off his back if you asked. It's amazing how caring and thoughtful he is after the shitty childhood he had. My uncle was an abusive alcoholic and beat him regularly. Alan always had bruises, but he never admitted where they came from, who gave the black and blue marks to him. But I knew.

It broke my heart as a kid. Breaks my heart now, as an adult, to see how he has refused to be destroyed by that painful past. He just keeps plugging along, smiling, offering kindness after kindness to others for every painful memory he still struggles with, probably.

If there's anybody I wish I could be more like, it's cousin Alan.

While I'm there, Alan tries really hard to get me out of my shell-- a little too hard. He always makes sure when he introduces me to his friends that he tells them I'm gay.

"Really, really gay," he says.

Everybody laughs sincerely, except me. I fake it as best as I can, like I'm comfortable in my own skin, when I'm really not.

Everything about being around Alan and his friends is awkward for me, but he's trying hard to "get me laid," as he says. I try to tell him it's not necessary, that I don't want to date right now, but he just laughs it off, can't believe that not everyone has a twenty four hour erection like him. "Man, little cuz," he says, "just let Alan work his magic, 'kay?-- get you some dickercise! I made that word up, by the way."

"You must be so proud."

"I am. Whenever you say it, you have to pay me a quarter. It's copyrighted."

"Alan, I can promise you, I'll never owe you a quarter, because I will never say the word *'dickercise'.*"

"But you just did."

I want to get mad at the blockhead. He's so annoying. But I know that he's doing it for me, earnestly looking out for me, constantly forcing me off the couch to take me to some weird, seedy bar in midtown. So I really can't be too irritated. I try to get into the city scene, I really do, more for his sake than my own, I guess. Alan makes me go out way more than I normally would, drags me out to every smoke filled dive bar in the city. It's either I go with him or I get an excruciating five minute noogie. I feel like a tag along, a fifth wheel. His friends are nice, but way too social for my tastes-- and loud. God are they loud. Drinkers. Party harders. The stay up 'til five AM and *drag-yourself-to-work-with-a-horrendous-zombie-hangover* type.

I go along with it, thinking it will take my mind off James and the past. But I just can't get into it-- the city. I need some space. Literal open space-- trees, peace and quiet. I can't count the number of times I've had to sleep with a pillow over my head to drown out the sound of Alan banging whatever blonde girl he has picked up that night at a bar. He has a thing for blondes.

But more than anything else, I need to see some old houses. That was my plan all along. I've been in touch with Buddy Haygood a few times. I've told him how excited I am to come visit Afton, how I'm planning on doing some writing-- a book on old homes of the south. I told him I was a nurse and when he found out I was looking to get out of the city for good, he was kind enough to recommend me to Abel Crickshaw, the local doctor. Turns out, they need a nurse in Afton. What are the chances?

I'm so excited I can hardly think straight.

I sit down on the couch, after gingerly removing a random bra out of the way and tell Alan I'm moving to Afton-- where I will never have to move strange women's undergarments off the sofa before sitting down.

"Afton? Never heard of it," Alan says, laying on his workout bench, breathing heavy as he struggles with the ba-gillion ton weights he's bench pressing. "And why would you want to live in some booneys place like that, anyways?"

"Houses," I say, brightening up. "Old houses are a passion of mine. I've done some research and Afton is supposed to have a lot of beautiful old Victorian homes. This might just be the change I need."

Alan's been giving me grief about my old homes tour book ever since I moved in-- *old home porn*, he called it, telling me I'd rather stay in and jerk off over old houses than go out and get laid by a living, breathing human being.

It may have been a little unsettling to him that I never denied this.

"Sounds boring as shit, man," he says. The weights clang down. He takes a breath in, heaves them up again.

"Maybe my step dad was right," I say feeling a little irritable with him for dismissing my passion.

"What-- let me guess, did he call me a knuckle head?" There's a strain in his voice as he keeps the weights suspended over his head a few beats. I can almost hear him sweating.

"Meat head, actually."

The weights slam down again.

"I have feelings too, y'know," he pants, turning to look at me. His voice sounds heart broken, but he's smiling. Alan is absolutely indefatigable at all times and impervious to insult.

I can't help smiling back.

"Man, I'm gonna miss you," he says and means it.

"I'll see you soon enough." It's a possible lie. "Just let me get settled and you can come up for coffee."

"Hell yeah-- and," he says with a mischievous grin, "bang me some small town chicks."

"You're such a troglodyte."

"What's that?"

"A cave dweller."

"Hey man, you're the one who never leaves his room."

"Fair enough."

"When are you moving out?"

"Tommorow."

I say it a little too fast and eager maybe.

"That soon, huh?"

He seems a little hurt. I guess he thinks I've been having the time of my life living here. I don't want to hurt his feelings, so I try to lie and say I've had a really good time staying with him.

He can tell it's not true and he hangs his head.

"I'm grateful for your hospitality, Alan, I am, really. Don't get me wrong."

And it's the truth, but I don't know what else to say to make him feel better so I turn all business like. "So, um, I'll need to pay you for letting me stay here."

"Not a chance dingleberry," he says, brightening up again. "If you even think about pulling out your checkbook, I'll punch you in the nuts."

He runs over, puts me in a headlock and gives me a playful-- yet, scalp abrading noogie.

"Quit!" I shout. "You're sweaty. It's disgusting!"

"Now, are you gonna try and pay me for living here?"

"No," I say, voice muffled by his gigantic arm. "Now let go."

"I can't hear you," he says in a sing song voice.

"No!" I shout.

He lets me go, laughing. "That's better."

Not only is Alan endlessly positive, he is generous beyond measure. He refuses to take a penny from me for staying here-- won't even hear about it. It's really annoying when you think about it.

I take a moment to smooth down my hair (he messed up my meticulous part) and wipe his gross sweat off my face. I straighten my glasses, too.

"You could have broken my glasses. They're not cheap, you know."

"You're such a nerd, Kevin. Man, I was *this close* to getting you laid, cuz."

"Shh," I say, dialing the number for Afton's roadside extended stay-- the Sleepy Time Motel. "I have to make a reservation for a room. Did you know they have extended stay rates." I sound way too enthusiastic.

He chuckles. "You get excited over the dumbest things, Kevie, you know that?"

He goes back to lifting weights, trying not to clang them as loud while I'm on the phone.

"Anyways, do you think that's really the best move for-- you know, someone like you?"

"Someone like me? What do you mean?" I say testily.

I know what he means, though.

"A gayfer-- duh."

He stops lifting weights. I can tell he is thinking how to say something without hurting my feelings. "Small town. Lots of oakies. You're repressed enough as it is. Haven't you ever seen *Deliverance?*"

"Oh, come on."

He sits up, shrugs, mops his brow. "Just saying."

"Anyway, I've already got a job interview with Dr. Crickshaw."

"Crickshaw? His name is Crickshaw? Creepy. Seriously, Kevin, you'd do a lot better in the city-- someone like you."

There it is again-- *Someone like you.*

"That's why I moved. I needed to get out of the city."

"You did. This is a whole new city."

"I need my own space. I can't listen to you screwing anymore random blonde sluts. Now be quiet, Alan, please."

"What's wrong with blond slu-- er, women? You just wish you had a chance with the Alan monster." He makes lewd thrusting gestures with his crotch and in a girlie voice cries, "Oh, cousin Alan give it to me-- forbidden love! Yes! Yes! *YEEEESSS!*"

He ends with a horrific squeal and starts laughing like crazy.

"Alan, you're disgusting."

But I can't help smiling a little. He's wearing a tank top that says, *'I'm with stupid.'* with an arrow pointing down towards his crotch.

"Ugh," I say. I dial the number for the Sleepy Time Motel, look away out the window.

Alan sees it's a lost cause, gets up, shakes his head. He leans against the fridge, gulps down what appears to be a gallon sized protein shake, wipes his mouth on the back of his hand, then says to me in an *oh-well* kind of voice, "You're gonna get butt raped."

PART III

AFTON, GEORGIA, JUNE 1993

The soul has illusions as the bird has wings: it is supported by them.
--Victor Hugo

I RENT A CAR the next morning, a beat up '85 civic covered with more rust than paint.

Alan drives me to the rent-a-car place, gives me another of his trademark gigantic, bone crushing bear hugs before I climb into the car. He looks genuinely sad and I realize I'm really going to miss the big goof. He's so large and full of life. He's a bright shining sun. I'm a gloomy cloud. I feel a little envious of him, his ability to be so positive all the time.

"Stay in touch," he says. "I mean it. Don't make me come up there and put you in the torture wrack."

I nod, check the atlas one more time. I already have the route highlighted.

He's wearing another cut off t-shirt. This one has a ghoulish, gore splattered zombie head on it. No text.

"Alan, do you even own any shirts with sleeves?"

Alan gives it a second's serious consideration. "No-- wait... yes, why?"

I just shake my head and drive off.

I leave the congestion of the city behind and head north about forty miles on I-75 before turning off the interstate onto a four lane highway. With the city behind me, I can feel the tension draining out of my shoulders. I let out a long building sigh. For all my expectations, though, the view around me proves disillusioningly bland, uninspiring and dismal. I pass a string of depressing, anonymous strip malls and the grandiose entrances to subdivisions with pretentious names like Plantation Oaks Estate-- where there's not a single oak in sight. Nor any other trees at all for that matter. The brainless, land developing, earth rapers have seen to that. Sight of those treeless streets lined with soulless, ostentatious brick monstrosities makes me cringe.

A wasteland.

Depressing. They tear down the trees, the old homes. They kill the spirit of a place. A big red mud nightmare, if you ask me.

After half an hour, I make the turn off to Afton.

It's a magic moment-- that simple right hand turn. A new world is just one blinker click away.

It seems like the rest of the world fades away when I leave the highway behind with its soulless modernity. The strip malls and cookie cutter houses vanish. The road is lined now with sweet scented pines. The hills close in behind me and suddenly I am entering a secret place, a land cut off from the rest of time.

A dream world.

The hills on either side are choked with kudzu. It strangles the trees and drips from their branches, spilling down towards the road like mother nature's salad flood. Up on my right, is an outlying farm, its field weedy and overgrown with shin high grass. An old tractor is sitting out in the middle of the field and behind it, a white farmhouse and withered, grey barn. The split rail fence is nearly hidden from view by a tangle of wildflowers and weeds-- black eyed susans, carolina tickseed and queen anne's lace. Butterflies flutter amongst the blossoms.

I roll down my window to catch a whiff of the sweet scented breeze.

I pass a run down junk store and an auto shop on the roadside, followed shortly by a scrapyard and a ramshackle fruit stand advertising garden fresh tomatoes and hot boiled peanuts. I've never had boiled peanuts. I didn't know they were boilable. So naturally, I have to stop.

It's going to be a hot day, I can feel it the moment I open the car door. But it's not quite there yet. Like an oven, this day is still preheating. Cicadas are trilling in the woods nearby, chorus swelling with the mounting heat. A muddy creek threads through the pine thicket, burbling in shadows. The place is pervaded by a mossy kind of quiet, like the kind you might find in an old graveyard.

There's a man sitting in a rocking chair out front. He's wearing overalls and a nearly shapeless grey fedora with about a million fishing lures stuck in the hat band. On his feet are a pair of worn out flip flops. He looks up at me, nods. With his olive complexion and long black hair he looks at least half Indian-- Cherokee, probably. His bright green eyes are a bit startling.

"Hey there, how's it going?" he says.

"Good," I tell him.

"They're a gift-- from my mother."

"Beg pardon?"

"My eyes. She had Irish ancestry."

"Oh."

"Gonna be a hot one."

"Yes, sir."

"Hot as pajamas."

"What's that mean?"

He grins. "Just something I made up. PJ's always make me sweat."

I tell him I've never had boiled peanuts before. He squints at me, gets up, scoops me up a styrofoam cup full of steaming boiled peanuts from a pot behind him then hands me the cup.

"What do you think?" the man says.

I chew thoughtfully for a moment. "They're interesting."

Earthy tasting.

He just laughs.

I pop another and then another. "Actually, they're really good."

This could be a new addiction for me.

When I offer to pay, he shakes his head, tells me they're on the house.

"The first one, you know, it's always free."

I say, "Thanks a million," tell him how excited I am about exploring this sleepy, little town.

"It's gonna be just how I pictured it. Fine, old houses. Barbeques at the beach. Games of horseshoes. Lemonade. Sweet tea."

"Just like Norman Rockwell?"

"Exactly. You read my mind."

"You know, kid, things aren't always what they seem."

Back in the car, I keep heading down the road. Up ahead it dips down between rising hills and a little ways off I catch a glimpse of sunlight on water. The trees thin out and I drive out of the woods into bright sunlight. A broad lake stretches out before me, its waters mottled greenish brown like a trout's back.

I cross a bridge over Lake Afton and looking out the window I see the waters sparkling in the early summer sun. The lake is speckled with fishing boats. There are people on the docks and also splashing in the water. On the opposite shore of the lake, beyond the forest of cattails and reeds, I can see, through the breaks in the trees-- the green, featureless uniformity of a golf course, with, here and there, a red gash of earth showing next to construction equipment where *'progress'* is being made.

And beyond, far away, I catch a glimpse of a barren hill just past the tree line, looming above the sloping golf course. And rising from the hill--

--a House.

It rears up like a dream, terrible, frightening and beautiful-- deep in shadow, even in the midday sun. It appears to be a desolate ruin. It broods in the distance, lurking like a beast… waiting to be fed a blood sacrifice.

Where did that crazy thought come from? A man eating house? Guess I'm just hungry is all and a little sleep deprived. I was so excited last night, I couldn't sleep. Tossed and turned all night, trying to picture every detail of my new and perfect life.

My civic rattles over the bridge and I crane my neck to get one last look at the house before it is lost to sight among the spiny treetops. Up ahead, I make one final turnoff onto a short twisty road which puts me out right onto Main Street, just a little south from the main part of town.

The guard rail here is dented pretty bad and there is a small makeshift white cross lying propped against it in a bed of dying handcut flowers, testament to some unfortunate car crash on this little corkscrew of a road.

Beyond the curve, a shady, tree lined street unfurls before me. It runs parallel to an old stretch of railroad tracks. And everywhere-- there's something green-- oaks, a few drippy willows, magnolias with white blossoms, spindly dogwoods. An old brick church appears on my right. The sign out front reads, *'Jesus is Alive.'* Next door is a big white house that has been converted into a funeral home. I keep driving, excitement mounting. I pass by house after house. Some real beauties. Grand old ladies sitting far back from the road, their pointed gables peeking out secretively through the trees. I have a hard time keeping my eyes on where I'm going. I've got a case of the butterflies already.

Farther ahead, Main Street is lined on either side with early nineteenth century brick buildings. The shops and stores have big glass windows with bright awnings. People are strolling lazily here and there in the midsummer day.

I've driven right into a living Norman Rockwell painting. This is it. This is an honest to God Grover's Corners. Anytown USA. I had no idea these kind of places existed anymore.

I feel my heart lightening and I smile.

Welcome home, Kevin Yoo.

I check in at the Sleepy Time Motel, drop my things off in my room and decide the first order of business is a walking tour. It's just after one o'clock in the afternoon. I was so excited the night before, I couldn't sleep. But I feel completely refreshed now.

The houses-- I gotta see 'em.

I'm supposed to meet Buddy Haygood at four that afternoon. That's three hours away. And I'm too excited to just sit in my room at the motel, so I decide to take a little stroll around town. I wander around, up and down random streets for about three hours, pausing here and there to take in the sights.

The railroad tracks run parallel to Main Street and I follow them north a bit, enjoying the beautiful, soul refreshing peace of this midsummer morning. The grass is high in places and dotted with fuzzy yellow dandelions and sprinklings of wild strawberries. I pass an old blue bungalow house. It's a pretty home, but badly in need of a repairs. The paint is peeling off in scabrous flecks. The grass is knee high in places.

There's a veritable jungle of growth surrounding it, a riot of weeds and encroaching azalea bushes badly in need of pruning have closed in around the house, threatening to swallow it whole. The yard is littered with trash, shreds of old newspapers, rusty tin cans and crinkled up plastic bags. A half dozen ancient pecan trees have dropped so many branches in the yard, it looks, in places, like somebody is building a barricade.

"What are you staring at?"

The rasping voice startles me and I realize there is an old woman, probably in her mid seventies, staring-- no, glaring at me from the front porch-- eyes brimming with gorgon flame.

"Sorry," I say, making a tentative apology, but she's having none of it.

She raises her arm, flings something at me. She's a damned good shot, too, because the projectile hits me in the side of the head, stings like crazy.

I look down at my feet.

A pinecone.

I'm so stunned I don't know quite how to respond. No one has ever thrown a pinecone at me before. I reach up, rub the side of my head, straighten my glasses which the well lobbed nature-grenade has knocked askew.

"Hey, what'd you do that for? You could've knocked my eye out! What's wrong with-- "

Before I can finish, she rears back again, aiming another pinecone.

I bolt. It's not worth losing an eye.

"That's right, run you little yellow bastard-- Run! You're all gonna burn." Her voice is a roar. "*AALLL YOU DIRTY FUCKERS!*"

Behind me, she goes on shouting, screaming at me in words I don't understand, almost like she's intoning the devil and attempting to bring a world ending curse crashing down on my head. I catch a few snatches including, "Agruun… Unglit… Old Ones."

It's the ravings of a crazy person. I glance back to make sure she isn't following me. She flings another pinecone, but I'm well out of range. She's still shouting, almost foaming at the mouth.

I run a few hundred feet, stop to catch my breath, decide to cut back across the railroad tracks and head to a safer part of town. I can't believe it, I've been here less than one day and I've already been attacked. How crazy is that? I have to admit, it's an ominous prelude to my new life and yet, for some odd reason, it doesn't bother me all that much.

Afterwards, convinced that I'm safe once more, I wander up and down another street just trying to take it all in, enforce some positivity after the unsettling encounter with that fiery eyed harpy. I pass by a much nicer looking lady. She is wearing a floppy, wide brimmed sun hat and watering her tomato plants. She must be concerned because she says on my third pass, "Excuse me young man, are you lost?"

"No ma'am," I say with a goofy grin on my face. I hold up my Afton old homes guide book. "Just admiring all the houses."

Her face brightens. "Ohhh, an old house lover, huh? You'll fit right in here. They're something, aren't they? Did you know that General Sherman stopped here during the Civil War, stayed right here, the scoundrel-- in Afton, overnight, before he made his infamous march to the sea. He tied his horse up, right over there, across the street-- at that tree. The one next to the railroad tracks by the depot."

I look across at the old oak. "Wow, I didn't know that."

"Well, it's true."

The woman looks suddenly unhappy. There's a flyer stapled to a tree at the edge of her yard. I glance at it.

IF YOU SEE A CAT-- KILL A CAT. YOUR LIFE MAY DEPEND ON IT!

I read it twice. Surely it doesn't say what I think it says... does it?

"Those rednecks," says the woman. She reaches out, rips the flier off the tree, wads it up. She smiles and tells me, "Nevermind that. Just some hoodlums."

I nod, but catch a seemingly nervous glimpse in her eyes.

"Oh my," she says. "Did you know you're bleeding."

I reach up, touch the side of my head. When I look at my fingertips they're stained with blood.

"Oh, yeah, a lady-- she, um, she threw a pinecone at me."

The woman looks suddenly exasperated. "Vera Griswick," she says through clenched teeth. "Don't mind her, she's the town crazy... well, one of 'em, anyway. Some towns have more than most, y'know. Lord knows we have our share. I am *so sorry*, sweetheart."

She pulls a kleenex out of her pocket, starts dabbing at the scrape on the side of my head-- very motherly.

"Ah, it's nothing, really. It just surprised me is all."

"That woman's just a crazy, old bitch-- pardon my language. I hope that doesn't ruin your impression of our town."

"No, really, it hasn't."

"Would you like a band aid."

"I think I'll be okay. But thanks anyway."

My stomach rumbles suddenly and I realize, other than the handful of boiled peanuts, I haven't eaten anything since the pack of cheese crackers I had for breakfast. I don't like to eat too much before traveling in case, you know, I have to poop. I say bye to the lady and head on.

Luckily I'm not far from Main Street and a few blocks away I see a silver sign that says, 'Birdie's Diner.' That's where I'm supposed to meet Buddy. I check my watch. It's almost four.

I can't help but notice that there are other fliers like the one I saw stapled to the telephone poles and taped to lamp posts all up and down the street.

IF YOU SEE A CAT...

What's more, there's a monster of a pickup truck parked diagonally in the middle of Main Street, taking up both lanes. It's as big as a tank and painted black, but there's so much mud spattered all over it, it looks brown at the moment. There are a pair of giant bull horns bolted to the grill. A few red necky types are standing in the street, including a red faced guy wearing reflective state trooper shades. He's giving orders to the other guys-- a kid with a marijuana tattoo on his shoulder and an older dude with a ponytail and a million jailhouse tats covering his arms. They're all three wearing work gloves and the jailhouse guy has a shovel. He scoops up a bloody cat's corpse off the roadside. The kid holds open a five gallon sized ziploc bag and the guy with the shovel dumps it in.

I catch a glimpse of the body as he shovels it in. It looks horrifying, more like a lizard than a cat with great clumps of fur missing from its scabrous skin.

"Careful, careful," says the red faced man. "Don't get any on you."

The kid seals the bag.

"Alright, let's get a move on," the guy with the tats shouts. "Some of these bastards got away."

"Man, I thought that was the last one," says the Marijuana leaf kid.

"Nope. Not by a long shot."

"Aw, shit."

"Aw, shit is right," says the guy with the ponytail. "Mildred Butters thinks she saw about half a dozen of these critters disappear down a manhole on Chestnut Avenue and you know what that means-- they're in the sewers."

They climb back into the monster truck. It roars to life and they drive off down the street, slowing down every few feet-- looking, I guess, for more dead cats.

There's a Japanese man in a tattered coat standing a little ways down the road, on the opposite side of the street from me, near the railroad tracks. He watches the truck pass, too. Then he turns and looks at me for a long moment.

Standing there in his heavy, dust covered boots and his weatherbeaten black trenchcoat, he looks like a lone gunslinger out of a sci-fi spaghetti western. A complete anomaly in this town. There's a white scar above his left eye, breaking his eyebrow in half. His hair hangs down to his shoulders. The black is streaked with grey.

I'm hit with a major wave of deja vu.

I can't help but feel like I've seen him somewhere before, but I can't place where. I could almost swear to it, though-- I know this man.

He reaches in his coat pocket, still watching me, pulls out a Spider-Man Pez dispenser and pops a Pez in his mouth. His expression-- it looks like he's trying to figure me out, too-- how he knows me.

Then he turns abruptly and walks away.

The eerie dream feeling I have fades and I shrug off the encounter, keep walking down the street.

I arrive at the diner a few minutes before Buddy, puzzling over the strange things I've seen this morning. I have the sneaking suspicion this town might not be as boring as people might think. It's burgers and fries and breakfast all day at Birdie's. I've already read about it in my guidebook. The smell of hamburgers frying wafts out of the front door and my mouth starts watering. But I resist the overwhelming urge to go in and order something to eat. I sit down instead on the bench outside and wait, thumbing aimlessly through my guide book all the while. About ten minutes later, Buddy pulls up in a rumbling blue 1964 Chevrolet with cattle rails in the back. The bed of the truck is full of haybales. He shuts off the engine and opens the creaky door. He catches a glimpse of me biting my lip, laughs, says, "Don't you worry. She's got it where it counts. I've had this sweetheart thirty years. She's lasted longer than both my wives."

I don't know if it's a joke until he laughs.

I have a good feeling about Buddy.

Yup, Kevin, you made the right decision coming here.

This is a fresh start.

And if anyone ever needed a fresh start, it's you.

"You must be Kevin Yoo."

"Yes, sir."

"You're probably wondering how I knew that," he says with a wink. "Well Kevin, welcome to Afton."

"Thank you so much. I really do appreciate it."

I shake his hand, tell him how glad I am to meet him, how glad for his generosity in taking time to see me. He waves it away.

"No trouble at all. Delighted to have you, Kevin. You don't find many young folks like yourself interested in these fine old homes."

My stomach gives another strained rumble.

He chuckles, says, "Was that yours or mine? C'mon, let me treat you to fine dining-- Afton style."

I can't argue with that.

There's a rustling from amongst the haybales and a pig thrusts its snout out from between the rails with a grunt.

I've always been a little jumpy and the sudden appearance of the pig startles me.

Buddy chuckles, scratches the pig's prickly chin. "Easy there, she won't bite. This is just Ruby. Say hello to Kevin, girl."

The pig snorts.

"Hello," I say awkwardly. I pause. "What about-- I mean-- should we--"

"Bring her inside? Naw, I tried that once, it didn't go so well. Don't worry, she'll be fine. I'll bring you a burger, sweetheart."

He opens the door for me and the chimes jangle. He exchanges *hellos* with all the locals at the counter and introduces me, too.

"This here is Kevin Yoo, future five star author of-- and expert on, old homes in the South."

I blush at the overly generous compliment.

"Welcome to the original greasy spoon," the waitress says cheerfully, coffee pot in hand. "Truth be told, it's not just the spoon that's greasy," says Buddy.

"That's for sure," the waitress agrees.

We slide into a booth by the front window, right in the sun. Buddy tells me to order anything I like-- his treat.

"I'll know if you're skimping," he says with a wink.

"I have a big appetite, just so you know."

"Fair enough, I've been duly warned."

I get a double order of hash browns, six sausages, two fried eggs a short stack of blueberry pancakes, a bowl of cheese grits, a glass of fresh squeezed orange juice and a cup off coffee. The waitress throws in a complimentary plate of fried green tomatoes-- another native delicacy which I am only too happy to sample-- um, wolf down.

Buddy looks at me wide eyed. "You weren't kidding."

"Nope," I tell him, then to the waitress, "Is there pie?"

Buddy shakes his head, chuckling, holds up two fingers, meaning a slice for him, as well.

The waitress frowns. "Buddy, you're not supposed to have sugar. Janice said so."

But he waves her away. "Beverly, what Janice doesn't know won't hurt her."

Buddy is not only the head of the Afton Historical Society, he also owns the local feed and seed. He's what you'd call an old timer. His family goes back four generations in Afton, right back to the founding in 1832. He's genuine, gregarious and full of local lore. And happy to share every one of Afton's old time stories with me. We talk town history a long time. Thank God, he's also a natural born talker-- like me! Nothing like that frigid woman on the plane.

"Us talkers-- we have to stick together," says Buddy. "Ain't nothing wrong with a little gab."

"Man, this is great," I tell him, one cheek chipmunk stuffed full of hash browns. "You should have seen the people on the plane. I couldn't get a word out of them. So harsh, y'know?"

Buddy shakes his head. "Unbelievable. All these people, y'know, they're in too big of a goddamn hurry. That's the problem. Too big for their britches, my daddy would say."

"I know, right?"

I take a big gulp of coffee.

"Well, you're in luck." He points at me. "I don't know anybody who's in a damn hurry around here."

"What a relief. You know Mr. Haygood--"

"Buddy," he says. "Mr. Haygood was my father."

"Yes sir. You know, Buddy, it's nice to make a friend." And I mean it.

Buddy slaps the table top, says, "Shoot yeah."

We clink coffee cups.

There's nothing like it, I tell you, breakfast for dinner and a friendly stranger to chat with about small town secrets. And Buddy, man, he knows everything about Afton-- every ghost story, every skeleton in every closet.

"Small towns are like that," he tells me. "Dull, mundane, at first, but once you scratch the surface--" He gives a low whistle. "Watch out."

"The most haunted town south of the Mason Dixon."

Buddy laughs when I mention the phrase.

"Well, we do have our share of ghosts. More than most places, I reckon."

He seems stoically proud of the fact in a Southern Gothic kind of way.

I remember the cat murdering fliers, figure there's an interesting story behind that. So I ask Buddy, "I saw some fliers-- about cats. And I couldn't help noticing-- well, a clean up going on outside. What's, um, what's that all about?"

Buddy looks a little uncomfortable, shifts in his seat, figuring the best way to answer my question. "That, ah, that's nothing. Just, uh, had a weird case of what you might call rabies lately, affected almost all the cats in town. Damndest thing. Outta the blue. But it's nothing to worry about. We got it all under control. Those signs are something Ray Riggs and his boys plastered all over town. He got a little gung ho about the clean up, if you know what I mean." He clears his throat and I can tell that he is anxious to change the subject.

"So it's houses, huh? That's your passion. Well, I'll tell you, Kevin, we've got us some nice ones here in Afton. Yes, sir. Grand old ladies."

I smile. He understands.

"Yes, I want to see every single one of them."

Buddy sips his coffee, when he speaks, his tone is full of distant memories. "Well, maybe not every one."

"Oh, but I do. I saw one as I was driving over the bridge-- just the tip of the roof in the sun. It was a big house-- big as a dang mountain--"

"A monster of a house," Buddy interrupts and then a little quieter. "A *reeal* monster."

It's an odd way to put it. *A Monster*. And it seems, for a moment, anyway, like there's a shadow across the table and Buddy's face. For a split second, I remember my dream on the plane. I can almost hear a thud like the beating of a dead, black heart, causing the coffee cups to rattle in their saucers. The moment passes and the shadow flies away. The coffee cups are still. But Buddy is right. Yeah, it was pretty gigantic. A monster. Even from that distance I could tell she was a big one-- a castle of a house sitting all alone at the top of that bare, pine ringed hill.

"Man, I'd like to get a look inside that one."

Buddy cuts me off quick. "Nah, you don't want to bother with that one. There's been some unfortunate disappearances up there through the years, sorry to say. It's a mess. Falling to pieces. Nothing to see there. Not anymore." He catches my eye, wants to make sure I've heard what he's said. He gets his wallet out, pays for our lunch. He won't even let me leave a tip.

We make plans to see each other again at the next meeting of the Afton Historical Society. He tells me I'll be the guest of honor.

"After all, it's not often we have a budding author in our midst. Enjoy your time here in Afton," he says, getting up. "There's plenty of lovely sights here in town. But take an old timer's advice, will ya? Don't go messin' with that house on Witcher Street. I don't want to sound gloomy, but it's got a bad reputation. Lots of bad memories."

I thank him, sit at the table a few minutes more.

Witcher Street…

…Of course, now that I know where the house is, I have to go find it--

--right?

PART IV

THE HOUSE ON WITCHER STREET

I am like a small creature swallowed whole by a monster... and the monster feels my tiny little movements inside
--Shirley Jackson
The Haunting of Hill House

S HE'S UNLIKE ANYTHING I've ever seen before. No house before, nothing else in Afton-- no house in my dreams, even comes close. If the Biltmore Estate and the Addams' Family Mansion had a child-- this would be it.

It's taken me over an hour and a half to hike across town and find her. I'm panting, out of breath, baked dry by the hot Georgia sun. Still, miserable as I should be, looking up at her, I've never been so happy, so intrigued, so overwhelmed.

So tempted with strange desires.

She reigns alone at the top of a hill, towers rising, gabled roofs tilted at crazy angles into the air. The sky behind blushes with the first hint of twilight. Far away, down the hill behind her I can see the encroaching edge of the Cobblestone Acres Golf Course and beyond-- the glimmer of late afternoon sun on the waters of Lake Afton.

It's hard to describe why she casts such a spell. It's not just her size-- the promise of numberless rooms waiting to be explored beyond those ivy covered walls. It's the way she stands there, aloof and proud, like a queen-- cold and cruel. No other houses are worthy of her company, so she stands alone.

"Quite a sight, is she not?"

I hadn't seen the man standing there. His voice startles me, snaps me out of my revelry, my trance.

He's leaning on the wrought iron fence, casting an adoring glance up at the house. His mistress. He looks at me, gives me a cold corpse's sort of smile. And his appearance? --stern, formidable, imposing, like a villain out of a Hammer Horror film. I swallow.

"Sorry to have startled you," he says, voice deep, like it's echoing up out of a deep mossy well.

He's a tall man, angular and sparsely fleshed as a living skeleton, dressed in a black suit like some sort of vampiric Edwardian butler. Hot clothes for this kind of weather, but he doesn't seem bothered. I'm sweating after the long hike across town, but his face is as grey and cool as clay-- gaunt as a vulture, too-- protruding cheekbones casting shadows on his sallow flesh. His iron grey hair is slicked back on his head, looks brittle like it might crack if you pressed on it too hard.

There's something regal about the man, imperious and cold, even-- like he is an extension of the house. Untouched, even at midday, by the warmth of the southern June sun.

"No, I was just-- it's just--"

"I know. She has that effect on some people."

"I saw it-- the house--"

"Her," the man is quick to correct me. "You must never be familiar or disrespectful to royalty. Houses, too. She won't tolerate it. She doesn't... suffer fools."

I know he's right.

"They're alive, you know. Some houses."

I know. Have always known. James didn't get it. This guy-- he understands.

"I saw... Her-- from across the bridge. Funny. She looked, at first, like a ruin."

He is quick to correct me. "A trick of the light, I'm sure."

"I'm Kevin."

I offer him my hand eagerly. He stiffens, looks at it as if the gesture is a distasteful one.

"Yes, I know. My name is Arthur Cranston." The coldness dissolves and he is friendly, welcoming again in an instant, salesman slick, almost. "I saw you admiring the house. I thought I would come down to say hello. We offer tours, you know."

It's a long way up that hill and I don't remember seeing him come down the path.

He smiles again, can see that I'm still under the spell.

"Houses," he says proudly. "You like them. I can tell. That's why you've come." He pauses then, as if deciding whether or not to let me in on a secret. He leans forward confidential now. "You heard her calling."

I nod.

I've got that dream feeling again, moving slow like I'm underwater.

"I heard about you from Buddy Haygood. You're Kevin Yoo, lover of fine homes. Well, sir, there's no finer house than this-- in Afton or elsewhere." He reaches up, strokes his chin as if he's just had a novel idea, looks up at me smiling, certain what he has to say will please. "Won't you come inside, young man?"

He opens the gate. The iron hinges groan painfully. I nod, step through. The gate clangs shut behind us. Cranston extends his arm motioning me on and I start walking.

It's a long walk up the hill, but I don't notice. It feels like the house is drawing me effortlessly up to meet her, tugging me along at the end of an invisible thread. Along the path, I notice spiders, lots of them, hundreds upon hundreds of the little bastards, crawling like they're on some sort of mass exodus, or a pilgrimage, rather, because it looks like the many legged horde is making its creepy crawly way up towards the house at the top of the hill. The line is almost unbroken all along the path.

There's a spider on my shoulder, not a big one, but enough to give me the heebie jeebies. I've never been a big fan of anything with more than two legs. I flick it off, and reflexively raise my foot to stomp it, but Cranston's hand falls on my wrist, clamps like a vice. I look up to see him staring at me with an *if-you-dare* look. His voice tolls like a iron bell.

"Be nice to spiders," he says. "And they will be nice to you."

I nod. The spider will live.

I turn my gaze to…

…Her.

I have never believed in love at first sight.

Until now.

I follow Cranston up the front steps. The house looms up, a mountain of timber and stone casting its gloomy shadow over my head. I shiver.

Cranston pushes open the huge oak door, stands back, arm extended once more, welcoming me, letting me step inside first.

What does the house look like inside?

It's hard to say. There are the obvious things, of course-- the grand staircase, just inside, sweeping up into impenetrable shadows above, high windows with leaded frames, dark wainscoting, heavy old furniture. The only specific thing I can recall is a large dark oil painting in a gilded frame. It's badly in need of cleaning, and I have a little trouble making out the figure of a dour looking woman, severe as sin, in a black dress staring down at me, her corpse pale hands-- fingers unnaturally long-- long as knitting needles with too many joints, clasped in front of her. It's almost like she wasn't there a minute ago, but now that I'm looking, she has materialized out of a netherworld miasma to chill my blood with her foreboding eyes. It's her eyes, alone, that show up startlingly clear-- bone white even, against the chiaroscuro shadows swirling around her. They seem to glow maliciously as I pass beneath, sparking with wicked life.

"Wow, she looks, um, pretty tough."

Cranston stares sourly at me. Maybe it's a painting of his mother.

Fearing I've offended him, I change the subject quickly. This place-- I want to know everything, the whole history of the house from the beginning-- the very, very beginning.

He chuckles, "All in good time, Kevin Yoo. All in good time." He leads me down the main hall into a room with an enormous marble fireplace, offers me a seat in one of two gigantic antique chairs that look like medieval thrones. About a hundred and fifty creepy ass animal heads are mounted on the walls. Lions, tigers, bears-- oh my. And also zebras, deer, an owl, a fifteen foot rattlesnake and even a giant crab. And I have the weirdest feeling that they are all staring down at me with their dead, glass eyes. But anytime I glance up at them, they seem to be looking the other way.

"So many questions. So eager to know. That's so nice-- so nice. I'll tell you everything, but first," he gives me a wink, "how about a drink?"

I think he means water, at first. And I'm grateful for the offer. My mouth feels like sandpaper after the hike.

"I am really thirsty."

Cranston smiles, takes a decanter off a shelf, fills two glasses, offers me one.

Brandy? Not exactly a good thirst quencher, but I'm a guest.

"You, uh-- you wouldn't happen to have a glass of water, would you?"

Cranston just smiles, raises his glass. "A toast. To new beginnings."

His smile is sharp as a knife, his teeth, yellow and long as pegs. I hadn't noticed that before. We clink glasses.

I take a sip of the amber colored brandy, wince at the burn as I swallow.

Looking over, I see that Cranston's glass is empty. If he drank, I never saw it.

He starts to tell me about the house, surface details only, the date of its construction, who it is named for, the families that have lived here. He says nothing, of course, about the disappearances. I won't learn about those until later. I will stumble into her many horrors on my own.

"Buddy Haygood," I say, "he told me not to mess with this place. Why is that?"

Cranston shakes his head, dismisses Buddy Haygood's advice with a wave of his hand, his skeletal fingers flutter before me, joints knobby and bulging arthritically. "Peasant superstitions."

And suddenly Buddy seems silly to me, a babbling, small town yokel. I feel ashamed at the thought but it's Cranston that knows what's going on. It's Cranston I can trust.

Right?

"No reason to feel guilty," he says guessing my thoughts. "Small minded people are like that." Then, in a confiding voice, he adds, "But we're not small minded people, you and I, are we, Kevin?"

His cadence is strange like he's making an intonation, summoning demons out of the basement and there's the hint of an accent. I think it might be British. But I can't say for certain, everything is going fuzzy.

"Where are you from-- originally?" I say.

He just smiles.

"Seriously, where... are... you from?"

Without a hint of sarcasm, he answers, "The deepest abyss of the underworld."

His face squinches up, an attempt at a grandfatherly smile. But the mock kindness veils murderous disdain. His nails scratch on the wooden arms of the chair. That's when I notice his hands. Long, thin fingers, tapered nails. It's like he has raven's feet for hands. A gold, spider shaped ring with ruby eyes glitters on his left ring finger. He clenches his hands and his finger joints crackle painfully like ten thick twigs snapping simultaneously.

"Who-- whose house did you say this is?"

"Why your house, Kevin," he says matter of factly. "Of course, no man is her master. She rules all. But you will continue to add to her magnificence every single day that you remain here. Isn't that exciting?"

The prospect, perhaps it's supposed to sound delightful, but there's a sinister undercurrent rippling just below the surface. I can feel an invisible, slippery mass wriggling in the darkness around my ankles, threatening to trip me up, entangle me and pull me under, devour me, leave my fleshless bones picked clean.

They're waiting, just within in the walls-- those worms.

I can almost hear them now-- slick writhing, twisting tirelessly with blood craving.

The brandy-- or whatever it is, has gone straight to my head. I look down at the glass, notice that it's empty. I don't remember drinking that much. I don't remember taking more than one sip.

Sitting in that ancient throne, long fingers clutching the arms, dressed as he is, in black, Cranston looks like the lord of all vultures. His eyes glow like red coals in deep sockets. For a moment the room seems to distend behind him, stretching out, creaking and popping as it does so, writhing like a serpent, shedding its skin.

Growing larger.

Alive.

And I hear a thudding sound. At first, I think it's my own heart pounding, brought on by the sweat inducing alcohol. But it sounds like it's coming from beneath the floorboards, from the vaults under the very foundations of the house.

"Do you-- do you hear that?" I ask weakly.

I rub my eyes, set the glass aside.

No more brandy.

When I look back up, Cranston is leaning forward, elbows arched, smiling at me, or at least giving me a cheap imitation-- a vulture mimicking a smile.

I rub the sweat off the back of my neck. "It's so hot in here. Can we-- may you, I mean-- um, I, uh, open a window?"

And Cranston, with vicious kindness offers, "Why don't you have another drink?"

I look back at the glass.

It's full again.

I feel hot, uncomfortable, a little dizzy.

"Who poured the--"

Cranston goes on talking in a disturbingly friendly way as if nothing is wrong. "It's actually lucky for me that you're here." He looks at me, traps me in the gaze of his hard, black eyes. The burning coals are gone now. The last flickering of hellfire drowns in twin lakes of darkness. There's not a glint of light in either socket now, just two black orbs, soulless as a shark's eyes. "You see, I have some pressing family business. I have to leave town-- tonight, even, if possible. Under the circumstances I would need someone to watch the house."

My head feels muddled. "But you don't even know me."

"Yes, I do. You are someone, like myself, who can appreciate fine things-- fine things like this house. I knew it when I saw you standing at the gate admiring her. Besides," he begins, with mock apology, "she's already made up her mind." He laces his long fingers together, leans back satisfied in his chair, regards me for a moment. "You're the one she wants."

"Who?"

He gives me a *tut-tut* smile. He knows I know. There's no reason for pretense.

The House.

"I'll tell you something, Kevin and it's not something I would tell just anyone, you understand? This house is not like any other. She keeps her secrets well. You keep your secrets, too, yes? You already have much in common. *Sooo* much pain in you. I can sense it." The way he says it, the way his eyes roll back, it's like he enjoys that fact, like he's feeding off my misery. "But she can make that all go away. Your family troubles... your deep seated repression... "

"How-- How did you know about that?"

"She knows an awful lot about you, Kevin. Much more than you think. She has an uncanny ability for insight into the human soul. Here you will find, Kevin, there is no more pain. She has dreams to offer-- for a price, of course." This last part he waves away as a mere formality with his raptor's claw. "But I can see you're willing."

"I-- I don't have much money. None, really."

Arthur Cranston seems painfully delighted at my naivete, gives a cold laugh. "No, no, the payment is not in money. How silly, Kevin, really."

"Then-- uh, how do I pay?"

"Nevermind that for now. Will you stay?"
Of course I will.
I nod.
I look at the glass.
Empty again.

"Excellent!" as if he's clenched the deal. "It will be a comfort to an old man like me to know that someone as eager as-- full of life-- as yourself will be here to keep her company while I am away. She has such a tendency to get lonely-- as most ladies do."

A *man-to-man's* knowing wink.

I don't know a thing about ladies, of course. But I don't bother embarrassing myself by saying as much.

"How-- how will I take care of it-- her?"

"Nonsense," says Cranston sternly, one fist suddenly clenched. "This house, you'll find... takes care of herself."

The world is fading away around me. I'm slipping farther down, being swallowed by the shadows, losing sense of things in the plunge. The feeling is unsettling, alarming, but also warm and delicious. Unavoidable.

"Please understand, she only wants willing participants." Almost an aside, he adds, "There's a good chance you'll perish. She has quite an appetite. I'm not trying to scare you, just letting you know the odds, fair and square, yes?"

"I understand," I answer dreamily.

"You must never, ever cross her, Kevin."

"Why?"

"Because she will kill you, devour you-- mind, body and soul."

I'm so dizzy, I'm not even sure what I'm agreeing to. Not even sure if this conversation is actually taking place or if it's all in my head.

"You still want to stay, even after everything I've told you?"

He sounds almost impressed, or maybe he's just mocking me and completely aware that I'm too sloshed to distinguish between the two.

I shake my head. It wobbles so much, I feel like it might topple off my neck.

"Very well. Don't say I didn't warn you."

"Where do I sign?" It's a half joke, an attempt to be brave in the face of Mr. Death. But Cranston looks mirthless, defeats me at a glance.

"No, no, dear boy, no contracts, no pens dipped in blood. Your word is all She needs. And now... She has it."

Another vulture smile. Triumphant. Victorious. The Devil dragging Faust down to hell. His previous smiles might have been cold but at least they came off as well bred. This one is hideous. And his teeth, yellow-- and long as antique clothespins, a demonic nutcracker's mouth-- why hadn't I noticed it before?

A monster? No, no. He couldn't be. He's just a harmless, albeit creepy, old man. It's the brandy-- it's screwing with my mind. And it's so damn hot in here. I'm all muddled, confused. When I glance at him again, he's just Arthur Cranston.

I look, in fear, out the window, dully terrified at what I've just done-- selling my soul and all-- and for what? Ancient furniture? Dormer windows? A hiding place for my wretched soul? The sun has set leaving a phantom trail of fire, far, far away down the hill on the waters of the lake.

I feel a sense of foreboding, say weakly, "I'll have to get my things, first."

My last protest. My last excuse to leave the house.

"No," says Cranston forcefully, again, his deep voice tolls like a bell. He pauses, smiles before going on more affably, "No need to leave. I'll have your things sent for in the morning."

I can't argue.

Cranston doesn't seem surprised that I accept. I no longer feel surprised that he has asked *me*, a perfect stranger, to house sit while he is away. After all, this house, it's like no other.

And the house--

--she chose me.

That thought fills me with fear and likewise with desire. "The tour-- you said--?"

"Best saved for the daylight. Too many... *shadows* here in the night. Wouldn't want you to trip and fall or... open the wrong door."

A shadow flickers in a corner of the room and I start violently, thinking-- for a second, anyhow, that it looks like a spider-- a giant eight legged horror, creeping up out of the darkness, ready to pounce on me, stab me with its fangs and hang me up, a bloodless husk in its web.

I look out the window again and can see nothing but blackness beyond. The sky is pin pricked with starlight now.

"How long have we--"

I turn around. The seat opposite me is empty.

"Mr. Cranston?" I whisper.

There is a burbling sound at my right hand. The glass is full again.

The world is swimming around me.

Darkness closes in.

My hand slackens. I drop the glass. It thuds dully on the thick oriental rug. I hear the fabric drinking down the brandy with a snake's hiss.

I start to slide forward out of the chair, but feel myself being tugged backwards. I hear the crack of the wood as the chair pulls me back in a stark embrace.

In the night, I have a strange dream-- a half awake nightmare vision, a bloodcurdling imagining of lethal, creeping, soul murdering doom.

I'm lying somewhere in the dark, sweating under heavy blankets that twist and slither like they are alive, sentient, pulsing with hideous life.

The air is heavy, so hot and thick it's almost unbreathable.

A shadowy figure is placing a bag-- my bag-- at the foot of my bed. I catch a glimpse of the stranger's face. It's a woman. I almost think I recognize her-- that merciless glare, those gorgon eyes, brimming with flame.

How did I get in a bed?

I may have muttered the question aloud, I'm not sure. The silver haired woman, she just gives me a scornful glance from beneath her hood before vanishing into the shadows.

Her face. I know her. Don't I?

It's the woman who lobbed the pinecone at me.

The crazy lady.

Vera Griswick.

I hear a sound downstairs. A door in the hallway opening with a prolonged creak.

And then... ticking footsteps. Something very heavy and unhuman is lurching up out of the darkness.

Something with what sounds like a lot of legs.

I hear it lumbering up from the cellar and then down the hall it goes, turning at last and heading up the main stairs, cautious, slow, dragging its heavy bulk behind it. The banisters creak and crack as the thing squeezes its way up to the first landing-- its gargantuan spider fat threatening to splinter the rails with every step.

I lie frozen, paralyzed like in a waking dream, barely able to draw a breath while I listen to the basement horror approaching in the night.

It's a dream-- a dream, I tell myself over and over again.

But my skin is crawling with pinpricks of horror.

It's coming down the hall, the sound of its stealthy steps breaks the tomb like silence of the house on Witcher Street.

Crick. Crick. Crick.

It passes outside my door, casting a long legged shadow which wavers across the floor. The shadow stops. The thing-- whatever it is, is just outside in the hall. I hear it snuffling at the door. I cannot breath. A wafting odor of death and decay seeps into the room-- a charnel house reek. Mingled with the stench of rot is the pungent odor of strange and evil smelling incense.

Oddly enough, I can almost see the monster in my mind's eye, even with the door closed-- a red, hairy horror with eyes burning like coals. I know the eyes are red because there is a faint, infernal glow showing beneath the crack in the door. And I know that those polished, red eyes are lighting its way as it climbs up higher into the house.

While it lurks outside my door, a faint pounding begins somewhere below, coming from deep under the house, making the gilt framed pictures rattle against the walls. And the walls-- they seem to warp and bulge with every beat of what sounds like a gigantic heart. It must be a trick of the dim moonlight showing through the branches of the tree outside my window, casting endless criss cross patterns on the wall-- but the shadows are making the walls appear laced with a forest of veins pumping dark blood with every beat of the half imagined, hideous heart.

At last, the thing outside my door turns, drags itself away down the hall. I hear it climbing up the stairs to the third floor and then on to fourth and finally to the attic beyond. The rough and hairy scraping sounds of the monster dragging its hide along the floor grows faint.

Only when it is gone can I breathe.

I sink down into darkness once more.

I wake in an upstairs bedroom, tucked in, clothes folded neatly at the foot of the bed. I'm even wearing my favorite pj's. Weird. Who undressed me? Cranston? The pinecone throwing gorgon? The House? Sunlight is streaming in through the tall windows. The house is utterly silent with a *you're-completely-alone* kind of quiet. The air feels stifled, heavy, suppressed. Not as bad as the night before, but there's definitely room for improvement. I climb out of bed, head for the windows.

I can't recall the nightmare from last night. I dreamed there was something in the hall, didn't I? A giant spider. How silly.

"What we need in here is some fresh air, Kevin."

The dusty drapes are covered with numerous little dark blotches and getting closer I see-- with skin crawling clarity, it's more spiders, dozens and dozens of them. I grab my shirt off the foot of the bed, twirl it up and start flicking the little hairy monsters into oblivion. My shirt snaps again and again-- *Ka-Pow! Ka-Pow!* Indiana Jones style.

"Be nice to spiders, my ass."

When the drapes are sufficiently de-spidered enough to approach, I tug open one of the large windows to let in some fresh air.

It's odd. On such a beautiful summer morning, I don't hear a single bird. Sure, they are warbling and chirping farther away down by the lake and in the greenery surrounding the golf course. But there's not a single bird singing anywhere on the grounds of the house. Not even in the tree outside my window.

After dressing, I go downstairs back to the room where Cranston and I sat the night before. I check the cabinet with the brandy decanter. It is full, not a drop missing.

And-- I have no hangover. Not a trace of a headache. No desire to barf. Nothing.

"Mr. Cranston? Mr Cranston?" I call out.

He doesn't answer.

I didn't really think he would.

I'm not really sure, in that moment, that there even is such a person as Arthur Cranston.

Oddly enough, this realization doesn't strike me as too crazy. It's not that I think Cranston is a ghost, exactly, though he might have been. It just doesn't seem important. All that matters now is the house.

She chose me, after all.

Cranston is inconsequential.

I can lie to myself, tell myself I don't know. But I do. Deep down I understand that the house wants me and I want her and nothing else matters as long as we are together. Sure, I try to rationalize it at first. I tell myself things like, "Oh, Cranston, he just went away in a hurry, like he said."

But somewhere deep in my heart of hearts, I know.

Cranston was a spirit.

I smell the aroma of fresh brewed coffee and crispy bacon on the air. I head down the hall to the kitchen and find a hot breakfast set out on the table for me. It's all very old fashioned. The stove and huge porcelain sink appear to be from the 1940's or even earlier.

"Thank you, house."

I sit down, feeling the delicious warmth of the sun shining in through the window above the sink.

Someone knocks on the back door.

I look up, see a young woman peering in through the window. Our eyes meet. She smiles, waves. She has a cheery look and bright brown eyes.

I go to the door, coffee cup in hand.

"Hello," she says when I open the door. "I didn't mean to interrupt your breakfast."

"No worries," I say.

"Oh, where are my manners-- I'm Holly."

"Kevin."

We shake hands.

She holds up a bouquet of scraggly wildflowers in one hand.

"I picked these for you."

"Thank you, they're lovely."

She shrugs. "Mostly weeds, I guess, but I think they're pretty... and they smell good. Do you like flowers?"

I've never really thought about it. "Sure."

We stand there a moment, she is smiling expectantly at me.

"Oh, uh, would you like to come in?" I ask.

It doesn't sound strange for me to act like this is my house.

She doesn't seem to think it's odd, either, that a total stranger is asking her inside. It's like she expected me to be here. Almost like we meet here for coffee every morning. She thanks me, says, "Golly, thanks, I could use a cup of coffee. I'll tell you most mornings, I'm up with the birds, but today I'm dragging. Got a real case of the mullygrubs, know what I mean?"

Her voice is bright and chipper-- no hint of dragging to my ears. If this is her with the mullygrubs, I can't imagine her chipper.

We sit at the table together. She is a sweet young lady, very quaint, a Grovers Corners kind of girl. I can already tell in the few seconds I've known her that she is probably the perkiest, sweetest person I'm likely to meet in Afton or elsewhere. There is something dated in the way she dresses-- very nineteen sixties with her pucci style print dress and her hair molded in a high volume bob tied back with a blue ribbon. It's not unusual for fashion to lag behind in a small town, but maybe retro is in even here in Afton. I think it's kind of charming.

"That's a pretty dress."

"Thanks a million, Kevin, really." And returning the compliment, she says, "What cute pj's."

And before I can get to the stove and the coffee pot, she's already there, opening cabinets to take out a cup for herself, moving around the kitchen like she knows the place-- which, she probably does, being a next door neighbor, I imagine.

"Don't mind me. I know my way around. Lived in Afton all my life. But you're a new face in town. So mysterious. We don't get many visitors here. It's a real thrill."

Her voice contains a hint of genuine excitement and it's clear to me there truly aren't many thrills in her life.

"Gosh, I've even got goosebumps, can you believe that? Sorry to drop in unannounced, but I saw you yesterday when you came up the hill. I was really happy-- a new neighbor, you know. Not much happens around here. I guess you can think of me as the welcome wagon, only there's no wagon-- it's just me," she adds *matter-of-factly* as if I might be waiting for an actual wagon to roll up.

She gives me an unexpected hug. "Welcome to Afton, Kevin Yoo."

I think about telling her I am just visiting, just staying a couple of weeks, but I don't say that. Instead I tell her, thank you. I feel a sense of unearned pride in her thinking the house is mine-- the pride of a commoner chosen as beloved by a queen.

She rummages around in the cabinet under the sink, pulls out a crystal vase, fills it with water. She places the flowers in the vase and sets it on the table. A large spider plops out, springing out in front of me like a hairy booby trap and I shove away from the table with a shout.

"Kevin, relax. It's just a little spider."

"You call that little? I thought it was an eight legged kitten." Glancing up, I notice more spiders on the kitchen cabinets.

"Where the hell are they coming from?" I ask, mystified. I'm about to pull off my house shoe, smash the assassin spider right where it's crouching-- in the middle of the table. But before I can execute my swipe and squash, Holly has already trapped it in a glass and is carrying it to the back door.

"Be nice to spiders, Kevin-- and they'll be nice to you."

She tosses the spider out, closes the door. What she said reminds me immediately of the human vulture-- Cranston.

"Holly, do you know anyone named Arthur Cranston?"

She looks puzzled, shakes her head.

"Never heard of him."

Holly sips her coffee, wide eyes beaming at me over the rim of her cup, as if she's waiting for me to fill her in on the details.

"Should I have?"

"No, it's not important."

"You okay, Kevin?"

"Oh yeah, fine-- fit as a fiddle."

Holly pours herself a second cup of coffee and we talk a little about the town, it's history. I tell her I have an interview that morning with Dr. Crickshaw.

"Are you training to be a doctor?"

"No, I'm, uh, a nurse."

She stifles a laugh, bites her lip. "Oh my goodness, Kevin, you're a hoot. Imagine that, a boy nurse. That'd be the craziest thing."

I'm not mad, because I can tell she is being completely earnest. Absolutely clueless that there are male nurses. She sees my face, blushes crimson.

"Oh, Kevin-- Kevin, I'm so sorry. I thought-- I had no idea. I didn't know that-- you know, boys were nurses. I must sound so old fashioned to someone like you-- coming from the big city." The last part is almost a whisper, as if the big city-- any city other than Afton, is something out of a fairytale. I might as well be from the Emerald City of Oz.

"It's okay, really." Holly's the type of person it's just not possible to be mad at. Maybe it's the extreme air of naivete that surrounds her. It's almost a palpable cloud.

"You must think I live under a rock."

"It's okay, I promise."

With new resolve, she says, "Well, I think it's great that you're a nurse, Kevin Yoo. And I think, if Dr. Crickshaw has any sense, he'll hire you on the spot."

Holly stays about an hour, has two cups of coffee. As much as I enjoy her company, I start feeling a little antsy halfway through my second cup-- a little anxious for her to be gone so I can start exploring the house. I don't want to rush it, though, so I take my time. Once she's gone, I go from room to room on the first floor, very slowly. I decide to do just the downstairs rooms in the front of the house that morning.

I step outside only once onto the front porch. There are extensive grounds surrounding the house, comprised mostly of an overgrown lawn and weedy gardens with a few pieces of broken statuary. Unkempt but still a sunlit world of wonder to explore. But no. I only want the interior. The mysterious passages and rooms within rooms.

And besides, when I step out back and look down the hill, I can almost swear I see something shivering in the tall golden grass near the foot of the hill. And the shivery thing-- it looks all hunched over with its clothes in tatters and its skin stretched tight over its bones. It has a skull for a face and it stares at me with two black pits for eyes.

But that's silly.

I've always suffered from an overactive imagination. When I look again, there's nothing there. No eyeless zombie. Just the morning breeze causing the grass to sway.

I make one foray upstairs, passing the second storey, pausing at the landing which leads up to the third floor. A stained glass window lets in scintillations of multicolored light from above, painting the floor in rainbow hues. Motes of dust swim in the variegated light.

And in the silence, it feels like there is something-- a malignant presence lurking in the cobwebby darkness overhead, listening for me just like I'm listening for it.

I look up the stairs towards the darkened third floor. A dim but powerful recollection comes flooding back. My dream last night. The stilt legged horror dragging itself up out of the basement, up the stairs, past my bedroom and on up to the third floor. In the silence, I think I hear floorboards creaking overhead. It's ridiculous. There's no one-- no *thing* up there, but still...

I've always been a little impressionable and the hair on my neck stands up followed by a creepy crawly feeling like a swarm of little bugs is crawling up my back.

Maybe She doesn't want me up here-- not yet, anyways.

I hurry back downstairs, telling myself that there will be plenty of time to explore the upper floors later. Really, I guess I just want to get back downstairs, into the sunlight, away from those lingering shadows.

Back on the ground floor, the wide hall and front rooms are filled with golden light. A return to sunshine makes me dismiss my jitters as just the result of an overactive imagination. I'm only slightly unsettled when I discover the basement door is open a crack-- carving a sliver of darkness in the wall. There's an odor of mildew and decay, like wet rotten wood, wafting out of the darkness and mingled with the unwholesome smell I catch the faint but unmistakable scent of pungent incense lingering in the air. I shut the door quickly and hurry off to explore the adjacent room. It's full of heavy antique furniture, expensive, and old. I'm pretty good at identifying antique pieces, but this stuff defies definition. It's reminiscent of many periods and styles and yet-- it's too bestial and grotesque to fall under any particular time period. A little unsettling, I have to admit. Almost pulsing with life. Totally unique. It must have cost Cranston a small fortune. He has good-- if not bizarre, tastes, the old vulture, I'll give him that.

Oddly enough, I don't feel like a stranger snooping around. I feel strangely at home.

She has been waiting for me.

Again, I tell myself-- I am home.

What do I love about her?

It's hard to say.

There are the obvious things, of course.

The wainscoting, built in oak bookshelves, the distorted tiffany chandelier in the front hall, the delicious sleepy feeling wafting through her sunlit hallways. The-- almost opiate laden sense of disorientation that pervades her rooms.

But it is more than that.

I have the uncanniest feeling that the house-- she senses my moods, arranges herself accordingly. If it is too hot in one hall, she cools down. Too drafty in another, she warms perceptibly.

Crazy, crazy, crazy-- but I know-- she's doing it for me.

It is hard for me to leave her that morning, I'll admit, on the brink of this dark mystery. She's contrived a million little diversions to entice and intrigue me. But I'm supposed to meet Dr. Crickshaw and afterwards it's on to City Hall for dinner with Buddy Haygood and the rest of the Afton Historical Society.

I get dressed, leave the house, start the walk to town with a giddy feeling like someone who has just fallen in love. Behind me I think I can hear a whisper on the breeze.

Hurry back. Hurry back. I'll be waiting, my love.

There's a stray dog sniffing around the gate outside. I stop to scratch her behind the ears. She's friendly enough and wags her tail. I'm telling her what a good girl she is when suddenly her hackles bristle and she starts growling. She gives a few vicious barks and I jerk my hand back, but realize she's not barking at me-- she's barking at the house.

"Hey, you there, what in the hell are you doing up here, huh?"

I look up, see a grizzled man standing on the road a few feet away. His jowly, bulldog's face is covered with stubble-- a five o'clock shadow, at nine AM. He is swaying unsteadily. Drunk, already this early in the morning.

I don't really know what to say.

"I said, what are you doing here?"

"Hi, I'm Kevin." I offer him my hand, not sure what else to do.

He looks at it, puzzled, suspicious, even that it might be contaminated. With a shrug, he decides there's no harm in shaking and grabs my hand. His hand is course as granite and rough enough to shave the skin off my own. He gives my hand a good, hard, shake and I do my best to control a wince, somehow managing to turn it into a smile. He stumbles a little, says, "*Whoooaaa*." Then, when he manages to regain his balance, he introduces himself.

"Will-- Willie Higgins, but my friends call me 'Bub'. Or they would-- if I had any friends. So it's Willie to you." His speech is slurred. He chuckles, steadies himself, looks serious all of a sudden, leans in close to whisper confidentially to me and I catch a nauseating whiff-- a stew of unpleasant smells-- beer and urine and there's a bitter tinge under it all of sweat and old puke.

"You stay away from this place, understand. It's no good. The house, it got her. It'll get you, too. So you stay away. You stay away from-- "

His eyes grow wide all of a sudden. He's looking over my shoulder up at the house. He starts trembling and sweating. I glance back, but don't see anything out of the ordinary. Just the house in the morning sun.

"No, no, *nooo*," he moans. He holds up his hands like the house is threatening him. Then he starts shouting, "The house! It got her! It got her!"

Looking at this sad train wreck of a man, I can't help but wonder how people get to this point. How did he fall through the cracks with no one there to save him?

I try and help him, reach out to keep him steady, but he bats my hand away, loses his balance, staggers sideways and ends up falling in a nearby ditch. He's wailing and crying now and I lean down to help him, but he crawls away from me. It takes him a few seconds to get back to his feet, but when he does, he's still got those crazy, rolling eyes. His face is glistening with sweat. He glances at me, then back to the house.

"It's okay, mister, it's gonna be okay."

A madman leer splits his blubbery face like a jack o'lantern. He cackles, "I warned you! I warned you! It got her-- it'll get you too!"

Witcher Street ends at a sort of dead end of busted pavement and broken asphalt just outside the front gate. The road leading back to town is paved. The other direction leads, by way of a long, winding dirt road down to the unfinished golf course.

He starts shuffling off down the dirt road side of Witcher Street, kicking up clouds of dust, laughing or crying, I can't tell which.

From the pine thicket nearby, I catch a glimpse of a man standing, half hidden by the trees and overgrowth. He's wearing a long black coat, tattered and weather stained. He looks almost like a living scarecrow.

It's the Japanese man. Same one. Same scar. Same weather stained look. Same inch thick coating of dust all over him. Must be. I can't imagine there would be more than one-- not dressed like that, anyways. At a Tokyo sci-fi convention, no big deal, maybe, but here, Asian gunslingers don't look like a common occurrence-- not in this town.

Am I being stalked? He's looking in my direction and I'm getting a major creeped out feeling. I call out to him, ask him what he wants. He ignores me, looks up at the house then turns and disappears amongst the trees, slipping deeper into the woods, ragged coat fluttering out behind him.

Dr. Crickshaw hires me on the spot.

Holly is a veritable psychic.

I feel relieved, even though I suspect there is little competition for the position.

I think it's mostly because he and Buddy have known each other for sixty years. I'm what you call a shoo-in.

"You understand, of course," Dr. Crickshaw says, eyeing me over his horn rimmed glasses, "that this is a temporary position. My regular nurse, Lori, is out of town for the summer. So you are welcome to stay through August-- after that I can't make any guarantees, understand?" He has the loudest damn voice I've ever heard. His booming basso takes up the whole room, threatens to bowl me over, push me out the door and into the hall.

"Completely, yes, sir."

"Yes, sir-- I like that. So many disrespectful kids these days-- pierced and tattooed. You see 'em all over the news. But I have a good feeling about you, Kevin."

"Thank you."

"No tattoos?"

"No sir."

He opens the top drawer of his desk, shuffles some papers aside, pulls out a pack of cognac dipped cigarillos, lights one for himself then offers me one.

"No thank you." I wave it away politely while he puffs a few clouds of sweet scented smoke into the air.

"You don't mind, do you?" he asks, in an affable Foghorn Leghorn tone.

"Oh no, of course not."

It wasn't really a question. He hefts one leg up across the other, leans back in his chair and heaves a long sigh. "All that's missing, son," he says, eyes half closed, "is a whiskey sour."

He can tell I'm a little puzzled. "I know, it's a bit of an irony. But I've always felt a little smoke is good for the lungs-- strengthens 'em, you know. Maybe I'm behind the times, as they say."

There is someone in one of the rooms down the hall-- two people, I can hear the muffled sounds of their conversation through the wall.

"Don't-- um, don't you have patients?"

"Yes."

"Should you-- I mean... The smoke?"

"Oh, hell son, in this town, we respect our elders. They can wait-- let an old man finish his smoke."

"But smoking-- you know... it-- "

"It what?"

"Causes cancer."

"*Bah*, never been proved. That lie was made up by the same limp wristed liberals that cooked up global warming. Do you know that last winter is one of the coldest we've had on record here in Afton? Didn't know that-- well, did ya?"

"No sir."

"That's right." He jabs the cigarillo at me for emphasis. "I'll bet you didn't."

He chuckles, expects me to do the same and I manage a weak little laugh, a squeak, really, even though I think this is completely insane.

"And what do they know anyway? Do you know how old I am? I'm seventy eight years young," his voice thunders with pride. "And the only damn thing I've been doing longer than practicing medicine is smoking. Never been sick a day in my life. Seen a lot of young folks come and go-- and who knows-- maybe if they smoked now and again they'd still be here, not pushin up daisies over at Oak Lawn Cemetery, catch my drift?"

I bite my lip, look back over my shoulder, wondering if this is some bizarre practical joke. But, no, Doctor Abel Crickshaw is in earnest.

"We've just got our own way around here, see. We don't need people from *out there* telling us what to do-- getting in our business. In Afton, Kevin, we take care of our own."

He pauses, eyes me, letting it sink in, waiting probably for an agreeable nod-- which I wholeheartedly give.

For a brief moment I wonder what century I'm in. I say nothing. Dr. Crickshaw doesn't look like the type that likes to be challenged. His stern expression is replaced with a more affable smile, but I can tell it's just thinly painted on. He's waiting to see if I contradict him.

When I fail to do so, he brightens, takes a couple of encouraging puffs, relaxes.

"No, Buddy wouldn't do me wrong," he says. "And if he says you're the one, well, who am I to argue?" He uncrosses his legs, leans forward now, opens the folder I brought him on his desk containing my resume and references. He mutters aloud a second or two as he reads over the top page. He looks up at me, puzzling uncomfortably over something.

"But still, it is a little odd."

"Sir?"

He squints at me, chin propped in hand, tip of his cigarillo still wispy with smoke.

"A male nurse," he says, eyeing me over his glasses. He pauses, strokes his silver goatee. Looking at him in his white doctor's coat and bolo tie, I am reminded of Colonel Sanders.

I feel a little knot tightening in my stomach.

You can't run.

"It's a little unusual. But it might be a nice change. Shake things up a little around here."

He chews on his lip a second. "You're not married, I see."

"Um, no."

The knot tightens. I tremble, knowing where this is going.

"Not, uh, queer, are you son?" he says with an awkward chuckle. "Forgive me for asking."

It's not something I'd get asked in the city. But I'm in the buckle of the Bible belt. I'm smart enough to know that things are handled here a little differently.

All the saliva has gone out of my mouth. My heart is thudding. I'm trembling, and I pray to God he doesn't notice. I know in that moment, my being hired depends solely on how I answer this question. If I don't get the job, I can't stay. If I can't stay, I can't see Her anymore. And Dr. Crickshaw, I can tell, is old school. A classic southern good ole boy. The smoking, drinking doctor. There is only one right answer.

"No, sir," I say with a nervous laugh.

It's just a little white lie, I try and tell myself. It's just for the summer. I can be me later.

He gives me a relieved smile, chuckles. "That's good, son, I figured you weren't." He leans in over his desk a little, confiding in me. "We just don't want that type up here, if you know what I mean."

"Yes sir, I understand."

I also understand that I have just sold my soul.

"We just can't have them here-- those uh, *bum humpers*, I call them. Understand?"

I nod. My mouth feels like it's stuffed with shreds of sandpaper.

We go on with the interview and it proceeds in a false but friendly enough way, but I can't help but feel I waited a second too long to answer. I feel like he might know. More than once while we talk, I catch a suspicious squint in his eyes. Maybe I'm just being paranoid.

"What brings you here, anyway?" he says, his robust voice subdued now.

"Just needed a change of scene, I guess. A little slower pace." I'm feeling fidgety, wondering if I gave him the right answer.

Is there a right answer?

Why am I sweating?

"Well, you've come to the right town. If things were any slower here they'd be dead." Another chuckle, this one, unreciprocated.

"Buddy says you've got a passion for old homes?"

"Um, yes, sir."

"It's good to see young people with respect for old things." He taps the desk with one finger for emphasis. "Very good."

He glances down at my references, mindlessly twisting a ring on his finger as he thinks it over. For a second, I think it's just like Cranston's ring, a gold spider set with the tiniest eight rubies for eyes. But no, I'm just imagining it. Can't be.

"You've got great recommendations, no doubt about it," he says reading over the typed pages. "Impressive schooling. Damn fine. But honestly, son, don't you think after all that big city hospital experience you might find Afton a little-- well, dull?"

"That's what I want, sir."

He chews his lip a moment before answering. "Well, then that's what you'll get."

He stands, shakes my hand.

Buddy is waiting for me at the steps of City Hall.

"Well, how did it go?"

His anticipation is genuine and I'm glad to see him.

I tell him he's looking at Afton's newest nurse. He claps me on the back, ushers me in to the meeting room where the rest of the Afton Historical Society is waiting. There is a folding table set up with horderves and a couple of bottles of wine. The board consists of twelve members including Buddy.

"We're missing a few charter members tonight-- Cecilia Jacobs, Emery Marsh, Walter Reeves and Harold Trout. They couldn't make it-- prior engagements; but I think we'll get along just fine without them. They send their warmest welcomes to you."

He introduces me to everybody else. They give me a warm welcome, make me feel really at home. The last bit of tension left over from my interview with Dr. Crickshaw fades away. I'm safe again. No one will ask about my being gay here. Buddy fills a glass of wine, hands it to me, taps a fork on his glass, proposes a toast in my honor. It's a happy occasion, though I'm not really feeling it. I feel a little dead inside after what I've done.

You sold out, Kevin, my boy.

You lied.

Welcome back to the closet.

The truth, I read once, *will out.*

My heart has gone crazy, beating too fast, then too slow with intermittent hiccups and bumps. *Kevin, oh, Kevin, what have you gotten yourself into?*

This innocent little town is going to eat you alive, kid.

"A toast," Buddy says, startling me, "to the newest addition to Afton, Mr. Kevin Yoo, resident nurse and soon to be pulitzer prize winning author.

Population was five thousand four hundred and thirty six. Now-- five thousand four hundred and thirty seven."

His announcement is met by raised wine glasses and cheers.

They have arranged a comprehensive old homes tour of Afton for me. I thank them, try to sound grateful but my thoughts are already turning back to--

Her.

The House on Witcher Street.

I can hide there. The House-- She doesn't care that I'm-- well, you know... I can stay hidden there. Unjudged. Unmolested.

Safe.

Yes. Safe and hidden with--

--a darker thought intercedes...

... with that long legged horror lurking in the attic, and that black heart beating in the basement.

"You're staying over at the Sleepy Time, aren't you?" a woman asks me, interrupting my thoughts. Buddy has introduced her as Dot Townsend, owner of the Red Oaks-- Afton's only bed and breakfast.

I nod absently.

"Not anymore. I'd be delighted to have you stay at the Red Oaks until you can find an apartment and get settled in. After all, it's not every day we get someone here interested our town."

I thank her, but say the Sleepy Time is fine for me until I can find an apartment. "I don't want to impose."

"It's no imposition, really, sweetheart."

I tell her I will think about it.

"What's to think about?"

She seems genuinely puzzled that I am not as excited to accept the offer as she is to make it.

"Hey, maybe the kid's got some business over there off the highway, if you know what I mean," a gravely voice says. "Maybe it's easier for him to have lady friends in a roadside motel."

The lewd suggestion comes from a fat little man leaning in at the open door.

When no one invites him in, he feigns offense and struts in. "What's all this? A party, and I wasn't invited? I'm hurt, really and truly, I am. Buddy, who's your new pal-- aren't you going to introduce us?"

Buddy sighs, doesn't seem too happy to make the introduction.

"Kevin Yoo, this is Scottie Allgood, head of the Afton Developer's Committee."

Mr. Allgood is a short, fat meatball of a man with dollar signs shining for eyes. He's got a gold chain around his neck, half hidden by his generous sprouting of chest hair. He also has a ring on every finger and a watch the size of sun dial on his wrist. His mustache and what little hair he has left on top of his head is dyed jet black. Dressed, as he is, in a green sports coat, he looks like a maniacal little leprechaun. He's sweating profusely, takes a second to pull out a handkerchief and mop his brow. His bald head glistens in the light. He stuffs the hankie back in his coat pocket, comes up, slaps a thick arm around my shoulders, leans sweatily against me, says, "Nice to meet ya, kid. Heard a lot about you from my old buddy, Buddy, here." He chuckles a little too loud at his own joke and I can smell the whiskey on his breath.

"Why in the world are you hanging out with these old fogeys anyways-- the free buffet? Listen, kid, if you want to get in good in this place, you just come sit in on one of our developers' meetings. We got plans for this stagnant little town. Buddy and I-- uh, we have differing views on preservation," he adds with a slick smile.

"Yes," says Buddy, not smiling. "I'm interested in saving houses. You want to tear them down."

Mr. Allgood shoves off from me, puts his arm around Buddy, says with used car salesman slickness, "It's all about balance, knowing which houses you can save and which ones it's better to let go."

Buddy shakes off Mr. Allgood's arm.

"It's about filling your pockets with money," Dot says.

"No need to be nasty," says Mr. Allgood, same oily smile on his lips. He picks up a cracker topped with cheese off a plate on the table, crams it in his mouth, goes on talking, spraying cracker crumbs with every word. "They're still upset, kid, because last year I got the vote to tear down an old run down dump on the edge of town."

Dot swells up in her seat. "The Harris House. We tried hard to save that jewel. It was built in 1832, the year of the town's founding. It was a beautiful old homestead."

Allgood guffaws. "For what-- the squirrels? Place was falling in."

"We were raising the money to save it." She turns to me, trying to stay calm. "It was going to be an art's center for the city. Pottery, drawing classes, that sort of thing."

Mr. Allgood snorts, helps himself to a glass of wine. "And now it's gonna be a hamburger drive through-- complete with playground."

"People could have had art lessons."

"Now they can have french fries." He says with a laugh, his little piggy eyes are shining.

"You've had enough to drink," Buddy says, taking the bottle of wine from him before he can refill his glass.

"The problem with you people is you lack vision. You're stuck in the past. Wake up! And boy, oh boy have I got plans for this town. There's a few more houses on my list. Starting with that dump over on Witcher Street."

Buddy's face loses its coloring, goes grey like pottery clay. "Not this time. We'll fight you, Scott. Honest to God."

"I hope so," and making a theatrical little bow, he adds. "May the best man win."

He offers his hand to Buddy. But Buddy just stares him down.

So he turns and slaps me hard on the back, says, "Tough crowd, huh? See ya around, kid." He stumbles away out the door singing an off key rendition of, *'We're in the money.'*

"The nerve of that man," says Dot Townsend. "We lost three houses to that weasel last year. Sorry, I know calling him a weasel isn't the Christian thing to do."

"No," says Buddy, "dung beetle would be closer to the mark."

"He doesn't come from here, so he has no respect for the history of this town. All he cares about is money," Dot says. "That man won't be content until this whole damned town is one giant parking lot. Oh, Buddy, what are we gonna do?"

Buddy puts his hand on her back, gives a gentle squeeze. "Well, there's no reason to get worked up about it. We'll deal with him when the time comes. Right now, we have an old homes tour to take-- a welcome to our new friend, Kevin."

Everybody's temper improves on the old homes tour, except, perhaps, mine. Buddy thinks it's a little strange that I don't take any notes, snap any pictures or ask any questions-- especially after I was all fired up the day before-- ready to write a book on the history of old homes in the south. I've brought a spiral bound notebook with me, but he only thing I see when I glance down at the pad in my hand is a forest of doodles, endless swirls, little whirling dervishes of nonsense-- an outer manifestation of inner turmoil, perhaps? A page of mini labyrinths. And in the center of one-- a little ballpoint scribble the size of a pea with eight stick legs.

A spider.

Looking at it, I feel more unsettled than I ought to.

I guess I do seem a little disinterested. I hardly even look at any of the houses. I don't remember drawing any of these swirls, either.

"You feeling alright, Kevin?" Buddy asks.

"Uh-huh."

"You sure?"

"Yup."

"Aren't you going to write anything down?"

"Not just yet. I'm thinking it through."

"You seem a little off. Didn't eat any lunch today?"

"I ate earlier-- breakfast at the hotel."

"The Sleepy Time doesn't offer breakfast, Kevin."

I feel suddenly and unaccountably irritable with the old man. "I'm just not a big eater, that's all."

"That's not what you said yesterday."

"Jet lag, I guess."

Holly would call it the mullygrubs, probably. It's a swirling combination of my little white lie, the nasty encounter with Mr. Allgood and also I'm thinking of the House on Witcher Street.

"You should think about Dot's offer. The Red Oaks Bed and Breakfast is the finest establishment in town— besides my hardware store, of course."

I smile weakly.

Come back, my love. Come back. I'm waiting.

"Yes," I say aloud.

Buddy shakes his head, smiles, thinking I was answering him.

Work goes reasonably well with Doctor Crickshaw that week. He's abrasive and bossy and operates with barely veiled bombastic condescension whenever he's around. But fortunately for me, he's rarely in the office. And true to his word, nothing much happens in Afton. A few people come in for allergy medication. An unusually high number for refills on sleeping pill prescriptions. And about seven people need to get spider bites treated, (one of whom is in bad enough shape to get sent to County General). It is an unusually high percentage for a town like this, but nothing to call the nightly news about. Dr. Crickshaw makes an awful lot of house calls that week I notice, more than I think would be necessary for such a small town. He comes back, more often than not, smelling like whiskey and cigars. It's a relief beyond words that he has very little interest in maintaining his practice. Mostly I sit at the front desk and I daydream about the House.

My house.

My love.

The mistress of my burgeoning affair, the house of my dreams which I can still maintain and control, no matter what Cranston said.

After all, a house has no control over a man.

I am its master.

Right?

For the first time in a long time I'm not thinking about funerals and death.

Amy calls once to check on me at the office. She's not happy.

"Daddy's not doing well, Kevin. I thought you should know," she says, her tone intentionally accusing.

I want to say, so what, he's not my dad. Instead, I say, "I'm sorry to hear that." My voice is flat, emotionless.

"You know that Jin is doing everything he can to help out."

"Ah, yes, the Korean Jesus. That's very kind of him." Another mechanical response.

"You asshole. It should be you. But you're traveling the world. Well, you picked a fine time to go on vacation. When are you coming back?"

"I'm not coming back, Amy. I live here now."

"How can you do this? How can you be so damned selfish. Did you know how hard it was to find you? I couldn't get you at that motel you said you were staying at. What did you say the name of it was again?"

"Oh, there's no phone in my room anyway. If you need to reach me, just call me here. But, to be honest, Amy, I really hope you don't need to reach me."

"You jerk. What do you mean you don't have a phone in your room?"

"Like I said, it's easier if you just call me here at the office."

"Kevin, what's going on? Where are you staying?"

"With a friend."

"A friend? You just moved there." She's starting to sound really pissed off. "Kevin, I'm going to talk to cousin Alan. I want him to drive up and check on you."

"Don't be ridiculous. I'm fine. Better than I've ever been."

"Something weird is going on, Kevin. Tell me what it is."

"Sorry, Amy, I have to go. Bad connection."

"Kevin, you're such a liar."

"Gotta go."

"Kevin, don't you dare hang up on-- "

I hang up.

Even though conversations between Amy and me are always a little tense-- this was more strained than usual. Typically, I don't come right out and say the kinds of things I just said. It's almost like I wasn't fully in control. And I wonder would She-- the House on Witcher Street, be proud of me? I'm doing it, after all, for her.

I need to get my mind off family issues, veer it away from guilt. The latest edition of the Afton Gazette is on the desk in front of me. I pick it up, skim the pages. An article by the local staff writer, Eunice Bailey, catches my eye.

Strange Days

Yes, gentle reader, they are here again-- those strange days, unfortunately not too uncommon for us here in Afton. We've become so used to weird goings on lately that strange, for us, is the new normal.

We are finally getting the last bit of mess cleaned up from that terrible occurrence which unsympathetic outsiders are referring to with mock horror as, Night of the Kitten. They may be laughing, but there was nothing funny about that nightmare to those of us who survived. And we owe a debt of gratitude to Mr. Ray Riggs and his boys-- who stand out as true heroes of that terrible night. And we mourn the loss of our good feline friends here in Afton. It will be a long, long while before any of us feels comfortable with a cat for a companion again-- not after the horrors of that night, when we all learned how frighteningly easy it was for us to become cat kibble-- a sobering truth to which only those of us who lived through the terrifying ordeal can attest.

Now there is a new rumor swirling in town, rumors of something walking the streets at night-- a giant creepy crawly, reported by several eyewitnesses.

And what sort of bogey are we talking about this time that has come to stalk the streets of Afton? Well, gentle reader, sources, who at this time wish to remain anonymous, are telling this hard nosed reporter that it is taking the form of a giant spider.

Unfortunately, this is not the first time such reports of abominable arachnids have been made here.

Will wonders-- or terrors, alike, never cease in this town?

This reporter, for one, wishes to high heaven they would.

Cannibal cats? Buddy never mentioned anything about that when we talked. He said rabies-- didn't he? An onslaught of flesh eating felines-- it doesn't seem like something that would just slip your mind. But what really sets me wondering and causes the hairs on my neck to stand on end is mention of a giant spider lurking in the darkened streets of Afton.

What kind of place is this?

The guy at the fruit stand was right.

Things aren't always what they seem.

This idyllic little town is holding a host of dark secrets.

I lock the door to Crickshaw's practice and head to Watson's Grocery off Main Street to pick up a new blue Mead spiral notebook and a pack of Bic ballpoint pens-- red and blue, determined to get some writing done. I came here to relax and write about old houses. I haven't made much progress with either, but now I'm puzzling over the hint of strange terrors in this town. And I want to know more. It might be against my will. Maybe I'm being drawn in like a bug in a whirlpool-- down, down, down to my doom. But I can't help it. I have to find out what's going on around here. I need to record this, write it all down, capture the bizzaro nature of this town. It might be the only thing that saves me. Because, right now, I'm starting to feel like I'm teetering on the edge of a deep pit.

"It's a damned shame, isn't it?" the lady in front of me at the checkout says.

At first, I don't know what she's talking about, then I see she's looking at the milk carton in her hand. There's a black and white photo of a teenage girl on the side of the carton with the caption, *'Have you see me?'*

And underneath, her name-- *Missy Harper*, followed by the date she disappeared.

Just two days ago.

"She was such a sweet girl. I hope they find her. It's a sad time when you're not even safe in a small town like this-- *Hell, your own hometown.* I remember growing up here, we used to leave our doors unlocked all night long. Not anymore-- No sir, not with all those crazies running loose. Did you see the nightly news the other night? I couldn't believe it-- "

She goes on rambling, talking to me like she's known me her whole life. And the whole time, I'm thinking, how does she know *I'm not one of those crazies?*

It's while I'm standing there, zoning out in the checkout line while the lady keeps on talking and talking and talking-- that's when I see him--

The Japanese man in the tattered coat. He's standing a few customers in front of me. I'm staring at him, but he doesn't notice me. And that's when it clicks--

--the kid on the plane-- the one who sat next to me hugging his skateboard.

This man, he has the same scarecrow frame, the same mop of scraggly blue-black hair (though his is streaked with grey) and most definitely the identical stoop shouldered stance as the kid with the skateboard. Looking at him, I think they could very well be related. This guy could be his brother, his cousin, his father, maybe.

Shit, if I were crazy, I'd probably say it could even *be the damn kid*-- just a couple of decades older.

He even has the same Spider-Man Pez dispenser.

What are the chances of that? It must be some new Japanese craze I haven't heard about-- *web-head* candy dispensers.

As I watch, he flips back Spidey's head and dispenses one of the pink sugar lozenges from beneath its red and blue chin, pops it in his mouth.

When it's his turn at the checkout, he lays down a fistful of Pez refills and then stands still as a stone while Debbie, the checkout lady, rings him up. She looks up once, smacking her gum, smiles, says, "Got a sweet tooth, huh, mister?"

He just stares, blankly, his thoughts a million miles away. His face is just as weathered as his coat. One look at this guy and I know he has traveled a million miles or more-- with very little sleep. The lines of his journeys are etched deep in his face. The white line of the scar above his left eye shows up plainly against his bronzed skin. He seems weary, but resolved-- determined not to let himself be broken.

I've seen pictures of faces like his before in National Geographic. People who have lost everything. But who resolve to go on. If not to live in the metaphorical sense then only to survive. His face may as well be carved from stone. His mouth is set in a grim straight line. His eyes--

--world weary, exhausted by what he has seen.

Who the hell is this guy?

It looks like he's staring at the bagboy, a middle eastern kid. The kid has a shy, bookish look and when he notices the Japanese man staring at him, he goes red in the face and looks away.

When Debbie tells him the total, the Wanderer, as I call him, glances at her, squints like he's trying to make sense of what she just said.

"Mister? Mister, you okay?"

He nods, emotionless as an automaton.

She repeats the total. He looks back at her now, then reaches into his coat pocket, scrounges around, pulls out a handful of very ancient looking coins and puts them down on the convey belt in front of her. From where I'm standing in line, I can smell the spiky scent of mildew wafting off of him, like his clothes are growing mold, like he's been sleeping in damp burrows and roadside ditches all his life and never in a bed. He bows slightly, grabs up the fistful of Pez refills and shoves them in his pocket.

He hurries out the door.

Debbie glances at the coins, calls for him to stop.

He doesn't look back, his coat trails after him, whipping and snapping like a living shadow.

"Sir-- sir! You have to come back! We don't take-- um, gold coins."

The manager has heard the shout, is leaning in beside her now.

"Do we, Stan? Do we take... gold coins?"

Stan Watkins picks up one of the coins, holds it up, gives a low whistle.

"What is it, Mr. Watkins?"

"I'll be damned. These are Spanish doubloons." He glances over at the bagboy. "Rabbit-- go, see if you can catch him, huh?"

Rabbit. The bag boy's name seems painfully appropriate to me. I've never seen anyone more uncomfortable in their own skin, unless, of course, it's me.

"Should I call the police?" Debbie asks.

Stan Watkins lets loose a little unintentional guffaw. "No, sweetheart, you should call *Sotheby's.*"

Poor Debbie stares blankly, born into a world of *Hee-Haw* and *Price is Right*, *Sotheby's* is not on her radar. Mr. Watkins scrounges for other words to convey his meaning.

"These coins are worth ten grand, at least."

Hearing this, the squirmy kid, Rabbit, nods, ducks out after the stranger.

I'm just a few seconds behind him. The kid is jogging along, calling for the man to stop in an *embarrassed-beyond-all-means* voice, when all of a sudden, a kid on a skateboard comes racing down the street. I catch a glimpse of him speeding by, realize it's the Japanese kid from the airplane-- the one who sat next to me.

What are the chances? Where in the world did he come from?

Rabbit doesn't see him, steps right out in front of him and the Japanese kid tries to skid to a halt, but it's too late. He slams into Rabbit and they land in a heap on the grass. The Japanese kid lands on his back, the impact is rough enough to knock the wind out of him. He lays there stunned for a moment as Rabbit leans over him, asking if he's okay.

The Japanese kid is clutching his forehead. He's cut it pretty bad in the fall and there's a big gash right above his left eye. The gash is oozing blood. It trickles out between his fingers and drips from his brow to his cheek. Definitely going to leave a scar.

Up ahead, I see the tattered man pause, turn back and glance at the two of them-- Rabbit and the Japanese kid. I can't be sure, but I think he gives a little smile, like he's remembering something from a long time ago. And his eyes look shiny like someone who wants to cry, but can't because the tears are long, long gone. He reaches up, runs his fingers lightly over the thin white line of the scar over his left eye. Then he turns, hurries and walks away, the shadow of his coat whipping behind him.

When I get back that evening, the stray dog is sniffing around the gate again. When she sees me, she wags her tail. I kneel down, scratch her behind the ears. She seems friendly enough.

"I've made my decision. I think you're okay, I really do," I tell her. "How would you like to come live with me?"

She pants in my face, tongue hanging out, tail swishing in the dirt.

"It's settled then. It will be nice to have a little company. You're gonna need a bath, though. And a name. How about Goldie?"

More tail wagging tells me she seems open to the idea.

"Come on," I say. "Let's get you cleaned up."

I open the gate, walk up to the house. Goldie trots along behind me.

When I enter the house, I know something is wrong. The air-- it's way too cool. Refrigerator cold, almost. She's unhappy.

The portrait of the woman in the black dress with the insanely long fingers-- she's staring at me. I look away quickly, unsettled as usual by its harsh gaze and pass beneath it, pretending that I want to look at the floor, that the floor is interesting beyond all reason.

There has never been-- nor will there ever be-- anything more interesting than this damn floor.

"Kevin."

The voice is quiet, barely a whisper, but venomous.

My heart leaps up in my mouth and I look back. I could almost swear that the woman in the black dress has shifted slightly. And there's the lingering hint of a fluttering in her fingers as if she has jerked her hand back quickly after trying to--

--what?

Grab me?

The painting is still. If not at rest, than at least under control. I try to be brave, look her in the eyes, subdue her. But she wins. Very quickly. I know, if I challenge her, she'll peel herself off that canvas and climb down out of that shadowy picture while I'm sleeping and-- I don't want to think what she will do. I never, under any circumstances, want to wake up and find her standing at the foot of my bed. I look away, hurry down the hall out of her sight, leading Goldie along behind me, very grateful for the dog's reassuring presence.

I bathe her that afternoon in the porcelain clawfoot tub in the downstairs bathroom. The room fills up with steam and I scrub her really good, get her all sudsy, then rinse her off. I wrap her in a towel afterwards, then turn to wipe the steam off the mirror.

A swipe of my hand against the glass reveals a sight that sends me reeling.

An eyeless horror staring back at me, mouth gaping, full of writhing worms.

I shout, stumble backwards, fall into the tub. I konk my head pretty hard. When I sit up, Goldie is staring up at the mirror and growling. I pull myself up out of the dog flavored water, heart pounding and climb out of the tub. I lean slowly forward, trembling as I approach the glass, terror squeezing me like a vice, wondering with an ever mounting sense of terror if that eyeless corpse is lurking just on the other side of the glass, waiting to reach out, grab hold of my hair in its leprous hand and pull me through.

To where?

The other side.

The land of the dead.

What made me think that?

I look in.

It's just me.

Kevin Yoo. Terrified, shaking and soaking wet.

I need a drink.

Afterwards, I go to the library to have a look at the books. I avoid the front hall. I tell myself I just want to take a meandering way back around to the front of the house. But, truth be told, I'm afraid of that woman in the black dress. I'm shaken up pretty bad after the bathroom fiasco. I can't handle anymore scares, real or imagined.

Reading will take my mind off the terrifying hallucination. Goldie trots behind me, finds a spot beneath a window and lays down to dry in the sun.

I browse the shelves. There are hundreds of volumes, all of them old hardcover books, seemingly untouched like Gatsby's library. For looks only. A decoration. A well executed detail to bring this imaginary doll house to life.

I am hoping for one particular book.

"Come on, library," I say. "Where is it? *Hasting Crumberdumb's Atlas of Architectural Studies.*"

It is a long shot, I know. The book has been out of print for decades.

Something thuds to the floor a few feet away.

I kneel, pick up the book which has landed face down on the floor.

Hastley Crubberdrums Atlas of Architectural Studies.

Well, the title is sorta right.

"Hey, what are the chances!"

I grab a glass from the liquor cabinet, fill it with brandy from the endless decanter that Cranston used on my first night here. I take a sip.

Good stuff. Just the right amount of burn.

I used not to drink, but the House, She has a way of always greeting me when I come home with a glass of brandy-- at least, I think it's brandy. Whatever the hell it is, it does the trick every time.

I sit down with the book and spend a few hours reading. I don't remember what I read. It is like when you try to read a book in a dream. The words don't make sense. They seem to dissolve and rearrange themselves on the page. But I pretend, I guess, that it all makes sense, that I am making progress in the book.

The glass refills itself once or twice-- or maybe I refilled it without realizing it. I'm starting to get a little fuzzy. I'm starting to obliviate, as I call it. I can feel the dissolution coming on, but can't stop.

Goldie is looking up at me-- a little accusatory, I imagine.

"What? It's medicinal," I tell her, "the house… she says so. Don't you, my dear?"

Guilt equals paranoia. I will feel neither guilty or paranoid. Not anymore.

If I drink-- I drink-- so be it.

"Dumb dog."

I look back at the book lying open in my lap. It's a different book altogether now. A heavy tome bound in some type of strange material. The cover feels dry and crackly like it's wrapped in brittle skin. The pages are filled with runic symbols and strange illustrations. The images, like the words, seem to swirl and dissolve. But I catch wispy glimpses of strange, babel like towers rising crazily into the air from barren landscapes and monstrous things-- a giant rat, centipede, moth and spider being worshipped with fire and human sacrifice deep inside the darkness of ancient temples. Surely, I'm imagining it.

The pictures and the revolting feel of the book itself leaves me feeling nauseated and I set it aside, unsettled by the bizarre nightmare images. I pick up my spiral notebook determined to get some writing done, instead. But the House has other plans. It's just like that afternoon on the old homes tour. Time and time again I put the pen to the page, but everytime I glance down I see that I've just ended up with a page of scribbles. Mindless doodles and swirls. Nothing else. I don't have time to get flustered because, my tumbler, I see, has just been miraculously refilled. That happens again and again, same as it did the night I met Cranston.

The House-- she's treating me right.

Isn't she?

I am bleary eyed and more than a little disoriented after imbibing generously from the cut crystal miracle glass. I spill about a dozen loose papers out of my lap. They scatter on the floor. I glance at them, irritated I will have to correlate them all. But when I look closer, it's just more mindless scribbles. I feel suddenly very angry. The House-- She's playing games with me. I fling the glass away in frustration, look at the dog, ready to shout at her. But she's looking up at me sweetly with her big brown eyes and I feel the anger melt away.

After all, it's not the dog's fault I'm drunk.

"Who needs to write, huh Goldie?" I say, tossing the loose pages aside. "No one's gonna read it, anyway."

I hear a gurgling noise, like a stomach growling.

"You hungry, girl?"

But Goldie is looking up, too, like she has heard it.

I look out the window. It is already dark. I hadn't realized I've been sitting there that long. It was early afternoon when I sat down with the book.

There are little specks all over the carpet at my feet. It takes me a second to focus my double vision. When I realize what the little blots are, I jump up, start swearing and stamping my feet.

"Dammit! Stupid spiders! Little bastards-- *DIE!*"

After eradicating the danger, I stumble to the kitchen, feed Goldie some table scraps-- leftover chicken from the fridge.

Afterwards, I take her out in the yard so she can pee and I can get some fresh air. I close my eyes, take a few deep breaths, trying to clear my head. Goldie trots off around the corner of the house and I wait. A few moments later, I hear her yelp.

I run down the steps, around the corner of the house, see that she has gotten tangled in the bushes at the side of the house. I don't know how she did it. It's like someone has tied knots around her legs. Odd as it seems, it looks like the bush has snagged her, like it is trying to drag her into the shadows.

It takes me a few minutes to get her untangled. I have to go back and get a knife from the kitchen. When I start cutting the vines they squirt black, foul smelling liquid all over my hands. It smells like roadkill.

I look up, wiping the sweat out of my eyes and am startled to see the two fan light windows in the high tower above glaring down at me. They are glowing orange and look like angry eyes. I haven't been in the tower yet and don't remember seeing lights on up there earlier. Behind the frosted glass, a shadow lurches-- something with crooked tent pole legs stalks back and forth behind the glass in the red light, insect like.

Maybe I'm just imagining it; I have, after all, drunk nearly a bottle of brandy. When I look back up a second later, the windows are dark.

I hear someone cough behind me. I jump up, turn, see someone a few feet off, standing in the grass smoking a cigarette. I can see the orange ember glow brightly as the person takes a slow drag. I recognize him, puzzled as hell, though, what he's doing here.

It's the Japanese kid from the plane. He has a bandage on his forehead covering the gash he got earlier.

"What are you doing out here?" My tone sounds a little accusing, not sure if I have any authority-- after all, *what the hell am I doing here?* It's not my property.

He blows out a stream of smoke, flicks the cigarette away, nods in the direction of the road.

There's someone standing there. I can't see the person, so much as sense that he's there. And I know, beyond a shadow of a doubt who it is.

The man in the tattered coat.

The Wanderer.

The kid must have followed him up here. I think about telling the man to come out of the shadows. But I know it won't do any good. And I don't feel like I'm in any danger. Oddly enough, I get the feeling that he might be trying to help me in some odd way. It's just a hunch I have. Call it intuition. But there's some reason he's following me, I just have no clue why. Instead, I turn back to the kid.

"You remember me from the plane?"

A nod.

"Did you move here, too? What are you, an exchange student?"

Another nod.

"That's what I thought. How's your head? That was a pretty nasty fall you took today."

He doesn't answer, just reaches in his pocket, pulls out the Spider-Man Pez dispenser.

Seeing it reminds me of the shadowy gunslinger-wandering-samurai guy.

"Hey, did you steal his Pez dispenser or did he steal yours?"

The kid scowls at me like he doesn't understand.

"Is that your dad-- in the black coat? Or your uncle or something? Why is he following me? What does he want? Are you following me, too? Well?"

He gives me another puzzled look, lips pursed, then glances back up at the house. He hitches his thumbs together-- same as he did on the plane and makes that creepy crawly motion with his fingers, like a spider scurrying up a wall. The gesture makes me shiver.

"How did you-- Did you see it? Do you know?"

He shrugs, grabs his skateboard out of the tall grass, starts off down the hill towards the gate.

"Hey, hey wait up!" I shout. "Wait a sec! Who are you?"

He just gives another shrug then walks through the open gate, turns back again, and pointing at the house shakes his head. His meaning is clear enough.

This place is no good.

He puts his headphones back on, hops on his board and skates off down the darkened street. The sound of the wheels scuffing on the pavement fades away into the night.

"What the hell?"

I don't know how to make sense of it. I look around, expecting to confront the man in the tattered coat, standing in the moonlight, staring at me.

But there is no one there, just a sparse cloud of lightning bugs drifting in the darkness down by the road.

But not a single one, I notice, on my side of the gate.

When I get into bed, I hear the stomach gurgling sound again.

"Still hungry?" I ask.

Goldie only whimpers.

She seems restless, unsettled. She keeps whimpering, getting up, pacing around the room.

"Go to sleep girl. We'll go on a nice long walk tomorrow."

I drift away, lured into a shadow land of fitful slumber where men in tattered coats walk side by side with red haired spiders. And looming on the cusp of it all--

--Arthur Cranston, rubbing his hideous, birds' feet hands together, plotting...

...plotting.

I wake up in the middle of the night to the high pitched yelp of a dog.

I sit up in bed, listening.

"Goldie?" I say. "Here, girl."

The bedroom door is open slightly. I can see a sliver of moonlight in the hall. In the silence, I hear a scraping sound like Goldie is scratching her claws on the floor.

I get out of bed, step out into the hall just in time to hear another yelp and then a clanging sound like a metal grate being slammed shut. I reach for the lightswitch in the hall, press the button, but no light comes on.

I start down the hall in the dark.

"Here Goldie," I whisper. "Here, girl," over and over again.

I step in something cold and sticky. I kneel down and can see dark splotches on the floor in the moonlight. I touch one with my finger, sniff it. It has a sickly sweet metallic smell.

Blood.

Beside me I can see a wrought iron grate, probably a heater vent connecting to a shaft which leads down to the furnace in the basement.

A sharp howl comes from the darkness beyond, startling me and I fall back.

My heart pounds in the silence.

A rattling gurgle breaks the stillness. This is followed by a series of clicks and pops as the house settles back, full, sated.

I reach up to try the lightswitch again. I touch the wall and it gives way beneath the slight pressure of my hand, starts to suck it in, like it's trying to devour me. The wall is no longer solid, but slick and slimy, and my hand sinks into what feels like a writhing mass of cold spaghetti.

Worms.

Thousands and thousands of slippery worms.

The living wall starts to slurp me up-- all the way up to my wrist, then my forearm, then my shoulder. And me screaming all the while. I can feel the slithery things twisting around my flesh, wriggling between my fingers. I even think I can feel them nipping at me with tiny, toothless mouths. I can hear the wet, slithering sounds as the worms twine in and around themselves, endlessly writhing.

I jerk back my arm and hand from the hideous suction, dislodging part of the writhing mass. A heap of worms spills onto the floor with a sickening splatter sound like ten people throwing up simultaneously. They flip and squirm, pop and snap at my feet like they're sizzling in a frying pan. I stagger back, my feet slipping and squishing in the middle of the mess. My arm is dripping with snot like strands of viscous goo.

My first thought is to make a run for the stairs.

But the house, it must know what I'm planning, because the second before I bolt, the entire wall bulges out and with a rattling noise like a giant belch, the entire side of the hallway gives way, vomitting thousands upon thousands of worms. The mass rears up like a tidal wave, looming over me, blocking the hall and then slowly-- but with ever increasing speed, closing in on me. As it slugs and slimes its way closer, I can see the worms twisting and turning frantically, propelling the entire reeking mass faster in my direction with their endless convolutions. And as the worm wall surges towards me, it churns up glimpses of yellowed bones in its midst; old skulls grin out at me and then get swallowed up, only to be churned up once more by the slick, seething mass.

I run back to my bedroom, slam the door.

I scrape the bottoms of my feet against the carpet, trying to scuff off the worm gut residue. I shake my arm wildly trying to fling off the gooey filth. I go for the windows, trying to yank them up, but they seem to swell up even as I touch them. There is no way to get them open. I am stuck in the house. Trapped. A prisoner. At Her mercy. I stand panting, wipe the sweat out of my eyes and reluctantly crawl back into bed, too scared to walk the darkened halls, too terrified to even attempt opening the door. I pull the covers up, like a scared little kid and lay very still, trying to sleep, but knowing I won't.

Beyond my door, I can hear the wet writhing sounds, slippery twistings and undulations. The worms are waiting on me.

Throughout the night, I hear a faint whimpering in the walls all around me. Poor Goldie. Her desperate cries sound far away, but it keeps me awake until morning.

"I'm sorry, girl. So sorry."

I should have known I couldn't bring anything into this house. Not even food. I tried two days earlier to get some things down at Watson's grocery-- a carton of ice cream and some bananas and deli meat. When I woke up the next morning, the ice cream was splattered on the floor like the refrigerator had spit it out. The bananas had turned black and putrid overnight, so had the meat. It was festering with maggots.

I can only eat what She provides.

She did let me keep the notebook. Of course, I haven't gotten a word written. It's her way of mocking me.

I guess I know I will never find Goldie. There's no use in hoping. I will try looking for her, sure, in the morning, when I am released from this room. I will even go down into the basement the next day but I know beyond a shadow of a doubt, I won't find a trace of Goldie in that cavernous, earthen cellar.

I don't expect I will ever see her again.

That's how I learn that the House does not like to share.

And the house, like any beast, has to be fed.

PART V

THE MOST HAUNTED TOWN

All houses are haunted. All people are haunted. Throngs of spirits follow us everywhere. We are never alone.
--Barney Sarecky

BREAKFAST IS LAID out again the next morning-- just as it has been every morning since my arrival.

I walk into the kitchen, greeted by Holly's cheerful voice.

"Well, good morning sleepy head."

Sleep deprived and still on edge from the horror of last night, I jump at the sound of her voice, spin around.

Holly is standing behind me.

"Dammit, Holly! You scared the shit out of me."

What? Are we married? What the hell makes her think she can show up any damn time she likes?

"Sorry, the door was unlocked. I just wanted to see how you're adjusting, you know, to small town life."

"Fine," I say, more testily than I realize. "Do people around here usually just walk into other people's houses unannounced?"

She looks hurt. My voice is harsher than I intended.

"Sorry, you just startled me, is all."

"I'll knock next time."

"No, no, really-- it's okay. I promise. I didn't sleep well, either. Hey, you didn't happen to see a dog outside, did you? A sandy colored mut."

I know the answer already, but ask anyway.

"No."

"I guess she got loose."

"Who?"

"Nothing."

I am still trying to fool myself. In the morning light, what I imagined the night before seems so impossible. Just a bad dream. The dog got out, that's all. After all, Holly just said the door was open.

"You look tired, kid," she says.

I'm thinking of Goldie and the house and also of James. The stress of the lie I told Crickshaw is weighing on me, too.

"Sometimes things are hard." I'm holding my head in my hands, feeling weak and a little hung over. I feel almost translucent.

"Boy are they ever," she agrees like she's relieved at what I said.

"Are you always this perky?"

"Not always. But mostly. I've never gotten anywhere being sad. What about you?"

"I never seem to get anywhere-- period."

"That's no way to be. You just have to believe in yourself, Kevin."

"Even if no one else does?"

"Even so, kiddo. You know, my daddy used to tell me, we don't get to choose the life we want. We just have to do the best with what we get. What do they call it?-- playing the hand you're dealt. After all, like Scarlett O'Hara says, *Tomorrow is another day*."

"Frankly, my dear, I don't give a damn-- Rhett Butler."

"You're funny, you know that Kevin Yoo. You've got a winning smile to boot."

"You really mean that?"

"I really do."

"That's sweet. Thank you."

I catch myself suddenly, get a little nervous. What if she likes me? It's happened before. I have to tell her. I don't want her getting hurt. I have no control over the fact that I can be adorable, at times-- what most people would refer to as *a real cutie pie*.

"Holly, listen, I like you, really, I do... But-- "

"It's okay, I know," she says before I can say anything else.

"What do you mean?" My stomach feels upset.

"I know that you don't-- you know, *go out with girls*." The phrase, it's so disarmingly old fashioned. "It's okay," she says suddenly, fearing she might have upset me. "Don't worry, it's not obvious, if that's what you're worried about. I won't tell anyone."

"I'm not worried," I say a little defensively and then wonder if I am. After all, didn't I lie to Crickshaw. Didn't I sell my soul in that office? I breathe, slow and deep, *be calm Kevin-- be calm. Don't project your anger on Holly. You did this to yourself, Yoo. You know that.*

"Maybe that's part of my problem. I guess I am scared. It would be nice, you know, to-- to let it go. Know what I mean?"

"Of course, I do, Kevin." She nods, understanding perfectly. "We all have things, you know-- things we carry around with us." She reaches across the table, takes my hand, a sweet and caring smile on her face. "Someday, Kevin, you can lay your burdens down."

I feel suddenly tired as Atlas holding up the skies.

"When?"

"When you're good and ready."

"Sometimes I feel like I'm-- like I'm not gonna make it. I feel like I'm lost, like in a labyrinth."

"Without a ball of twine," says Holly with understanding. A shadow passes over her face and for a moment she seems infinitely sad.

"You know the feeling, huh?"

"I've felt like that for years. How can you beat the monster at the center of the maze without Wisdom's thread?"

I can see the dark twists and turns of stone tunnels in my mind. But maybe some labyrinths look different. Maybe some appear quite nice at first. But in the center, there's a monster waiting... maybe not a Minotaur in this case. More likely a spider.

A red spider with eyes of fire.

"He left me," Holly says all of a sudden, her voice almost a whisper. Quiet as it is, it startles me. Visions of spiny red haired horrors melt like fog in the sun.

"You were married?"

She's looking very far away. "Briefly. Then-- one day... he just left. No explanation. I guess, the thing is, you just have to keep going. Pull yourself up by the bootstraps, as they say."

For the first time I see a look of true sadness on her face. But it passes in a second. She wipes a tear off her cheek with the palm of her hand and she smiles at me. "What are you hiding from, Kevin Yoo?"

I can't decide if I should tell her or not-- about Mrs. Lebowitz and the ax wound and all the funerals I have attended under false pretenses. I've never told anyone. But Holly has opened up to me. She trusts me. It's time for me to trust someone, too. I swallow the lump in my throat.

I tell her. Slowly, painfully, awkwardly.

She listens.

When I finish she sits for a moment in thought, bites her lip then smiles.

"Well, sure, you could go around being a negative Nellie about it, or you could see it as a glass half full."

"Are you from Green Acres?"

"Good heavens no," she says.

We're both laughing now.

"Holly, if someone walked out on you-- they're an absolute fool. I mean it," I add sternly, before she can duck the compliment. "You are truly the most lovely girl I've ever met. Honest to God."

It takes her a moment to speak without tears. But then she tells me in her no nonsense, determined way, "It sounds to me like you did a lot of good, brought a lot of folks comfort when they needed it. But it's probably good that you don't do that anymore. You're alive, Kevin Yoo-- " Her voice is as soft and as promising as this early summer day, full of hope and the assurance of old sins forgiven, new days ahead. "Don't you know that? Aren't you glad?"

"For what?" I ask, flinging off the last sludgy residue of gloom that has so stubbornly gooped itself to my spirit.

"You're breathing, silly. That's more than you can say for most of the people who have ever lived on this planet. And the sun is shining on you. The world, as they say, is your oyster."

"Maybe I'm allergic to shellfish."

"There you go again, Mr. Mullygrubs. Stop it. Stop it right now," she says with playful but stern insistence. "And look... look up... "

A beautiful beam of sunlight is shining down on the table through the window. Countless motes of dust are swimming in it, spinning and spinning in an endless and uncomplicated waltz. Holly lifts her hand, lets her fingers tickle through the beam of light. Then she leans, chin resting in her palm and stares dreamily across the room at nothing in particular.

We sit in peaceful silence after that, finishing our coffee. I look at her and wonder, how does someone come into your life, a complete stranger, and with just a few words and a smile make it all better? Sometimes the right person just seems to come along.

"Kevin, when the time comes, you have to fight-- do you hear me? No matter what."

"Even if I lose?"

"Yes. Sometimes you succeed, even if you can't see it. Even, if it seems, at the moment, that you fail. There's a bigger picture, y'know?"

"Holly, thank you. You've really cheered me up. I mean that."

She blushes at the compliment, lingers at the door a moment. "You're gonna be just fine, you know that, Kevin Yoo. Don't give up. It's-- what do they say, a big world out there."

She gives me another smile and slips out the door.

And I believe it, too. It is a big world out there. It's wide open before me.

Or, as Holly says, *the world is your oyster*, Kevin Yoo.

It's not too late to change.

This just might be the day.

I'm feeling so positive after seeing Holly that I intend to get right out there in the sun and go for a nice, long walk, but the house, she has a way of stalling me. It's hard to explain just how she does it. But time seems to flow differently inside these walls. She can stretch or compress the minutes according to Her mood, Her desires.

I find myself counting light fixtures, stairs, doors, trying to get an exact measurement of the house; but it is impossible, because whenever I go back and recount anything-- the numbers are never the same. I don't know how she does it.

And there are always whispering voices and a hint of music, upstairs, downstairs, at the end of every hall, the sound of stealthy footsteps and doors softly shutting. It's never flat out horrifying, unsettling, maybe-- like She is teasing me, luring me further and further in. But whenever I think I'm about to discover the source-- there's nothing there.

I start to think it's all in my mind.

Did I imagine it? The laughter? The music? Is it here? There? Anywhere? Nowhere?

I realize I'm going in circles, trying to break the loop of repeating thoughts. But it is no use.

Things start to get a little hazy. My head is clouded by a sudden rush of fog. It's almost like I'm drunk-- or I've been poisoned.

And I hear Her voice whispering to me, promising to show me dark wonders, better than any encouragement Holly could ever give me.

Why seek the sun, when I can hide you in glorious shadow?
I can make you the servant of a living god.
If only you will submit to me, my will and the will of Unglit.

I'm drawn by her voice and I wander further and further back into the house, passing rooms within rooms and endless corkscrew hallways that twist round and round upon themselves and always delving down. The walls stretch and contort like melted wax. The woodwork and stone pulses, expands and contracts. I'm feeling a little claustrophobic, almost like She's swallowing me whole and the power of her contracting muscles is forcing me against my will deeper down into her gullet.

At some point, She guides my hand up along a stone wall in some part of the house I have never seen before. My fingers trail along until She gives a command and I press my hand against a protruding stone set in the wall. A panel swings inwards and a gaping black hole looms before me. I'm drawn deeper down into the bowels of the house. The light grows dim behind me, fades to a dismal twilight grey. The smell of earth and mold is strong in my nostrils. I don't remember going down into the basement, but that's where I find myself, hand trailing along a damp, moss covered stone wall for support.

I'm alone in the dark.

The stink of mildew and decay grows stronger, clogging my nostrils.

What am I doing down here? How did I get here? And-- where the hell am I going?

Down, down, down. I'm walking in a dream like stupor down long flights of crumbling stone steps, slick with water. There's no way this can be part of the house. It feels like I'm miles underground. Surely, I'm dreaming.

How much time has passed in the descent? There's no telling. It feels like hours, but it could be only minutes. The sounds of my shaky breathing is unsettling in the dark. The pounding of my heart sounds loud enough to draw out any number of lurking horrors from the impenetrable shadows. I feel like numerous blind eyes are turned in my direction.

I think about turning, fleeing back up the stairs, but my attention is captured by a faint glimmer up ahead. A pale, red light flickers in the darkness at the bottom of the stair.

A gust of cold air rushes up from below and in the dim light, I realize that there is an open gulf gaping wide on my left side-- a bottomless chasm. An abyss.

Thoughts of plunging into that blackness makes my head reel and I reach out to steady myself, lean back against the stone wall on my other side. Looking up, I can see tier upon tier of shadowy pillared niches, swimming into focus in the red light. Thousands of columns, supporting thousands of arches, all decorated with grotesque and bestial statues. How could anything like this have been carved here? It would take thousands of men, hundreds of years to carve what I am seeing. It's impossible. An opium vision is the only explanation. Surely such a sight as the one I'm seeing could not exist in the waking world.

I hear a scream from below. My heartbeat quickens.

A few minutes more and I reach the bottom of this portion of the stairs. I see that the stone steps turn and plunge downwards, deeper into the hideous darkness. But I go no further. The red light is coming from just beyond the nearest alcove. I'm trembling and sweating, despite the cold air, as I duck beneath the nearest arch and peer into the red litten cavern beyond. The rock is carved with more columns. Bestial statues, sculpted from black rock, adorn the walls.

That's when I catch a familiar whiff of the noxious incense, same as I smelled the night the eight legged horror was lurking outside my bedroom door. I put my hand to my mouth trying to block out the reeking stench. Massive, black tallow candles burn in recesses along the walls. The guttering light casts a forest of flickering shadows around the chamber.

Across the cavern, I can see several figures, their bodies draped in long tattered robes, hunched over, prostrating themselves on the floor before one of the grotesque statues. I gasp when I see the object of their adoration and my breath catches in my throat.

A terrible spider, big as a boulder. Red as hell.

The hooded figures are chanting, intoning some earth bound evil. I can't understand the words and for that I'm glad. They are still huddled close together and I can't make out just what it is they are doing, but their movements consist of violent tearing and jerking motions-- like they are cutting and slicing and ripping something apart. A muffled scream comes from beneath the huddled mass. The black robed figures shift suddenly, and something comes loose with a wet, ripping sound. That's when I see it-- the pale, lifeless arm sticking out from the huddled mass. One of the figures raises a pair of bloody hands clenching a still quivering heart. I nearly swoon, but catch myself. All that keeps me from collapsing is me doubting my sanity, not truly believing that I'm seeing this horrible rite acted out.

"It's a dream," I mutter over and over again. "A dream, a dream."

More bloody hands reach up, pieces of flesh clenched in their fingers. And on the ring finger of each hand, a golden spider-shaped ring catches the light and the numerous blood red ruby eyes glitter cruelly. They lay the meat on an altar before the image of the spider god. My heart is racing wildly. My vision goes blurry a couple of times.

And I see the face of the dead girl, the one whose heart they have torn out.

It's Missy Harper-- the girl from the milk carton.

The priests, if that's what they are, go on chanting, raising their voices in unison and at certain parts of the rite, pausing to drizzle blood over a mouldering skeleton which lies on the ground before them. And I am able to pick out a few frighteningly familiar words from amongst the otherwise indecipherable demonic intonations.

"Agruun... Unglit... Azgaroth..."

I have no understanding of their meaning, but I know I've heard these words before.

And as the blood drips on the bones, I hear a hissing sound, see steam rising from the skeleton. And then red, veiny sinews begin to thread themselves around and around the bones, twisting, winding like newly sprouted vines. Bloody sinew is growing back on the bones before my very eyes.

"*Rise. Rise-- RISE!*"

These witches, warlocks-- whatever they are-- they are giving life to the dead by taking it from the living.

The last echo of their conjoined voices dies away, followed by a death knell of silence.

And then the skeletal fingers, glistening with gore-- twitch with a spasmodic jerking motion.

The dead thing-- It's coming to life.

The hooded figures lean in, draping the rising corpse with a black tattered cloak like their own.

Dream or no dream, this is enough, more than my mind can handle. My thoughts are reeling. I stagger drunkenly back, trying to get out of the cavern unseen.

That's when it moves.

The red idol, carved in the likeness of a spider, rears up with a hiss. It's many jointed legs arch up and the abomination rises to life. It descends slowly, one thorny leg at a time, making its way down from the pedestal.

I clamp one hand to my mouth choking back a scream. But too late.

They've heard.

The hooded figures rise up, start to turn slowly towards me. And one of them-- I recognize, even with her face half hidden by the shadow of her hood. As she turns around to glare at me, I recognize the old cruel face and the burning Gorgon's eyes. It's her. The one who cursed me on my first day in town. The one who tried to knock my eye out with a pinecone.

Vera Griswick.

I turn to flee, stumbling back between the columns and through the rock hewn arch. In my terror, I have forgotten about the chasm and nearly run off the brink into the black abyss. I skid to a halt, kicking a shower of loose stones into the blackness. For an instant, I stagger on the edge, arms cartwheeling, nearly pitching headfirst into the abyss, but manage to pull myself back from the brink. With my balance regained, I turn and rush up the stairs, stumbling once, twice, on the second fall banging my shin against the hard stone. I draw in a painful hissing breath, but am on my feet again in a second. Behind me, I can hear a bull-like snuffling and snorting. The red spider is stalking me, lumbering up the stairs, pulling its hairy bloated belly along behind it. For all its massive girth, it moves fast. I glance back once, see it gaining, smooth, soulless eyes lit with inner fire. It's going to pounce on me. There is no way I can out run it.

It's going to catch me, skewer me on those lethal, sabre length fangs and drag my body back to the red litten cavern where those black hooded figures will carve me up on that gore drenched altar.

And when I turn back...

A black cloaked figure is standing before me, blocking the stair. It reaches out one skeletal hand. Threads of gore drip from its fingertips showing where strands of muscle and veins have started to thread around the newly reanimated bones. I see no flesh. The fingers come crawling towards me, spattering blood at my feet, all over my shoes. It it the thing from the altar. The corpse newly raised from the dead. I cannot see its face, only two eyes burning like embers beneath the shadowy hood.

Cranston.

It reaches out for me, grabs hold of my wrist with its withered hand, squeezing my flesh with grave rotted fingers. My flesh burns beneath its touch and I feel painful blisters bubbling up on my skin. I pry furiously at the hand. It lets go, then grabs hold of my throat, lifts me off the ground. I hear a sizzling sound, smell the stench of burning flesh as those talon fingers leave their mark on my neck.

The grave ghoul throws me aside, as easily as if I was a ragdoll. I land stunned on the stairs, head lower than my feet. I hack and gasp for breath. My throat is on fire.

I feel my senses splintering. Everything is going dark. I try to raise myself up, but collapse, the back of my head hitting the hard edge of stone. As my vision spirals down into blackness, a shadow falls over me and I see the light of eight globes of fire as the many legged abomination closes in over me, drenched in the smell of blood and the horrible incense...

...My eyes flutter open and I find myself lying on my back in the front hall. Overhead, the chandelier sparkles in the sun, the tear drop crystals tinkle in a cool draft. I sit up.

It was a dream. I got dizzy, light headed and I must have fainted. Low blood sugar, maybe? I sit up, rub the palm of my heel in each eye. That's when I notice the fading blotches on my wrist, like subtle traces of burn marks. It looks like the faint remains of long, thin fingers pressed into my flesh.

And my throat is sore and raw. I reach up to touch it and wince at the pain.

There are more spiders swarming all over the floor around my head. It's no longer a shock, but enough of an irritant to make me swipe at my hair over and over again to make sure there are none nesting there.

I shake my shirt out, too, pat my pants down roughly. There's a glob in my mouth and I hock once, spit the wad of bloody phlegm out on the floor. The mucus contains a black blob-- the crushed corpse of an arachnid.

I hack violently, spitting again and again, knowing there can't be anymore spiders in my throat, but unable to stop, nonetheless.

I get to my feet, walk down the hall towards the back of the house, feeling frantic but resolved. I run my hands back and forth over the numerous walls, tapping, knocking, prying, searching for the loose stone that marked the entrance to the secret passage. And what will I do if I uncover the stairway to that hideous vault? Run screaming from the house, perhaps? Or run screaming down into the dark?

I spend an hour dragging my hands here and there, over and over again, until my palms are sore, searching for the passage that opened into the abyssal darkness. I find nothing-- just one ordinary wall after another. No secret doors or hidden stairways leading into eldritch horrors, no doorway to crouching spider idols or red litten caverns where necromantic corpses are being reanimated with offerings of flesh and blood.

Just solid walls of stone and wood.

It is past three o'clock when I finally leave.

My good mood from earlier has drained away. It doesn't improve when I look down the path and see Mr. Allgood hurrying up towards me, in a burgundy jacket and blue polyester pants. He's puffing like a steam engine. He stops to swipe his forehead with a handkerchief, then pops his cremieux pork pie hat back down on his head.

"Well, well, well," he says, running his thumb and forefinger over his mustache, "If it isn't the budding author. Good morning, kid."

Good morning? It's past three o'clock in the afternoon, isn't it?

Did I lay in the hallway all night?

Is it the next day?

I feel disoriented, uncertain what time it is-- or what day, even.

"What are you doing up here? Getting material for that pulitzer prize winning book of yours." He gives a gravelly, smoker's laugh. "Well you better work fast, 'cause this house is about to be history. You're in luck, though. This morning, you're about to see history made. I'm taking a survey of the area, making arrangements for the newest phase of construction of the Cobblestone Acres Golf Course. You may have recognized my handy work."

He smiles at me, nods down the hill in the direction of the golf course. I can hear the rumble of machinery and the shouts of construction workers as the golf course expands inch by inch and yard by yard, encroaching on the woods and the fields bordering Lake Afton. There is a construction truck parked down by the gate with a logo painted on the side: *Garcia and Son*. I can see a Mexican man and his teenage son taking a survey of the land, jotting down notes, making preparations for the destruction of my house. Scottie Allgood smiles with satisfaction, seeing the ever expanding Cobblestone Acres growing ever larger in his mind's eye, filling his pockets with even more soon-to-be cold, hard cash. I have an immediate, overwhelming, gag-reflex dislike for this man.

I think of Buddy, what he would say. "What about preserving the past?"

"What about paving the way for the future," he counters. "You know, you've been hanging out with those old fuddy duddys too much. You've really gotta learn to broaden your perspective. And this--" he says pointing up at the house. "--this ramshackle mess is next. Jeez, what a dump, huh?"

Ramshackle? A dump? What is he seeing? My face flushes angrily.

"She's beautiful."

"Maybe if you're a bat or a possum. But I guess beauty's in the eye of the beholder, like they say, huh, kid?"

I can feel my face redden. I'm grinding my teeth.

"You see, kid, this house is owned by the city. It's a prime piece of real estate, what with the golf course just down the road. Man, oh man, a person with the right plan comes along-- that person being me, of course, he could make a fortune. Strange thing, all the deals to bulldoze this place through the years-- they always seem to fall through. But not anymore. I've got a deal that the people of Afton won't be able to pass up. The town council is sure to vote in my favor."

"I can't talk right now," I tell him but he doesn't care.

He starts to push by me and instinctively I reach out, grab him by the arm, pull him back.

"Hey, what the hell, kid? Listen, there's a reason I'm the richest man in Sprig County. I have vision."

"But no soul."

"Ouch," he says playfully and jabs me in the shoulder. "You got spirit kid, I'll give ya that."

"You can't go up there."

"What? Why the hell not?"

"She doesn't like you."

"Who? What are you talking about? The house? Are you crazy, kid. Hands off." He jerks his arm away, straightens his jacket.

"You've got no right to come up here. This is private property."

"The hell it is. I just told you the city owns it. This house, she's not yours, kid, that's for damn sure. And if it was private property, what the hell are you doing up here, anyway, poking around? You know, maybe I should give a call to Sheriff Sadler. He might be very interested to know we've got another thrill seeker up here-- coming to exploit the past-- coming to conquer Demon House! Where exactly did you say you were from again?"

"None of your business."

"I could very well make it my business."

"It's best if you don't stay here."

"You threatening me?"

"No, but she doesn't like you. You've been warned. It's for your own good."

"I've been warned." He laughs. "You're off your rocker, kid, crazy as a koot just like that good for nothing drunk Willie Higgins. He says the same kinda crazy crap, too. 'The house, it got her!'" He puts his hands to his cheeks in mock terror then chuckles. "You might just be cracking up, hanging around here all the time. That's what happened to him. This house-- it drove him crazy."

"Back off," I shout.

There's a cracking noise overhead and a piece of the overhanging eave breaks loose, comes crashing down, nearly on Mr. Allgood's head. He jumps out of the way, lands flat on his stomach in the dirt.

"I warned you."

He stumbles to his feet, leans back down, grabs his hat. "You're crazy, kid, that's what you are, you know that? Absolutely nuts."

He turns to hurry back down the path. "I'm gonna talk to the sheriff about this. You're in for it-- just wait and see! And this stupid ass piece of shit house is slated for the wrecking ball! When that day comes, I'll give you a front row seat, you looney."

The bricks in the path shift suddenly. I see it. He doesn't. The tip of his shoe catches on the upturned angle of a brick and he falls forward with a shout, lands face first again, this time busting his chin open. He gets up, hand cupped under his bleeding chin. His hat has landed in the grass. He doesn't bother to retrieve it, just stumbles back down the hill, clutching his chin, glancing back over his shoulder once to give me a vicious look.

He shoves his way through the gate. The Mexican kid asks if he's okay, offers to help him sit down, but Allgood elbows him out of the way, gets in his station wagon, slams the door and drives off. The wheels peel out throwing up a cloud of gravel dust as he speeds down the road.

Across the street, I see *him*-- sitting at a stone picnic table in the little neglected public park. The Wanderer, draped in his ragged black trenchcoat. He watches Allgood drive off. When the dust settles, he looks up at me, then stands, pops a Pez and walks away down the road, hands stuffed in his pockets.

Halfway down Mainstreet, I see a woman come stumbling out the front door of Aggie's Salon. She is clutching a cardboard box to her chest. She tosses it down on the sidewalk, pulls a container of lighter fluid out of her coat pocket and douses the box and its contents with fuel. She turns back to the salon, starts raving, shouting, spittle flying from her lips.

"Sinners! Whores of Babylon! Painted Harlots!"

The box is crammed full of beauty supplies-- makeup, fingernail polish and at least one can of hairspray.

"Burn it all! Burn it all!" she screams. "You're all gonna burn, too!"

A rather large bosomed teenage girl is coming down the sidewalk with her mother. They are about to go into the salon, but the girl stops to have a laugh at the old woman's crazy display. Her mother, a little unsettled, tries to hurry her along.

"Becky, hurry up, sweetheart."

The girl, Becky, just laughs and the sound of it causes the crazy old woman to turn her venomous gaze on her.

With a sneer, she says, "Getting gussied up for your whoredoms, *BITCH?*"

The girl's mother gasps, drags her teenage daughter inside the salon.

Vera tosses the lighter fluid aside, pulls a book of matches out of her pocket, strikes one and tosses the flaming match into the box. It flares up with a *WHOOSH!*

A woman, presumably Aggie, has rushed out the door of the salon, trying to save her doomed beauty supplies, but she's too late.

"Goddamn it, Vera, that is the last straw!"

A group of women watches her from inside, faces pressed against the glass, their hair done up in curlers. A small knot of people has started to gather on the sidewalk as well.

"Repent you children of perdition," Vera screeches wheeling round on them, turning round and round like a beast held at bay, like she is ready to pounce and rip out the throat of anyone foolish enough to approach her.

Vera Griswick, the crazy pinecone throwing bitch, has her hands raised, fingers curled like claws.

"The hour of your doom is at hand. Soon, Unglit shall come forth and spin a web around the earth and snare you all like blood fat flies! And what a joy," she hisses, "it shall be for Him to suck the juices from your wretched, bloated corpses."

She stops suddenly when she sees me. Her eyes narrow and she coils like a serpent ready to strike. I catch a glimpse of gold on her finger.

A spider ring with ruby eyes, just like the one Cranston wore. I'm sure of it.

It's the same damned ring.

"It was you," I say, the horror of another recollection flooding back now, "in the red room, pouring blood on the bones. I saw you. What is Unglit? Is that its name? The spider?"

I glance again at the ring.

Her eyes flash fire and I can't tell if she is looking at me with contempt or with mockery. Her lips twist into a cruel smile touched with a shadow of secret knowing. The smile curdles in an instant and she clenches her teeth, growls like a rabid dog. She lashes out, jumping towards me with preternatural swiftness like she's possessed and rakes her nails down the side of my cheek.

It burns like a mother fucker.

"Blaspheme not thy lord and master, lest it displease him and he hang thee up as victuals in his web!"

I clutch my bleeding face, stumble back, doubling over at the burning pain-- just like the lich's choke hold.

The knot of people standing a few feet away gives a unanimous gasp. A man pushes through the gathering crowd.

I hear him ask, "What in God's name is going on here?"

Aggie, still standing on the front stoop of her salon says, "The damned harpy is burning my beauty supplies-- Again! And she just tried to scratch that poor kid's eyes out, Sheriff Sadler."

"Dammit," says Sheriff Sadler walking forward. "Vera-- Vera, come here, right now!"

From his exasperated tone, I can tell this is an ongoing battle. But a daylight battle, nonetheless. They know nothing of Unglit, these regular citizens of Afton-- or the other horrors, I have begun to imagine, that are lurking just under these streets.

The light burning in her eyes dims and she shrinks down, a crazy but harmless old woman again, no longer a fiend of hell. It's a clever ruse-- just like her Old Time Religion bullshit. The charade is well acted, but I can see right through it. I know what a hellspawn lurks just beneath the surface. I've seen those basilisk eyes unveiled, burning like twin windows into hell. I saw her in that red litten cavern offering sacrifices of human blood and flesh to the true god of her heart.

Unglit.

At that moment, the can of hairspray in the burning box ignites with a heart stopping *KA-BOOM!* --like a Fourth of July firecracker going off unexpected and half the onlookers scatter, shielding their eyes and faces, amidst cries of *"HOLY SHIT!"* and *"GOOD LORD!"*

Vera throws her arm across her forehead in a melodramatic display of losing consciousness. With her other hand she clutches her chest, screams out, "My heart! My heart!" She sways on her feet, staggers sideways and collapses.

"Vera! the Sheriff shouts, then turning to the crowd behind him, "Somebody call an ambulance."

In response, the only voice I hear is Buddy Haygood, just arrived on the scene. "Do we have to?"

I'm supposed to talk to Sheriff Sadler. He wants to know if I want to press charges. Maybe I should, maybe I should see to it that the old bag gets locked in a cell under the jail, but I have other things on my mind.

Did I see her in the crypts underneath the house on Witcher Street? If so, how could she have been there? I couldn't have seen what I saw-- flesh and blood growing back over dry bones.

Nevermind the giant spider.

It's all madness.

How in the hell would I prove it, anyway?

And the human sacrifice-- it was the girl from the milk carton. I feel suddenly enraged that such a lovely girl has lost her life in such a dark and terrible place and at the hands of those vile monsters. No doubt about it. Vera murdered her, slit her throat, poured her blood out on the bones--

--Cranston's bones.

I'm sitting at the front desk at Dr. Crickshaw's office, after daubing my wound with hydrogen peroxide and covering it with a bandage. I dip my fingers into a can of vaseline, daub it on the blisters on my wrist and throat. The phone rings. I wipe my fingers off.

I pick up the receiver, and before I can finish saying my customary, "Dr. Crickshaw's office," my step sister interrupts. She sounds nearly frantic.

"Kevin, it's-- it's dad. He's not doing well. He's at the ICU. You have to come home."

I want to be childish, petulant, say, "Why in the hell should I come home. You're there, princess."

He's not my dad, after all.

Instead, I swallow down my anger, go for the easy lie-- tell her I'm making plans to fly back as soon as possible.

But I'm not. The House-- it won't let me.

After a brief and terse monosyllabic conversation with Amy, I hang up. Dr. Crickshaw is standing nearby, watching me, stroking his goatee and peering at me over those jagged looking horn rimmed glasses.

"Is everything alright?"

"Yes, everything's fine."

"Because to be quite honest, son, you look a little rough."

I must look more tired than I thought.

"Well, you look a little drunk," I mutter.

"What was that, son? What did you say to me?"

His face has reddened, *snap-of-your-fingers* quick. His hands slide down, he plants them firmly on his wide, hall clearing hips. His voice has a sudden touch of thunder to it.

"Nothing."

He huffs and puffs a minute, clearing his throat a few times, wondering if he should give me hell or let it go. With his snorting and snuffing and frantic foot stamping, I can almost picture a bull getting ready to charge. "That's what I thought you said. Let me tell you, boy, you are walking a fine line with me-- showing up late to work-- hell, not showing up at all, even. I've about had it with your big city attitude. I will not tolerate any disrespect from a goddamned-- "

"Goddamned what?" I say, standing, surprising myself, realizing my right hand has clenched itself into a fist. I tremble, in a cool voice, say, "Go on, say it-- a slope? A gook?"

Normally, I'd say I was way out of line. But I know what type of man he is. I know what he thinks of me-- people like me. I doubt there's a white robe in his closet, but it wouldn't surprise me.

I can tell I've caught him off guard standing up to him like this, calling him out. When it comes to it, I'm starting to see he's just a blusterer. A wind bag, full of hot air. He pats down his hair, twists his goatee in his fingers, seems a little calmer now, but still uncertain how to deal with me.

"Son, I'm going to ask you something," he says darkly, "and you better sure as shit be honest with me. Do you understand?"

"Sure."

"Are you on drugs?"

"I wish."

"Because over these past two weeks I've noticed a difference in you. A change-- for the worse. I can't have a dope head working here. I won't tolerate it, understand?"

"I understand."

I stare at him sullenly. God, I'd love to punch his lights out-- and all he represents. Dammit, Holly, where are you when I need you?

He nods, but I notice the squint-- same one he gave me the day of the interview. He doesn't believe me and he's starting to think I'm a bad investment-- probably a-- what did he call it? --a bum humper, too.

"And you're mighty lucky that I don't have a replacement for you-- or your sorry ass would be out on the street. Now I'm going out for a moment. I have to uh--"

"--make a house call, I know-- at the liquor store."

He swells up again, but I give him the stare down and he turns and thunders off up the hall, blustering and cursing to himself.

When he leaves, I put the closed sign on the door, turn the lights off. I rummage through the top drawer of Crickshaw's desk, pull out his cigarillos, then sit back down out front in the waiting room and have a smoke in the dark.

This town-- it just keeps getting weirder and weirder. But it's not just me. It's not just in my mind. There's something strange going on here. It's lurking... just under the surface. Just waiting to break out. The air weighs down on me, heavy, oppressive just like it does before a thunderstorm.

This whole town is drenched in blood.

Less than an hour and three cigarillos later, I get a call from cousin Alan.

"Hey, dingleberry, where are you? Your family is worried sick. You know your stepdad isn't doing so great, dummy. I talked to Amy, she said you sounded weird on the phone. She also said you hung up on her. I called the hotel, you're not even staying there. And the car rental place calls me ten times a damn day asking what happened to the car you rented. I'm not the type to get pissed off, you know that-- but if I don't start getting some answers out of you, I'm gonna beat the hell outta you. Kevin, what's going on?"

"Nothing's going on, Alan. Just back off."

There's a moment of silence, then, "I'm coming up."

"Don't come up." I feel suddenly frantic. "I'm fine. I already have a ticket. I'm flying back."

"When?"

"Day after tomorrow."

Another pause.

"Bullshit, Kevin, I can always tell when you're lying."

He sounds upset with me. I've never heard him upset before. But he has no right. Wasn't it Alan that kicked me out? Hadn't I begged him to stay in Atlanta and he said, "No fucking way, dweeb." Wasn't that how it happened? Isn't Alan the real problem here? Or is the House-- is she twisting the truth in my brain like a corkscrew, weaving a new reality inside my head? But it seems so real.

"You shouldn't have kicked me out. None of this would have happened if it weren't for you, Alan."

"What are you talking about? I practically begged you to stay."

"Liar."

"That's it, Kevin. You're getting the goddamned torture rack, you hear me?"

It sounds almost like he's crying. Why in the hell would he be crying?

I guess I asked it out loud without realizing, because he answers in a tear choked voice.

"You don't get it. You just don't get it, Kevin. You have the dream life, a college education, a family that loves you, a future. I would give anything to have that, you know that? And you're throwing it all away. Me, your mom, Jin Woo-- even Amy, we're worried sick about you. You made your sister cry, Kevin. You are dishonoring yourself and your family."

"She's not my sister. And how do you know I have a dream life? You don't know anything about my family or me or what I've gone through."

"Jesus, you'll never be anything, Kevin, you know why? Because you're too goddamned busy being the victim to be anything else. I'm coming up to get you, like it or not-- even though I know for a fact your sorry ass doesn't deserve it. And if you so much as lift a finger to stop me, I'll punch your lights out-- I swear to God, I will."

God, even in the midst of my anger, I want to say I'm sorry. I do. I would never hurt you, Alan, not for a million dollars. You're the coolest guy I know. I want to tell him, but the only thing I hear on the other end of the line is a dial tone.

Too late.

I sit at the front desk, feeling fidgety, trying to decide what to do. Alan can't make me leave. Can he? I think it over, can almost picture him picking me up, forcing me into his car, driving me back to Atlanta and putting me on a plane for Seattle. And if I know Alan, he'll fly out with me to make sure that I actually go.

Truth be told, I almost want him to come and carry me away... to rescue me. Part of me is screaming, *Hurry Alan-- Hurry! For god's sakes, before it's too late!*

But the other half...

It wants to escape, to get away, before he gets here-- to make it safely back to the house.

Alan's right. I've hurt my family, my friends. At the core of it, I'm no good. Like an apple with a worm gnawing at the center. If I can't save myself, I can't be saved.

I can't risk it. He can't tear me away from--

--Her.

I won't let him.

Besides... She'll make it all better. She'll make it all go away. She'll fill up a beautiful amber colored glass of brandy or whiskey or whatever the hell it is. Just for me. There'll be time to deal with it all-- with my family, with myself-- later. Right now all I need is Her.

She knows it too. She is calling.

I jump up from the desk, leave a lame excuse for Dr. Crickshaw, tell him I need to leave early-- that I'm having stomach problems-- and that's the reason I've been a little off lately. All the fight has gone out of me after our confrontation and once again, I'm a scared little boy, unable to face the truth, to stand up to the bullies, real and imagined.

In my haste, I don't even bother locking the door.

I'm halfway down Mainstreet when I see Alan's sportster, ragtop down, zooming down the street in my direction. Shit, he didn't call from Atlanta. he called from a payphone just outside of town-- probably at the Bait 'n' Tackle over by the highway. He is trying to get the drop on me. Good one, cousin Alan. I want to be mad, but I know what he's trying to do...

...he's trying to save me.

Sorry, Alan. So, so sorry. It's too late.

I duck down a side street and risk peering out. Alan has parked in front of Doctor Crickshaw's and has just gotten out of the car. True to form, he's wearing a sleeveless t shirt. He hasn't seen me, thank God. I have to get back to the house-- my house. If I can get safely inside, I know he can't get me.

Alan hurries inside Doctor Crickshaw's, but is back out a few seconds later when he sees that no one is there.

I may be safe. He has no idea where I'm staying.

But as he is coming out, Mr. Allgood, a bloody rag pressed against his chin, is heading in. Alan nearly knocks him down. I see Alan apologize, then stop and ask him something-- probably, "Do you know Kevin Yoo?"

Yeah, I'm pretty sure that's it, because in response, Mr. Allgood starts shouting and waving his arms, gesticulating wildly with one hand, clutching the bloody cloth to his chin with the other. I've got to run. Mr. Allgood will certainly tell Alan that he's seen me hanging around the house on Witcher Street. That will be Alan's next stop-- no doubt about it.

I race across town, running as fast as I can. I run right by the Japanese guy in the tattered coat, nearly knock him down. I think maybe he shouts something at me, telling me to stop, but I can't be sure. I can't stop-- not now, not even to solve that little mystery. I can find him later; after all, he's been wandering around town as long as I've been here. I doubt he's going anywhere. I'm bound to see him again. Panting, gasping for breath, I make it across town and up the front steps of the house. I throw open the door, slam it shut behind me.

I stand, back against the wall, panting heavily, trying to catch my breath. A few minutes later I hear a car drive up outside. I hurry up the stairs to the second floor landing, pull the heavy curtains back, sending down a shower of spiders, and peer out.

I see Alan get out of his car, open the gate and start up the path.

At first I feel angry-- irrationally so, angry that Alan wants my house. Then I hear the house start creaking and groaning-- coiling up, getting ready to strike. It tried to kill Mr. Allgood earlier, what's to stop it from trying to kill Alan, too? It's responding to my emotions. It's my fault if Alan gets hurt-- or worse. And suddenly, my anger turns to fear.

"No Alan, go away. Go away. Please. There's nothing you can do."

Alan stops, looks up at the house, must see something he doesn't like. He looks puzzled.

A loud pop makes me jump. It's her, she's getting ready to strike. "No, no, no, not Alan, please. Just let him go."

Alan stands for a moment looking up at the house. He walks around back, disappears from view. It seems like an eternity. I can't see him. What if there's some creeping horror lurking unseen in the tall grass out back? A few moments later he comes back around, clutching his arm. It's bleeding. Some little accident happened back there, not much, but enough for the house to show me that She wields all the power-- that she will not, as Cranston said, suffer fools. Below, Alan paces back and forth, breathing heavy, looking for something to break, something to smash to get the rage out. He looks really pissed off.

"Fuck!" I hear him shout and then "Kevin! *KEVIN!*"

His cry, so anguished, lances my heart. I almost stand up and shout back. *Alan, help! I can't get out-- climb up and pull me out of here-- SAVE ME! PLEASE!* The cry is unspoken, of course. She'd never let me utter a word of it and live. And if I try to make a run for it? Forget it. I'll never make it. If I try to escape, she'll stop me. Kill me, even... and Alan, too. I can't let her do that. I can't live with that on my conscience.

"I'll stay, do you hear me? I'll stay."

It takes every ounce of willpower I have to not move, to not respond to my cousin, whom I can hear down below, crying now.

Alan gives one last look at the house. Then he turns, walks back down the path, gets back in his car and drives away.

My last hope is gone. But Alan is away and safe.

I breathe a sigh of relief.

She did it.

What did she do?

She threw an illusion at him, of course.

And because of it, I'm hidden here. Safe and sound. I never have to go back now.

What did she show him? I don't know.

A ruined house probably.

Shadows and rust and splintered wood.

She's clever.

I'm safe.

Alan is safe.

"Thank you," I tell her.

The house is quiet, but somewhere down below I think I hear a dull thudding.

And in the darkened attic above, a half imagined scraping sound, like thorny legs being dragged over a dust covered floor.

--the house's wicked, eight legged brain, contemplating endless treacheries in the gloom above me.

I feel like I'm gonna crash and burn. This town. This house. It's all driving me crazy. Maybe I'm driving myself crazy, too. I need to get away, to get my mind off my misery. I need to get out of the house. I want to get out, but I don't want to be in the light. I want to hide somewhere in the dark.

Before I go, I promise Her that I will return.

Of course you will, my love.

Why do I always seek the dark? Reject the light?

Whatever the reason, I'm in luck. The Old Standard Theatre on Grover Square is showing a series of summer matinees.

CHILLER HOUSE

--the marquee announces.

It's the last and probably worst film by seventies schlock meister Jeremy Shaftrick. I've seen a few minutes of it once on a late night horror movie marathon. Mercifully, I have never been unfortunate enough to endure the whole thing... until now.

"Great, just great."

It's about a haunted house at an amusement park which turns out to really be haunted, killing everyone who goes inside-- in the most insidiously disemboweling ways.

It's disturbingly ironic. But it's the only thing playing. At least it will give me a place to hide out.

There's only one person in line at the booth-- a tubby, chinless kid wearing calf length skater shorts. He's arguing with the kid inside the ticket booth.

"What do you mean you can't throw in a free popcorn?" the fat kid says.

"If you want popcorn, then pay for it."

"Look, Salzburger, don't be such a stingy Jew."

"I'm not getting fired over a bucket of popcorn, Wade."

"Oh, wow, Eric, you're so dedicated to your future career as a ticket taker. Your parents must be *sooo* proud."

"Besides, the last thing your fat ass needs is more junk food."

Wade snorts, glares at Eric, then shrugs, the fight gone out of him. "You're probably right. Besides, I don't really wanna see it anyway. You still coming over later?"

Eric sighs. "Of course. You sure you don't want to watch the movie. I'll give you the free popcorn."

"Yeah, I'm sure-- Julie's in there, right?"

"Unfortunately, yes."

"If she's in there, I think I'll pass. She hates my guts. Hey, when you come over tonight, don't forget to bring my ten-sided die back."

"Fine. Okay. Just go," says the kid, embarrassed suddenly that his buddy has mentioned the unmentionable-- He's a faithful Dungeons and Dragons player. "You're holding up the line."

"Line? What line? No one wants to see this crap." He turns to leave, sees me, adds, "Oh. Well, almost nobody."

He pushes his nearly shoulder length hair back behind his ears and slumps away down the street, a sweaty human cloud of gloom.

"It's about time," I gripe, irritated from having to wait on the fat kid and unaccountably crabby because of the bright sunshine.

Eric looks at me unenthused, says, "Welcome to the Old Standard. You seeing Chiller House?"

"Is that all that's playing?"

"There's only one screen."

"So that's it?"

He looks at me like I'm an idiot. "Yeah, that's it."

"It's just-- I really don't like horror."

"Oh, I'm sorry. Why don't I go buy a video camera, write a quick script for a romantic comedy, shoot it and bring it back here and show it. Would that work for you?"

"Just gimme a ticket."

The smart ass kid has this snarky smile plastered across his face and I really want to punch him out through the glass. Instead I slap down five dollars, snatch the ticket and go inside.

I walk away exasperated. From behind, the kid says, "Enjoy the show."

The lobby is dimly lit. I stop at the concession stand, decide to treat myself to some popcorn. I have to wait on the smart ass kid to walk over and scoop the popcorn for me.

"You want butter?"

"Yes, please."

"Oh, damn-- we're all out."

He's got that snarky smile again.

"Shouldn't you be in school, jackass?"

"It's the middle of summer-- jackass."

He tells me the total, but I stop him.

"I want a drink, too, twat."

He goes to the soda fountain, fills up a cup, glaring the whole time.

"And some Reese's Pieces. Not that box-- it's dented. The other one."

"You forgot the magic word."

"Oh, sorry-- *Now*."

Just giving the kid a taste of his own medicine. It's something I never do. But it feels good-- to get back at him, to take out all my pent up aggression on this snarky little shit. Well, that's the surface feeling. Underneath, I feel ashamed. That will come to the surface later. And I'll regret acting like this. But right now, I can't help myself. I'm feeling shaky crazy.

"Hey, why don't you relax?"

"There's an expression, y'know-- something about the ability to dish, but the inability to take. Do you know that one?"

"Yeah, I know it. You know the one about the asshole who pisses off too many people until somebody finally runs him over with a car."

"I don't know that one. But I do know this one-- about the kid who fails at life and ends up punching tickets at a run down movie theatre until he goes home one day and shoots himself in the head."

That was a little too harsh. I feel equal parts guilty and devilishly delighted. This town-- it brings out the worst in me-- a combative, aggressive, suspicious side I never knew existed-- or maybe always tried to ignore.

Eric, reaches in the glass case, pulls out the orange box of candy, shoves it at me along with my popcorn and the fountain drink. "I hope you puke."

The theatre is almost completely empty.

There's maybe a dozen people waiting to see this god awful, blood and guts epic. All but two of them are teenagers.

I sit down in the middle row in an aisle seat.

There's a group of four kids sitting in front of me, a little off to the side. Two of them, a red headed guy and a girl with hair spiked up like a blowfish are making out hardcore. I can hear the slippery interplay of their tongues.

Behind me, I hear somebody whisper, "That's him. Yeah, yeah, I'm almost positive. That's the guy that punched out Scottie Allgood."

I turn around, see a kid sitting one row behind me.

It's the Mexican kid I saw the other day working construction with his dad-- that day the house-- not me-- almost killed Scottie Allgood. I'm guessing this is the *son* from *Garcia and Son*. He's sitting with a pale, redheaded girl. She's wearing a ratty looking army jacket and way too much mascara. There's another couple sitting with them. A tall, skinny black kid slurping a Coke and next to him sits a plump, bright eyed girl with a mountain of bleach blonde curls piled up on her head like a mound of pasta.

When I make eye contact with the Mexican kid, he looks away.

"Aim, girl," says the plump girl. "I cannot believe I let you talk me into seeing this trash."

"Joy, what else were you gonna do today?" Racoon eyes asks. "Watch soap operas and eat Haagen Daz?"

"Maybe," Joy answers, a little snippy.

Her date, the Coke slurping kid, tries not to laugh, but Joy catches it, glares at him. "What's so funny, Austin?"

"Nothing. It's just, what could be better than watching Sara Schleck scream her way through a two hour gore fest? Did you know the director was investigated for murder when this came out because everyone thought it was a snuff film. Classic."

"Agree," says the Mexican kid. "And you get to see her tits-- twice."

Joy grimaces, rolls her eyes. "Lord, give me strength. I'm surrounded by idiots."

"C'mon, Joy, lighten up," says the Garcia kid. "Think of it as a nice, summertime double date, yo?"

Joy is not amused. "Matt, the four of us going to *Fernando's* for shrimp scampi is a double date. This is pure torture."

"Speaking of torture," says someone sitting a row in front of me, "I can't wait to see that screaming bitch get cut to pieces."

It's the ferret faced kid with scraggly red hair and cheeks festering with acne. He's stopped making out with the pixieish girl with spiked hair. Julie, I guess. She gives a few fist pumps, chants, "*Cut her up! Cut her up!*"

Two other kids, big oafish looking dummies, sitting next to her, both explode with, "*Hell yeah!*" and "*Ohhh, shiiit!*"

Even from where I'm sitting, I can smell the marijuana wafting off their clothes.

Maybe coming to the movies was a bad idea.

Maybe I should have stayed home.

Maybe I--

That's when I see him. The Japanese, road warrior guy in the trenchcoat, sitting by himself in the front right corner of the theatre near the emergency exit.

I start to stand up. I'm going to put a stop to this. Confront him. Find out what he wants from me.

I'm just standing up when the lights go completely dark and the protector rattles to life.

The teenagers cheer.

The rat faced kid shouts, "It's about time, Jew-burger!"

And from somewhere up above in the projection room, I hear an answering shout, I'm guessing it's Eric from the ticket booth. "Shut the fuck up and enjoy the movie!"

More cheers.

Then silence.

Cue creepy music and a shitload of ever mounting, incomprehensible schlock.

It's actually not too bad. It's so corny, so completely ridiculous. The dialogue is so stupid it's funny. And Austin was right, it's a nonstop scream fest. Sara Schleck is a pair of lungs with legs-- and tits. The slavering, hormonally driven, pot reeking teenage horde is loving it. Cheering, throwing popcorn, the collective teenage beast screams in unison with Sara Schleck. One of the goons in front of me lights a joint.

The girl, Amy, with racoon eyes, leans over me to take the joint from Julie, squashing her teenage breasts against me as she does so.

I hate to admit it, but I'm almost enjoying this stupid movie a little. The dumbass kids with their adolescent worries and cares. Innocent, high school summer days. God, what I wouldn't give to join them. I was a kid, once, too. I wasn't always so uptight and haunted. It's taking my mind off things, this grade B horror movie diversion.

Until the worms.

There's a scene near the end of the film where Chiller House disgorges a wall full of writhing worms that comes crashing down on Sara Schleck, silencing her screams and devouring her bare breasted body down to the bone.

It's too much.

I've seen those worms.

My stomach rolls. I'm going to be sick. I jump up, stagger out of my seat and up the aisle.

But it's too late.

I clutch my stomach and puke right in the middle of the aisle-- all to the resounding cheers of the weasel faced kid and the girl with the blowfish hair. It splatters all over the place and looking down at it, I think I see the vomit writhing, like I've just puked up a bucketful of worms. I heave again. This time when I look all I see is a lake of half digested popcorn, Reeses Pieces fragments and Coke. No worms. Just my crazy, out of control imagination again.

"Hey, Eric," one of the goons shouts, "Get a mop!"

A rectangle of light appears at the back of the theatre as the door opens.

"Aw, shit," says Eric. "I am not cleaning this up."

I feel perversely satisfied. It's payback.

As I walk out of the theatre, wiping my mouth on the back of my hand, I see Eric, give a weak smile, and a friendly reminder, "Be careful what you wish for."

I'm sitting alone in the room with the big fireplace in the dark.

There's a drink in my hand, of course. I don't know how many I've had.

How did I even get here? No clue. The last thing I remember is throwing up in the movie theatre.

It feels like I've been sitting here forever, like I'm a part of the chair. I have a hazy memory of getting up once and pissing in the front hall because I was too wasted to make it to the bathroom. I think I might have peed in here, too because it smells like urine.

From the shadows, the animal heads mounted on the walls seem to be glaring down at me with their glass eyes. I try not to look up at any of them-- the deer, the zebra, or the owl in the corner with its wings spread wide.

I feel disgusted with myself, just like I knew I would. I'm not cruel by nature but this House is bringing out the worst in me. I can't believe how I acted today. Whether or not the kid deserved it is beside the point.

I'm talking, muttering, answering the whispering voices that seem to be coming from the accusing animal heads. I can't look at them, even though they want me to. But I know they've changed. The glass eyes have clouded over. The taxidermied skins have sloughed off revealing rotting sinews beneath and all the beasts bear mouths full of fangs-- even the deer.

They are snapping and champing with those razor teeth.

I hear the flapping of wings as the undead owl thrashes violently in the corner behind me.

The rattlesnake lashes its tail back and forth.

Mingled with the whispers is a rising cacophony of reptile hisses and wild animal snarls and growls. It's reaching an unbearable brain splitting crescendo.

And they keep accusing me, this evil menagerie, telling me what a vicious brat I am.

"No, no-- I'm a nice person. I'm a nice guy. That was an accident today. I didn't mean it."

But the whispers keep getting louder, more accusatory.

Wicked, wicked Kevin Yoo. Wicked, wicked boy.

"Why are you doing this?" I sob. "What do you want from me? Stop. Stop. Please, stop."

And I clap my hands to my ears so I don't have to listen. But it doesn't do any good. Then I'm hitting myself in the sides of the head with my fists, shouting, "Shut up! Shut up! *SHUT THE FUCK UP!*"

I shut my eyes, hide my face in my hands.

From the front hall, I hear a heavy picture frame rattle against the wall. It's the portrait of that wicked old woman in black. Something thumps heavily to the floor. It sounds like she has jumped out of the painting.

My throat tightens. The room starts to spin.

I'm still babbling, trying to exonerate myself for my behavior today-- to silence my accusers. Who am I talking to? All the animal heads have gone silent. I open my eyes to find I am no longer alone. Crouching in the chair opposite me is the woman from the painting-- or a grotesque parody of her. It's hard to tell, my vision is so blurry.

But the thing hunched over across from me is draped in black fabric, not so much a dress as a burial shroud. I can see multiple sets of hands slithering in and out of the voluminous folds in the cloth. At first, it looks like the thing is holding fistfuls of knitting needles. But, no. The fingers on each hand are eight inches long, at least, and each one tapers to a fine pointed thorn.

And the face--

--there is no face, just a pale white blob of flesh, nearly shapeless like a half deflated basketball with two sunken depressions where the eyes should have been. There are several black marble sized moles scattered across the featureless lump of head-flesh. I think these might be its eyes, after all. Spider eyes.

I start to lose consciousness, fall to the floor.

I feel myself being lifted up.

The thing is carrying me upstairs, humping it along. I'm draped in one pair of its spindly arms, head draped back, like a corpse bride being carried by a demented groom in some Jimmy Whale, role reversal horror classic.

I'm too afraid to open my eyes more than a sliver. I catch a glimpse of one of its hands with those long, twiggy fingers trailing along the bannister. Thin, dental floss strands of *red-web-gore* trail out from its fingertips, sticking to the stair rail, stretching and snapping as the thing pulls its hand away from the rail.

The next thing I know, I'm lying across my bed in my underwear, snockered out of my mind. The bottomless glass still clutched in my hand. Through the window outside, I can see the light of the nearly full moon shining in gibbous and red-- a blood pearl in the black sky, painting my body crimson. I'll black out eventually, only to wake up, sweaty and exhausted, crawling with spiders, just in time to do it all over again. I could make a stand against her. But no. *Fuck it.* I will destroy myself one more time. What harm can it do?

Commence obliviation!

I'm frittering away my life-- minutes, hours, days in a drunken debauch. I just can't get it together. I don't even remember how long I've been in Afton anymore. It's still summer, I think. Yeah, 'cause those kids were at a weekday matinee. School must still be out.

I'm learning that this red eyed demon of the glass only comes out after dark. The House, she has a million horrors, but the night monsters are different from the day time ones. They gorge on different flesh. And every night, I tell her, *"No,"* but she doesn't listen, just fills up that glass-- *glug-glug-glug*. And me? I take it. I'm disgusted with myself. Yes, just one more, dear. I'll hate myself for it in the morning; but I can't-- *won't* stop.

Maybe I never got out much, like James always said. Maybe I have always spent too much time in my head; but I at least took care of myself. I used to jog, to eat mostly vegetarian, to meditate at the Buddhist center. But not anymore.

The House is my meditation now.

How did I get to this point, descending slowly down into madness by way of a hundred unremembered little steps? Now I find myself shut off from the rest of the world.

Why? Why are you abusing yourself like this, Kevin-- destroying your mind, body and soul?

Because I have not had the willpower to fight her. I have let her instill me with a thousand little festering fears. I have let her seduce me with a thousand more tempting fantasies and diversions. And now-- She is my master. And I? Her willing slave.

She is trying to flat out kill me, to drive me mad.

I despise her.

And I love her.

Cranston was right, after all. I was a fool to think I could conquer… *Her.*

All that matters is pleasing Her, giving myself wholly to my mistress, offering to pour out all my blood.

Why can't I stand up to her? Scream at her to stop? I'm scared, I guess and still fully under the spell of the House on Witcher Street. Captivated.

You can never beat me, because, love, you are a scared, little faggot.

"You wanna talk dirty to me? Go ahead, bitch, talk dirty. See if I care."

The alcohol is making me brave. I tell her I'll leave-- that I don't need her.

But we both know, I will continue to endure these torments and despairs and the mounting indignities she heaps on my head in the form of a thousand and one midnight horror movie scares. And the pain, I know-- in some ways, is desirable. Unavoidable. Inevitable.

I could end it. I think for a moment, I can drag myself up, run to the window and throw myself out-- impale myself on the spearhead points on the wrought iron fence down below.

No, love. Don't do that. Let me kill you slowly.

Is there another way out? I remember when I was little, my parents used to take me to Korean church and I wonder-- can God or Korean Jesus help me in here?

Her answer is swift and vicious and maybe a little too anxious.

No. No one can help you here. Not even your God.

The glass gurgles in my hand refilling hastily-- sloppily.

I tell myself, it's just a little problem. I'm somewhat tightly wound, I'll be the first to admit it.

And this little amber colored elixir? It just helps me unwind a bit. Takes the edge off. Helps me to deal with the fact that this entire town is drenched in blood.

And I keep telling myself--

--You're just great, man. Never been better. Looking good, doing fine. Yup, that's me, Kevin Yoo, the picture of perfect health. Fit as a fiddle. If you were to look in the dictionary under the term Healthy, whose picture would you see? Why, mine, of course.

And those lurking shadows? Well, we just won't mention those.

That's what I tell myself. But at times like these, a thousand doubts are flitting like a flock of sparrows through my mind. And the tidal forces lashing inside me are tearing me apart.

You're trapped, Kevin.

I'm a prisoner. And like any prisoner, I tell myself that I'm free, these walls are only an illusion. Anything to make my incarceration more bearable. I keep waiting for someone to break me out, but at moments like these, it's pretty clear that I'm self convicted.

I'm sacrificing myself to this Beast, willingly, it seems. And isn't that what Cranston said? She only wants willing victims. That's all too clear now. It's crushing me, like a boulder. Even when I'm away, the touch of her shadow is heavy as a *grind-your-bones-to-dust* mountain weighing down my shoulders.

My thoughts turn to James. I reach out, pick up the picture of me and him off the night stand, touch his face. It's the only photo I kept of us, the last memento I have of our relationship.

Lonely. So lonely.

Maybe I'll call him. Of course there isn't a phone in the house. She doesn't want me having connections with the outside world. But still, I could get up, stumble to town, use the payphone just outside the bowling alley, couldn't I? Of course I could-- *should.* I could call James, pour my heart out to him, tell him everything. Be honest and open for once in my life.

And just like that-- the rain starts, falling lightly at first but quickly turning into a downpour. Thunder rumbles in the distance. Is she summoning a storm to convince me to stay in bed?

No. No. It's a long way to town. I don't want to worry about you, dear.

She sounds more jealous for a moment than concerned.

Rekindling an old flame? Tomorrow, love, there will be time for all that later.

Yes, tomorrow and tomorrow and tomorrow.

If you call him, you'll just end up making a fool of yourself. After all, he doesn't love you anyways. Remember?

Besides--

--my glass is full again.

I dream of James. We are making love. He is on top of me, caressing me, kissing my throat, squeezing my thighs. I tell him I want him. He tells me, he's mine. He presses my head back-- a little violently, starts kissing my throat. I hear him growling like one of those possessed animal heads. It's a little unsettling. And his kisses have turned into cruel bites. His body feels cold like clay. I think about pushing him away, but he isn't going to budge and there is something thrilling in the bestial energy pulsing out of him. So I go with it. I'm moaning and calling his name over and over again, "James, James-- James."

It's ecstasy-- until I realize he's caressing me with too many pairs of hands-- six hands with long, deadly fingers. I wake with a start. It is the middle of the night. I am gasping for breath. There's a weight on my chest and it feels heavy as a boulder.

The faceless thing with long fingers is crouching on my sternum. It is groping me with six of its hands, rubbing my thighs, my stomach, squeezing my crotch. My legs are tangled around its legs. I try to scream, but I can't get any air into my lungs. It starts poking those dagger fingers in my face and dripping those strands of red, webby gore, drizzling them like honey in my mouth. I want to scream, throw the thing off, but it's no use. I twist and jerk under its weight. Its fingers tick faster, twitching and jabbing at me, cutting my cheeks and forehead with scalpel precision slices.

It leaps suddenly, flying back into a far corner of the room, flattening itself against the wall. It skitters backwards up the wall, then darts in a zigzag pattern across the ceiling out the door and down the hall.

I hear it flying down the steps, leaving the rustle of its death shroud in its wake.

Then… silence.

I reach up, touch my face. It's bleeding but not too bad. I want to get up, wash my face, clean my whole body where that thing touched me; but I'm too scared to get out of bed. My heart is pounding. My skin crawls with disgust. I shudder. That thing-- it was trying to rape me.

The House tried to rape me.

I sit up, listening to see if the thing without a face is coming back.

A drop of blood from one of the cuts on my face drips from my chin plopping onto the carpet. Then another and another dribble down.

I see the dark blots dissolve into the fabric without leaving a trace.

The House is not content to break my spirit, it also wants to drink my blood.

She wants to devour me completely.

Mind, body and soul.

I wake in the morning to the sound of breaking glass. I find the framed picture of me and James-- the snapshot of us cuddling on the ferris wheel, lying face down on the floor. I pick it up, turn it over. The glass is shattered. The crack runs right down the center of the photo. It bisects James face. I have been holding on to this one picture, have kept it on my nightstand since the first night I came to Afton-- last memento of our love.

But I need to let it go-- to let James go.

It's time.

She's telling me so.

She's trying to help me.

Also, she has no intention of sharing me.

Ever.

I dress in a hurry and head to town. I've got to find out about her. I need to know the truth about the House on Witcher Street.

Come back. Come back and stay with me, my love. I will show you wonders.

Her voice is almost pleading this morning, like she doesn't want me to know.

I'll be back-- but first, I have to find out the truth about you.

I shake off the urge to turn and go back. It's hard to do, but I force myself to walk faster.

I can't ask Buddy Haygood about Her. He told me to stay away from the house. If I ask him about it, he'll just get suspicious. I go, instead, to the Afton Public Library. Surely they will have some old papers I can look at, a historical register, a book-- something that will shed a little light on this mystery.

"Can I help you?" the man behind the desk asks pointedly. He's Kermit the frog skinny, with his unkempt hair swept over in a left sided part, whether kept in place with hairspray or grease, I'm not sure. I do know it's shiny. His chin and cheeks are dotted with spotty stubble, a hallmark sign of someone who will never be able to grow a full beard. He's wearing a green button up shirt and darker green sweater vest and a red tie-- pulled way too tight. I can't imagine how he breathes like that. He scowls, making it clear his helping me is a great imposition. A mangy, one eared tabby cat is curled up on the desk near his elbow, the tip of its tail dipping in the guy's coffee cup. It's a huge surprise-- the cat-- first one I've seen since coming to Afton-- well, live cat, anyway.

IF YOU SEE A CAT...

I thought the fliers had made it clear.

"Hey, you have a cat."

The man is alarmed by my surprise, reaches over clutching the cat defensively, as if he's ready to fight me to the death if I make a threatening move against the feline.

"What do you want?"

"Yes, I wanted to ask you if you know anything or have any books or articles about--"

I pause, realize I don't know what to call the house. The other houses Buddy has told me about on the tour all had names-- the Armstrong House, the Chandler House, the Willow Plantation and so on. I don't know what name *She* goes by.

"Yes?" says the snarky librarian, staring at me. He has already identified me as a time waster. His chin is resting in his left hand and he's drumming his right hand fingers on the top of the desk, chewing the inside of his cheek. His eyes have gone heavy lidded and dull, a *bored-out-of-his-skull* look.

"Do you have any information about the house on Witcher Street."

He sighs. "Oh, I see. You're *one of those*."

"One of what?"

"A gawker. A rubbernecker."

"What do you mean?"

"You're asking about that house and you don't know? Why would you be asking about that house unless you didn't already know?"

"I'm confused. I don't know what you're talking about. Honest."

He rolls his eyes. He obviously thinks I'm lying.

"The call number is SCH 173.64," he says. "Non fiction is all the way back."

He points vaguely down an aisle past the stairs.

"Of course, if you ask me, it's all nonsense."

He looks back down at his magazine. I am dismissed.

I stand there a few seconds, thinking I might ask something else. "I was wondering--"

He looks back up, sighs, tugs at his tie. "You again. Yes?"

"Could you show me where it is-- the book?"

A portly, middle aged woman with amber colored curly hair pokes her head around the corner. "Andrew Verner, you get up and show this nice young man where that book is."

"He's got legs," says Andrew Verner.

"Really, Andy. Don't mind him, young man, his bark is worse than his bite." She walks over, shakes my hand. "I'm Cecilia Jacobs, head librarian here at the Afton Public Library."

"Kevin Yoo."

She thinks it over a moment, realizes she knows my name from somewhere, then remembers. "Oh, yes, you're interested in houses. And what's this I hear about you writing a book?" She sounds suddenly proud of me, like a kind old aunt. "My sister told me. She's on the Afton Historical Society. Dot Townsend."

"Oh, right-- the bed and breakfast."

"That's right," she says, delighted I remember.

The cat stretches, meows pitifully, drawing Cecilia's attention.

"Andrew, if I've told you once, I've told you ten thousand times to get that damn cat out of the library."

Andy flips the tip of the cat's tail out of his coffee, takes a sip. "How could I possibly do that when that numbskull, degenerate, inbred Ray Riggs and his maladapted hell spawn are out patrolling the streets of our fair town, killing every cat in sight?"

Cecilia pauses, thumb to her lip. "Well, that is a conundrum, I guess; but what am I supposed to tell the overlords from the county office if they show up here?"

"They'll never know."

"Andrew, you keep a litter box in the restroom."

"Just tell them it's for me. I'm collecting fecal samples for Crickshaw."

"That is not funny. I want to see you in my office-- right after you finish helping this nice, young man."

Andy looks back up at me, chin resting in one hand now, squishing the right side of his face up. In his mind, I'm already half forgotten. There's a jaded lackadaisical look on his face.

"This *fine, upstanding young man*, as you say, is not interested in houses anyway. He's interested in a particular house." He glances at her.

"*The house.*"

"Oh," says Cecilia, the smile fading a little from her face. "What do you want to know about that old house for? It does have a dark past."

"What do you mean?"

"Um, Andrew, why don't you go get the book for him." The way she says it is kind of exhausted, like she's had to give in like this a million times before on just the same subject. And then to me she says, "Mr. Yoo, you should probably see for yourself. It's easier than my trying to explain it to you. I was never very good with ghost stories. But, between you and me-- it's all a bunch of bunk. Frankly, I wouldn't waste my time."

Andrew Verner gives another rumbling sigh as he slides out of his chair, walks around the counter, grumbling. "Follow me," he says.

I follow him down the dim aisle. He stops halfway down, muttering the call number to himself over and over, trailing his long fingers over the spines of the books until he finds the one he wants. "Ah hah, there you are," he says. He pulls a fat, well worn paperback off the shelf, hands-- or rather, shoves it at me.

"This is it. The names are changed. But that's the house. This is the town where it all happened." He throws open his arms in mock pride at the infamy.

I look at the cover. It shows a gloomy mansion looming beneath a full moon. The windows in the house are glowing with an otherworldly red light. Dripping, squid like tentacles are writhing out from the house's foundations.

Demon House.

"Jeremy Schaftrick?" I say when I see the author's name at the bottom of the cover. "The seventies schlock meister? The guy who did *Chiller House* and *Vampire Whores of Modesto*. Right?"

"Yeah, same guy. Here's a footnote you won't find in there," says the librarian. "He went missing, too. Her seventh to last victim, so they say."

"Sixth to last," Cecilia Jacobs calls out from the front of the library.

Andy gives an exasperated sigh. "Whatever."

He turns, walks back to the circulation desk.

I read the summary on the back cover.

In the heart of small town southern America...

A house of horrors. A house of terrors. A house that eats flesh and drinks blood. A house where the dead walk and where YOU are the next victim! You still want to see

inside-- even after everything I've told you. Well, if you insist. I shall open the gate. Come in, brave fool, come in. But don't say I didn't warn you. Go ahead, turn the page and find out if you are brave enough to survive the horrors of--
--DEMON HOUSE!

Total schlock. But still, I can't help feeling unsettled. Because I know that underneath the corny horror, there is a grain of truth buried within the covers of this book. Shaftrick probably had no idea what he was getting into. He was just out to make a buck.

I sit down at a table in the corner, tug the chain to turn on the green shaded lamp and open the book...

The names have been changed as the librarian said. But it is her. No doubt about it. It is my house-- the House on Witcher Street. I know it. What happened in that house? It doesn't matter, really. It is impossible to say how much of what Shaftrick wrote is true and how much of it he made up. But it has a long and bloody history. There have been a string of disappearances through the years, culminating with the one in the summer of 1963. The House plays host to a million horrors. Bleeding walls. Screams in the night. Floating apparitions. All your traditional haunted house stuff.

It has a bad history, that house.

Why?

That's what Jeremy Shaftrick had been trying to figure out.

What makes a house bad?

He never could answer that.

"Some places," he writes, "are just evil."

I glance up once while reading and see the librarian, Cecilia Jacobs talking to a man in a grey fedora. I recognize him as the half Cherokee guy who sold me boiled peanuts on my first day in town. Maybe I'm being paranoid, but the way they're whispering and glancing over where I'm sitting, I can't help but get the sneaking suspicion they're talking about me.

I am still reading when the assistant librarian makes the ten minute closing announcement. There is no one else in the building. He is looking down the aisle at me, making sure I understand my presence is about to become intolerable.

His announcement, "Attention, ladies and gentlemen, the Afton Public Library will be closing in ten minutes," causes me to sit bolt upright. I'm so bunched up-- nothing unusual about that, maybe-- so lost in the horrors of this book, that the sound of his voice suddenly breaking the silence almost causes me to yelp.

I leave the book on the desk, unfinished but with no desire to take it with me. I know enough about it now. I turn off the lamp and leave the library.

You're just making a mountain out of a molehill, Kevin.

It's not the first time, y'know.

There are absolutely no supernatural goings on here in lovely, little Afton Georgia-- jewel of Sprig County.

I'm trying like hell to convince myself.

But who am I kidding?

The harder I lie to myself, the tighter the steel knot twists in my stomach.

The next day, I decide to pay a visit to Eunice Bailey, the postmistress here in Afton and a lifelong resident, as well. She's been writing for the Afton Gazette for nearly forty years. And if that article on the killer cats and the spider are any indication, she must know about some of the strange things that are going on here. Does she know more about the spider? Does she know more about my house?

Of course, maybe Eunice Bailey won't want to talk to me. She might not want to share things with strangers-- an outsider like me. Afton, after all, seems like a place cut off from the rest of the world. Part of me hopes she won't tell me a thing, because I'm really afraid that if she does talk to me, I won't like what I'll hear. It will confirm that the horrors in Afton are real.

And how can I face that?

I find her sitting behind the front desk at the post office. She's the only one there, other than a fly that keeps buzzing around the room. Eunice, I notice, is battling it unsuccessfully with a rolled up newspaper.

She makes one last swat at the fly, and when her hand comes down, the gold ring on her finger makes a *tock* sound as it strikes the counter. She shakes her hand, winces as she adjusts the ruby studded ring and then looks up at me. Suddenly, she sits bolt upright, startled by my unexpected appearance, jerks her hands back, hides them in her lap.

She is a thin wasp of a woman. Her head ticks this way and that, almost insect like as she stares at me for a moment. I can tell she is taking it all in, studying me, absorbing every detail. She's wearing gigantic octagon frame glasses with lenses that are coke bottle thick. She peers at me, her eyes magnified by the thick lenses. In addition to her twitchy movements, her disturbingly magnified eyes give her a distinctly insect like look.

"Hi," I say.

I stand there a moment in awkward silence as the humanoid insect studies me, head ticking.

She rubs her thin hands together, licks her lips and I can tell she's already thinking who she will call first to spread this latest snip of gossip.

"Well, well, well," she buzzes, "if it isn't the new kid in town."

"Yeah, I'm Kevin, it's-- uh, nice to meet you."

"Yes, yes, yes, I know who you are. I'm Eunice Bailey." She offers me her hand, fingers twitching as she does so, squints at me. "What can I do for you, Mr. Yoo?"

She's cordial enough, but there's a hint of suspicion in her voice that tiptoes on the borderlines of paranoia.

When I tell her why I'm there, to learn about the history of Afton, and that I would like to have a look at her articles, she brightens up immediately, then realizes she may have given too much away and quickly resolves to be stern again. She is about to say something, but her mouth snaps closed and she leans away from me, puts one fingernail to her lip and chews on it tentatively.

She's waiting-- for me to convince her.

"I'm a big fan of your column, Mrs. Bailey. I've been reading it ever since I've been in town. I figured that if anyone would know the history of Afton, it's you."

Maybe I'm laying it on a little thick, but I'm desperate to get some answers.

She chews the tip of her nail with a *tck, tck, tck* sound, wiggles her chin as she thinks it over.

"I normally don't talk about these sorts of things, you know-- not with locals... and certainly not with strangers... You see, it's hard to tell who's making fun and who's serious, who really believes and who's just mocking poor, old Eunice Bailey. I've been telling the truth for forty years in this town and if there's one thing people don't want to hear anywhere-- but especially here in Afton-- it's the truth, young man. You say you're interested in the history of this town?"

"Yes, ma'am."

"What historical aspect, exactly, would you like to know about? Don't lie to me. I can read people like a book, you know. You don't report the news for nearly half a century without being able to see through the bullshit-- if you'll pardon my French. So come on, out with it. What do you want to know-- about the UFO sightings over at the Cartwright farm or that white squid that lives at the bottom of Lake Afton or the more recent horror of Afton's very own man eating cats? What did you come here to mock Eunice Bailey about this morning, hmmm?"

"I'm not here to-- "

She crosses her arms. Her head tilts on her thin neck. I have the sudden fear that at any moment, I could very well get stung by this human wasp.

I swallow. This will make it or break it. There's no point in lying to her, that much is obvious. I have to tell her the truth.

"Spiders. *The spider.* The one people are seeing in the streets at night. I've seen it, too. Do you know anything else about it? Please."

She stares at me for a long hard minute, stiff as a board. Her eyes have narrowed on me again. Then they open wide and she sits back, relaxed.

"You know something, don't you, kid. You believe. Or maybe, you want to. Yes. Come with me."

She slides out of her chair, and she's so short that I almost lose sight of her behind the counter. She scurries around, takes me by the arm and leads me to the door. She flips the open sign to closed, steps outside. I follow her out. She locks the door just as a man comes up with a box tucked under one arm. He has a fancy gold ring on his finger and maybe there's nothing strange about that, except that this guy looks like he crawled out of a garbage dump. I can't imagine somebody in his condition would ever have a ring like that-- solid gold and studded with tiny rubies.

"Eunice," says the man, "where are you going?"

"Oh, hey Jasper, we're closed."

"It's one thirty in the afternoon."

"Uh, emergency. Back in five."

"Dammit, Eunice, I need to mail this."

He gives her a stern look, shakes the package. It's a small box wrapped in brown paper. The wrapping is covered with little swirling designs, just like my labyrinth scribbles.

"It's very, very important, do y'hear me?"

"Oh, that. Yes, I remember. Hold your horses, Mr. Dupree, I'll be right back." Then she says to me with a smile, "One of the perks of this job."

We leave Jasper Dupree grumbling on the sidewalk behind us and Eunice half leads, half drags me down the street to the front door of the Afton Gazette. Like the post office, it's empty except for one guy dozing at his desk in the front room, half a sheet of paper sticking out of the typewriter in front of him. The sound of us coming through the door causes his eyes to open halfway. He mutters something, probably a 'hello' to Eunice, then shuts his eyes again. She buzzes a response to him and ticks her finger at me. I follow her to a back room, which must be her office because it its stacked floor to ceiling with banker's boxes, dozens and dozens of them. The desk in the middle of the room is nearly hidden from view. One glance at the place and I'm convinced that Eunice Bailey is-- without a doubt, one of the most prolific writers who has ever lived.

"Impressive, right. These are all my articles," she says proudly with a wave of her hand. "Most of them wouldn't be any interest to you, but a few," she says, shoving boxes aside, checking one label after another, "might be right up your alley."

I can't imagine what sort of filing system Eunice Bailey employs. It makes no sense to me, but it must work for her, because a minute later she exclaims, "Ah-hah," and yanks a bulging box out of the far corner. She heaves it up and drops it down with a heavy thud on her desk. The label is peeling off the box. I see two words scribbled in Sharpie marker:

WEIRD SHIT

"To be honest, I can't believe anyone is interested in all this," she says, but I can tell she is secretly delighted. "I get so much crap from people in town. It's because they're afraid-- afraid to know the truth about what's really going on around here. And I am all about the truth, Kevin. But in here you'll find out what you want to know. Night terrors and monsters. Things most people in this town would just as soon forget about. Things most folks around here don't believe-- or tell themselves they don't believe. But you can't live here long, certainly not your whole life, and not have seen a thing or two yourself. If you were to ask Dr. Crickshaw what medication he prescribes most to the people of Afton-- it's sleeping pills. People want to sleep. They want to forget. And they sure as hell don't want to dream. But this town, it sits on top of something-- exactly what it is I don't know. But it's big-- and it's rotten to the core."

"So you're telling me that this town-- Afton, Georgia is... what? A nexus for all evil?"

"Yes," she says flatly.

"Oh, okay."

She pulls off the lid and I see the box is crammed full of old clippings and articles, fragments of handwritten interviews she has made over the years. The papers are yellowed. It smells musty and old.

"You'll find what you want to know in here. You have to dig deep for the truth, you know. Literally in this case," she adds noting the mountain of papers crammed in the box.

"Would you mind if I photocopied some of these?"

"Be my guest-- there's more where that came from, got a whole garage full of material on this fucked up town at my house-- again, pardon my French. You just let me know. We'll get together and crack this case wide open-- and a bottle of wine, too, while we're at it."

I pick up the box, thank her, tell her I'll be back for more later and head across town to the library, lugging the goldmine of mystery with me.

I find a table in the reading room, flip the lid off the box and start digging through it.

"Oh, you're back. Got a project, huh?"

I look up to see Cecilia Jacobs smiling at me.

"Um, something like that."

She glances at the articles, her smile fades. "Oh, you've been to see Eunice Bailey, hmm?"

"Yes."

"Those are her articles?"

"Most of them. I think so."

"What are they about?" she asks, a little too interested in my opinion, almost nervous about what I might be reading.

"Well, I think they're mostly about-- "

I want to say-- they're about all the crazy ass shit that goes on in this weirdo town. But I mind my manners and instead, I say, "--the... um, unique history of Afton and her houses."

The 'houses' part gives Cecilia pause. She purses her lips. "Eunice Bailey, bless her sweet soul, is a busy body-- talented writer she may be and full of imagination, without a doubt, but she doesn't have a clue what's going on around here... not really."

The remark puzzles me.

"*Do you?*"

She shakes her head, snapping out of her thoughts, gives me a smile. "Oh, don't mind me, dear, I'm just prattling."

Before I can ask her anything else, she gives a startled cry that makes me jump. I glance up. There is a man staring in at me through the window. It's the sci-fi gunslinger in the black coat. He's staring at me, squinting, biting his lower lip. He looks up at Cecilia Jacobs, nods his apologies and turns away. He pushes through the shrubbery growing beside the building and walks off. I see him pop a Pez as he goes.

"Heavenly days, what was that about? He scared the daylights out of me."

"Yeah, he'll do that."

Andy Verner is at the door a second later, gripping the wall with one hand to steady himself, shushing us with his finger to his lips and commanding us to be quiet. The mangy cat is twining in and out around his ankles.

"Oh Andy, piss off," says Cecilia with a glower at the snooty assistant librarian.

Andy scowls, leans down, scoops up the cat, coos lovingly to it like a baby. He stands there rocking the orange, one-eared flea bag in his arms.

"I've been up all night, just so you know, trying to keep that fool Ray Riggs from murdering my goddamned cat." He is nearly shouting. He's staggering a little too, from exhaustion, I figure.

"Andrew Verner, you better watch your language. I will not hesitate to fire your nasty little butt."

Andy scoffs. "You've been saying that for years."

"I mean it," she warns, but her voice lacks conviction. She is like an aunt scolding a beloved, if wayward, nephew. "And get that damned cat out of here."

Andy saunters back to the circulation desk, grumbling, clutching the cat in his arms.

When he's gone, Cecilia whispers to me. "He is the biggest pain in the ass."

"Don't talk about me behind my back," Andy shouts from the next room.

She has picked up one of the articles and is skimming it unhappily. "Giant moth carries off man near County Line Road," she mutters. "My, my, my." She puts the clipping down, shakes her head, manages a weak smile.

"Enjoy your reading, Kevin," she says walking back to the circulation desk. "If you need anything, just ask. I can certainly recommend better material than what Eunice has given you."

Once she's gone, I take a deep breath and dive in, pulling out papers, scattering them out on the table in front of me, trying to organize the mountain of material as best as I can. It's no easy task. Story after story comes to light of the bizarre and otherworldly happenings in Afton through the years. These stories involve strange horrors lurking in Afton's shadowed places. Every article is a goldmine-- an insight into the little known tales of weird happenings in this seemingly sleepy hamlet. Eunice Bailey is right. Night terrors and monsters abound. Things most people around here would like to forget about.

It all comes bubbling up at me out of the box, one strange tale after another. It could just as easily be pulp fiction, lost material from Weird Tales magazine. I wouldn't be surprised to learn that these articles were actually written by H. P. Lovecraft.

One story concerns the giant moth that was rumored to live in Hattie Mae Daniel's barn. Another-- the giant, hairless rat Mrs. Dribbly worshipped in her cellar. She kept it, the article says, for years, feeding it on stray cats and dogs-- and worse things, too, it seems. Until one day, she fell in the pit and the rat ate her, too. Whether she fell in or was pushed, Eunice never was able to discover. Another article tells the story of a giant centipede that carried off Alvin Duggs and his family. Another relates the tale of the cult that Obadiah Stalks started over on the east side of Lake Afton, where he officiated as high priest in the worship of something that looked like a white squid until the whole compound was drowned by a flood. That was in the mid 1800's. Afton's strange history, it seems, goes an awful long way back.

Strange stories. Dark stories. Nightmares.

As if this supposed reality is actually transposed over another darker reality where monsters roam free.

And then, near the bottom of the box, I see the one that really catches my attention, makes my flesh crawl.

AFTON'S EIGHT LEGGED HORROR!
Giant spider spins a web of terror around the people of Afton, Georgia...

According to Eunice Bailey, the giant spider was rumored to live in the furnace room of the old Afton High School, before it burned to the ground in the spring of 1984. The article mentions a kid, Sean Neely, a freshman that year, who survived the school fire, was in the hospital for weeks afterwards being treated for burns and raving about seeing a spider with red fur and fiery eyes.

There's more...

I glance at another brittle, yellow paper snippet from the Afton Gazette, this one dated April 15th, 1984. A week after the fire.

I feel my pulse racing as I skim the article.

... with the recent destruction of Afton High, we are all left wondering what happened. In three years, six students went missing. Lastly, on the day of the fire, beloved science teacher, Arthur Cranston. Dr. Cranston was last scene in the vicinity of Afton High. After the debris from the fire was cleared, the remnants of collapsed tunnels were

found in the sub basement of the school. It is yet unclear whether the burrows are natural or manmade. Regardless, Cranston's body was not discovered in the rubble.

Incidentally, Arthur Cranston was the last owner of the most notorious house in Afton-- the infamous House on Witcher Street. Also known by derelicts and trouble makers as Demon House. According to the authorities, Cranston has now been named as a person of interest in the disappearances of the six students due to evidence found in his home. This reporter, for one, cannot believe that such a claim has arisen against one of Afton's finest citizens. However, Sheriff Sadler has said that he is very interested in speaking to Cranston-- when and if he returns. A search of the premises on Witcher Street has been made. None of the missing teenagers has been found.

I glance at the accompanying black and white photo. That's the second my blood runs cold, frigid with a bagillion instantly formed ice crystals.

There's no mistaking the image in the paper. I recognize the vulture, Cranston in his black suit and slicked back, brittle looking hair. He appears oddly unchanged. The same ten years ago as today. Cranston was a biology teacher at Afton High in the eighties. The House-- the spider... did it get him, too?

And when I finish reading all these things, I'm sweating. Things are coming together--

--things are also falling apart.

This town-- it's like a giant, evil onion. But instead of peeling layers away to find the truth, I feel like layer after layer of eye stinging peel is being laid down, concealing the truth, making it harder for me to see things clearly. A mess of squirmy thoughts like worms is wriggling in my feverish brain.

I feel suddenly shaky, not just because I haven't eaten, because I'm having withdrawl, too. I havent' seen Her in almost two days. I slept on a bench in the park last night. I haven't been back to the House on Witcher Street and she is calling... calling...

But I cannot go back there. Not yet. I have to know. I have to find this kid. Sean Neely. I have to talk to him, find out what he saw. My sanity depends on it. We have both seen it-- the same creature. I've never been so sure of anything in my life.

"Well, how did it go?" Cecilia asks as I leave the library.

"Good, I guess. Can I leave this box here until tomorrow?"

"Of course, I'll keep it in my office. Andrew, will you take this and put it on my desk."

"I have to do everything around here," he grumbles, grabbing the box from me.

"You poor, poor baby," Cecilia says.

"Mrs. Jacobs, what do you think? Do you think it's possible that there are strange and evil things going on in this town?"

"Let me answer a question with a question-- what do you think, Kevin?"

"I think-- yes, maybe. It's quite probable. After what I've seen."

"What have you seen, exactly?"

Andy is back now, he says disdainfully, "Yes, Kevin, tell us what you've seen. We're waiting with bated breath."

"Quiet, Andrew."

I clam up suddenly. "Maybe I'm just imagining things. Maybe all these weird occurrences have a perfectly reasonable explanation."

"Maybe," says Cecilia. "Then again... "

She shrugs.

The kid. He doesn't want to talk to me.

Says he doesn't live here anymore-- he won't. He can't.

Not after what happened.

I can't say I blame him. I understand why he doesn't want to dredge up those old horrors. I tell him this. I also tell him I really need him to reconsider.

"My life, y'see-- it depends on it."

He clenches his jaw, sighs, looks at his feet, struggling with the decision. I hate to put him in this position, but I really don't have a choice.

I've found him easy enough, just asked Cecilia where the Neely's house was.

It's my lucky day, I guess.

Sean is just here for the afternoon visiting his parents. He's driving back in a few hours to Athens where he practices law.

I don't know why he agrees to talk to me, a total stranger, to tell me the things he does. Maybe he can tell by the desperate look in my eyes. Maybe he understands. Maybe he needs to let it go, too.

"I'll tell you," he says. "But you won't believe it. Shit, most times I don't believe it, myself. I've tried to convince myself through the years that I imagined it. It's so-- so damned crazy, y'know."

"I know."

"When I'm away," he says in a shaky voice, "it starts to fade away and it all seems so unreal, but when I come back here, that's when I know-- it wasn't a dream. I didn't imagine it. It happened. Some real *X-Files* shit, y'know what I'm saying? That thing in the furnace room-- It was-- It was-- "

Real.

He swallows hard, and it takes him a minute to stop trembling.

"Can you tell me about it?"

He takes in a slow, seemingly painful breath.

"Sure. I'll tell you. But not here. Let's take a walk."

We head down to the lake, to find a park bench by the water's edge. Along the way, I notice someone following along behind us. I don't even need to turn and see who it is. The Spaghetti Western Samurai in the tattered coat sits down on a nearby bench, folds his arms across his chest, kicks his long legs out in front of him, lets his chin droop down. It looks like he's wandered down here to take a nap, but I get the feeling he's eavesdropping, taking in every word Sean says. Fine by me, let him listen. He's obviously interested.

Sean and I sit down on a bench by the water.

Looking out across Lake Afton I can see--

--Her.

She's looming there at the top of that barren hill, beyond the golf course, on the other side of the lake, casting a dreadful shadow that seems to fall over me even where I sit, weighing me down, threatening to suffocate me. The day is bright and sunny, but I can't help but shiver. I turn away, trying to avoid looking at the house, fearing that she knows that I'm delving into her secrets, trying to piece it all together.

And I know… She won't like it.

Come back, my love. I have mysteries without number for you to explore.

Her endless pamperings and promises of mysteries to uncover in incense scented halls, once so enticing, has started to make me feel ill, bloated, hungover. But still, I know will go back. It's unavoidable.

I almost get up off the bench right now, leave the kid alone.

Fortunately, Sean starts talking and I can turn my attention from the looming horror across the lake to the horror from the past that he's telling me about.

"It was the end of April. Spring semester. 1984. That's when I found out what evil truly is."

He takes another shaky breath, getting ready to go back. I can't imagine how it feels. When he looks up again, his eyes are clear, his tone determined.

"My sister, she went missing the previous semester. She was the last of six kids at the school to disappear in five years. For a town like this, that's an astronomical missing persons rate, as you can imagine. I was in Cranston's class. He taught biology. He had a real hard on for spiders. He had some bug hunter's club that met once a week after school.

"I didn't give a shit about bugs, but Melissa Joyner was in the club. And if she liked bugs-- so did I." He gives a little laugh, remembering the girl fondly. "You know how high school crushes go. Well, we stayed later than everybody else that day to help clean up. Cranston had shown us some boring-ass National Geographic filmstrip and we all brought snacks. I remember it so clearly, because when it was over, I asked Melissa if she wanted to go to Birdie's for a burger, but she said she wanted to stay and help clean up. I was heart broken until she told me she'd meet me there on Friday if the offer was still good.

"So I left school, got about halfway down the street when I realized I'd left my math book. So I went back. I didn't really care about the book, y'know, but it was a chance to see Melissa again, right? That's when I figured out math was good for something, after all. The school was dark when I went inside and I thought it was weird that someone had shut all the lights off so soon.

Then I heard the scream. It was Melissa. It was coming from the basement. The door was open and I went down the stairs into the furnace room underneath the school. That's where I found them-- and... It. Cranston had Melissa cornered and I thought maybe he was trying to rape her or something. But then I saw--

"--The spider. It was... It was a nightmare... a living nightmare. Big as a damned Volkswagen. Cranston, the sick bastard, he was gonna feed her to it. He had this staff in his hands and he was chanting and waving it, like he was hypnotizing the spider, trying to control it the way a snake charmer charms a snake. I remember the staff had this golden medallion on the end of it and in the center of the disk there was a ruby. And I felt like somehow Cranston used that medallion on the staff to control the monster; because the whole time he was raving about the Old Gods and whenever the spider would get too close, he would poke at it with the staff and it would hiss and back away into the shadows and become docile as a kitten. But I could tell from its eyes, it meant to murder him if it got the chance.

"And Cranston was also telling Melissa she should be honored at the part she was about to play-- a meal for Unglit, I think that's the name he used. He kept raving about the Old Ones, whatever the fuck that is, and how he had to make sacrifices to appease them. How he had found Unglit's tiny withered husk in some temple in South America and how he brought it back to life by making blood sacrifices to it. And how, when the time came, he was going to open a gate to the land of the dead and usher in a new age of the Old Gods.

"I tackled him, thought it would be easy enough because he was so old, y'know. But he was strong, way too strong for an old man like that. To this day, I'm not even convinced he *was* a man. I think, crazy as it sounds, he might have been a monster in disguise-- just wearing a human skin. We wrestled on the ground, knocked over a heap of old chairs. The wood was dry as a bone and when it fell against the furnace it caught fire in a second. The flames blazed up all around us. There was black smoke everywhere.

"Anyway, Cranston-- he got a stranglehold on me and I thought that was it, he was gonna kill me and feed me to that spider, too. It was there in the shadows, glaring down at me with those red eyes like hot coals.

"But it was Melissa, she saved me. She grabbed the staff Cranston was using off the ground, picked it up and cracked him over the head with it. She brained him good-- so hard, in fact, the staff snapped when she hit him and the medallion on the end flew off. She was strong as an ox-- star softball player back in the day. Cranston didn't know that, I guess. He thought she was just another easy victim.

"Well, the spider, it looked like it wanted to kill Cranston, like I said, but it couldn't as long as he had that medallion. But now, with the staff broken and the gold disk gone, it got it's chance. It pounced on Cranston. He scrambled like mad to get hold of that medallion, but it was too late. The thing-- it had him, bit him with those saber length fangs and dragged him gurgling into the dark.

"The fire was all around us. Melissa pulled me up and we ran. I didn't wait to see what happened to the spider. I just assumed it perished in the flames. Of course, by the way you're looking at me, I can tell that's not the case."

He shivers, hangs his head. "Jesus. It never stops, does it?"

By the time he finishes his story, the sun is setting in the west, turning the waters of Lake Afton to fire.

We sit in silence a moment. A mosquito drones dismally in my ear and I bat it away once, twice, three times.

"The mosquitoes around here are murder, huh?" Sean says, managing a smile. "We better get indoors before they drain you dry."

Sean stands up, shakes my hand.

"I want to thank you, Kevin."

"Thank me, for what?"

"For listening. I've been needing to get that off my chest a long, long time. It's nice to know that someone out there doesn't think I'm crazy. If I can return the favor, let me offer you this little piece of advice. Leave this town. Get the hell out of here. Pack your bags and go. Better yet, if you want to save your life and your sanity-- forget the bags and just go. Leave tonight."

I head back to town, make it a block from Doctor Crickshaw's office before someone shouts my name.

I turn back. It's Doctor Crickshaw. He does not look happy. His voice is trembling with barely controlled rage.

"Kevin, I'm going to put this as polite as possible. Where the hell and on God's green earth have you been?" He says, voice booming like thunder.

"I'm sick. I took the day off, remember."

"That was three days ago, Kevin."

He has his hands on his hips. His angry expression is slowly dissolving into one of complete puzzlement.

"Three days?"

The House-- She's playing with me. Time. It doesn't make sense anymore-- atleast, not to me. Time, I'm starting to realize, in Afton anyway, is completely relative... *if* it exists at all.

"What are those marks all over your arms and neck?" He leans close, bringing with him his aroma of brandy dipped cigarillos and whiskey.

"Are those spider bites?"

I hadn't noticed, but my arms are freckled with little red dots, swollen puncture wounds from dozens of sets of tiny arachnid teeth. Maybe the poison is making me crazy.

"You should have those seen about."

"I don't need you to check on them," I say sullenly.

"I didn't say me," he snaps. "I said *someone*. I'm done for the day. I don't do *pro bono* and especially not for combative little ingrates who don't show up to work."

I guess I should have known Crickshaw wouldn't do me any favors.

"Come inside, Kevin. You need to hear something."

I've been fired before. I get it. Right now I could give less than a shit.

But I follow him inside, through the darkened empty waiting room to the front desk.

"You'll need to sit down. I'll leave you alone."

He points to the answering machine. "There was a message for you yesterday morning. I didn't know where in the hell to find you so I could tell you."

He leaves me alone.

I think I know what the message will be.

I press play.

I hear Amy's voice, she is sobbing.

"Kevin, it's me, daddy-- daddy passed away this morning. Where are you? Why are you doing this?"

I don't listen to the rest. I hit stop, then erase.

I'm sorry Amy, really, truly. I am. But I can't leave here now. It's too late for me. I try to tell myself it will all be better when I get back to the house.

How do I feel about the news that my stepfather has died. I don't really feel anything.

Just numb, I guess.

"I understand that you'll be needing to go back to Seattle, right away of course," says Doctor Crickshaw, standing in the door once more. I can tell he's glad to be rid of me. This will be an adequate excuse.

"No, I'm not going anywhere."

The answer surprises and irritates him. "Kevin, your family needs you."

I don't answer, just walk towards the door.

"You can't stay here."

"I can stay anywhere I damn well please, you drunken bafoon."

"It's really not a request, boy-- You hear me?" Crickshaw is nearly shouting now, remembering how I stood up to him the other day, angered beyond belief at my standing up to him once more. "You goddamned yellow monkey!"

I turn, feeling the rage boiling up inside me, fed up with the good doctor. "What did you call me?"

"You go on now, get out of here, you little slope!"

That's when the world turns red. That's when I snap. That's when I let Her work through me. I channel all the whirling, netherworld darkness of the House on Witcher Street and unleash it on my boss, Abel Crickshaw. I rush at him, grab a scalpel off the desk, leap at him like a wild beast.

He cries out, stumbles back, completely caught off guard. I'm on top of him when he hits the floor and he is holding up his hands trying to ward me off, stop me from murdering him. His palms and fingers take the brunt of the slices. And I'm shouting-- without even realizing I'm shouting.

"I'm gonna cut you up, you fried chicken eating, racist, redneck bastard! You hear me? I'm gonna cut your ass all up! And I'm gay! I'm gay! I'm a faggot! A four star, butt fucking queer! How do you like it? How do you like it, huh?! So deal with it, *MOTHER FUCKER!*"

He's squealing now, shielding his face by wrapping his arms around his head, squealing like the proverbial stuck pig. His white coat is streaked with red.

I unleash one particularly violent, bone cleaving slice, but it glances off Crickshaw's gold signet ring. Lucky him.

The cigarillos have spilled out of his coat pocket. I grab a handful, cram them in his screaming mouth.

"You want a smoke? Here! Have a smoke! Have the whole goddamned dozen!"

The House pulls the plug. The dark energy gushes out of me. I fall back, collapse, panting, shaking like mad.

What have I done? What have I done?

I am going insane.

--have gone insane.

I fling the bloody scalpel away, sit shaking on the floor. Doctor Crickshaw lies nearby, curled up in a fetal position, sobbing, panting, barely able to get the words out.

"Good lord," he says, spitting fragments of tobacco from his mouth. "Good God almighty!"

Dusk is settling over Afton. I am not really hungry, but I can certainly use a drink. I've left Dr. Crickshaw lying panting on the floor of his waiting room. I walk down the street to the local bar, The Oasis.

All I can think is--

I'm fired...

... and I'm probably going to jail.

Reality is crumbling around me.

I have gone officially off the mother fucking deep end and now I'm over my head in crazy.

Yes, I need a drink.

The place is pretty empty except for a few regulars including the half Cherokee guy who sold me the boiled peanuts my first day in town. He's still wearing the worn out flip flops and the grey fedora with all the fishing lures. He shakes my hand, introduces himself as Harold Trout. There's also a woman with a cumulous cloud of red strawberry colored hair piled on top of her head. She's sitting at the bar, busy flipping tarot cards over, one after the other, then shuffling the deck and doing it all over again.

There's a couple sitting at a table in the corner. The man has a craggy face and thinning salt and pepper hair. The woman has a late 70's, Farrah Fawcett doo. She also has a gigantic fish bowl of a drink with entirely too many umbrellas in it. This is obviously not the first one she has had, because she is laughing super loud. The man is laughing, too.

They are certainly having a time. I wish I was. Seeing the lovers-- what else could they be?-- heads leaned together, holding hands, looking so damned happy, lost in each other's eyes-- it makes me feel empty and alone inside. God, what I wouldn't give to drink a neon colored cocktail from a gallon sized glass bowl with the man of my dreams.

James-- James, where the hell did you go? Why did you leave me?

"How is your stay in town coming along?" Harold asks.

"Good," I lie.

He's not convinced by a longshot. I'm drenched in sweat and still trembling a little.

"Kevin, this is Margie Dobbs. Afton's premiere psychic."

"Nice to meet you," I say.

"Likewise," says the woman, flipping another tarot card, too engrossed to look up at me.

I sit at the bar, order a beer. The bartender takes one look at me, gives a low whistle.

"Rough day, huh, son?"

What is he talking about? I glance in the wall length mirror behind the bar. It is quite a shock to see my face looking so thin and haggard, hollow cheeks, purple bruises beneath my eyes. My hair is a crazy rat's nest of tangles and-- holy shit-- it's not just my imagination or a trick of the light-- it's streaked with grey. How can it be? I have been getting plenty of rest, haven't I? --sleeping late every morning. A big breakfast waiting for me in the kitchen every day. And I have looked in the hall mirror every morning before leaving the house. I had looked fine then.

Of course, that's what the house wants me to see, I guess.

The house has wrecked me.

There's also the red scratch marks on my cheek-- courtesy of Vera Griswick. Along with the still painful blister marks on my wrist and throat where the thing in the crypt grabbed me. And on top of it all-- the numerous little red marks dotting my arms and face and neck.

Spider bites.

I look like a damned train wreck. No wonder everybody is staring.

"You're the Korean fella, right?" the bartender asks.

My mind is such a mess, it takes me a second to answer. Am I a Korean fella?

"Yes, sir."

"Emery Marsh, owner of the Oasis-- Afton's longest continually operating establishment-- besides the Baptist Church. Pleased to meet ya."

He reaches across the bar, shakes my hand.

"I'm very familiar with Korea, beautiful country-- *land of the morning mist*, they call it. The most decent, gentlest people I've ever met. Served there during the war. The Forgotten War, they call it-- Shit, I never forgot it, that's for sure. What part do you hail from?"

"Well, I was born in-- uh, just outside of Ichon, but I grew up in Seattle."

"No shit. I know Ichon-- too damned well. Became very familiar with it, in fact, between September 15th and 19th of 1950. What'll you have? It's on the house."

I thank him, order a beer. He sets it down in front of me and as I sit there drinking, I try to rationalize the situation, work it all out in my favor, convince myself I'm still on top of it all.

Maybe the house isn't so good for me. But I'm not in any real danger, am I? I'm in control of the situation. After all, when it comes down to it-- it's just a house. It can't come after me, can it? I can leave any time I want, right?

"--any time I want," says a slurred voice next to me.

I look over. Sitting a couple of stools down from me is a sad looking man, hunched over a tumbler of whiskey. It's Willie Bub Higgins.

"I'm cutting you off," says the bartender, not cruelly. He sounds sympathetic.

"But I can quit, Emery," the man insists, pounding his fist on the bar. "Any time I want."

"No, Willie, you can't. That's why I'm cutting you off. You have a drinking problem."

"I do not have a drinking problem... I have a stopping problem."

Bub Higgins tries and fails to laugh at his own joke. He pleads, instead, a few more times, but Emery isn't having it. He shakes his head sternly. Willie, defeated, staggers off the stool and out the door still mumbling-- "... any time I want."

I watch him go.

"Poor bastard," Emery says as he sets another beer down in front of me. "If ever a man had rotten luck it's that one."

"Is he the town crazy?" I ask.

"This town is full of crazies," says another local, Eddie 'Tater' Turner, owner of the Afton Scrap Yard. He's sitting a few stools down.

"It must be something in the water," says Harold Trout.

"Yeah, the gene pool," says Tater.

Harold Trout gives a deep laugh.

"What happened to him?"

"The summer of '63 happened to him. Drove him mad-- crazy as the proverbial koot. You know, Willie used to be the best fiddle player in Sprig County."

"Boy, could he make those strings smoke," Tater says. "He could out fiddle the devil."

"Had a new contract with some big recording studio in Memphis before his life fell apart."

"How'd it happen?" I'm a little afraid to ask because I know… *She* had something to do with it.

"Had a tragedy in his life, years back," Eddie says. "His wife disappeared. Thirty years ago. When he goes on a bender-- a really bad one, he still wanders up and down the streets at night, shouting about how the house got her."

"The House on Witcher Street," I say instinctively. I know.

"That's the one."

"They never found her?"

"Nope."

Harold Trout squints at me, asks me in his slow, easy way, "What's on your mind, kid?"

"That house-- " I've lowered my voice so that only Harry can hear. Emery is talking and laughing with Tater about something else. The rest of the barflies are out of earshot. "The house, you know something, don't you? Can you tell me about it?"

Am I just getting fuzzy drunk. Or does he really know?

The look I cach…

He knows.

"You don't want to hear it, kid-- trust me. But do me a favor, huh? Stay away from that place, will ya? We don't need tourists poking around up there."

For a second, I feel a surge of irrational anger. Harold is just jealous-- jealous that She loves me and not him.

They're trying to keep us apart, my love.

"No we don't," says Emery, listening in now. "But we still get 'em. I try to warn as many people as I can to stay away from that place but there are still some people-- gawkers, thrill seekers that come around from time to time to have a look at the infamous *Demon House*. They just won't take no for an answer. Just can't keep 'em away. No matter what we say. And somebody *aaalways* gets hurt."

"Like that kid that fell off the roof up there last summer," says Tater. "He and some friends went up there on a dare. They bet him a hundred dollars he wouldn't go in. Well, he climbed up onto one of the roofs. But he fell. Broke his neck. When they found him they say he had scratches all over his arms-- not from the fall-- like something had been reaching out from one of those dark windows and clawing at him, like it was trying to drag him inside."

Margaret Dobbs, sitting next to Tater, nods forcefully in agreement, causing her cotton puff of strawberry colored hair to wobble back and forth. In a twangy voice, she says "That's what his friends down below reported to Sheriff Sadler;

said the kid was screaming his head off when he was trapped on the roof-- saying there was something-- a dead thing without eyes, trying to pull him inside."

"Nonsense Margaret," says Emery, polishing a beer stein. "The kid was drunk and stoned. They all were."

But Margaret isn't convinced. "They also say, when they found the body, it had the most terrified expression still frozen on its face. Now what did he see, I wonder, that made him jump off a roof like that? What made him climb up there in the first place? I guess some people are doomed to die. It's in their stars."

I drink my beer in silence, listening to some more of the local gossip as told by Emery, Harold, Tater and Margaret. The talk drifts from *Demon House* to other strange things that have happened in town. I've heard it all before-- weird things wandering the streets of Afton after dark, people disappearing in the woods without a trace. Three beers later, I thank Emery, plop some change on the bar for a tip and leave the Oasis.

Outside I see Mr. Haygood coming up the sidewalk, probably on his way to join his pals at the Oasis. "Hey there, young fella, I haven't seen you in a while. Been worried."

"I'm fine. I've been busy."

"With what?"

"Nothing, just private stuff."

"I heard about you and Scottie Allgood." He gives me a wink and a playful jab in the shoulder. "You showed him, I guess."

"Showed him what?"

"Allgood said you busted his chin. If you ask me, the little porker had it coming."

"It was the house. I warned him."

But even as I say it, I wonder if that's true. Did the house do it? Could it possibly have attacked someone? It's just wood and stone, right? And me? I've never harmed anyone in my life. Right? Excepting the fact that I just tried to carve Abel Crickshaw into little quivering bits of ham. Otherwise, I'm a very nonviolent person. Allgood, that little porker, he was lying. Then again-- I'm the one with bloody scabbed knuckles, same as I would have if I had punched Scottie Allgood. The Mexican kid, he said it was me, too. I feel dizzy. I've been reading all day-- all those articles by Eunice Bailey and then listening to that story by Sean Neely, then the unexpected part where I nearly murdered Dr. Crickshaw-- and once again, I haven't bothered to eat. Now, hearing what Buddy is telling me I don't know what's true anymore.

In all honesty, I guess I haven't known what the truth is in a very long time-- certainly not since coming here to Afton.

Buddy looks puzzled at me, decides to change the subject. "How's the writing coming along, Kevin?"

It takes me a second to remember what he's talking about. Ah, yes, my glorious masterpiece-- *The Complete History of Old Homes in the South*-- by Kevin Yoo. Who in their right mind would wait in line for a book like that? I laugh at the foolishness of it. What a stupid dream, to think I could create something worthwhile. All I can picture are the whorling arabesques, the mindless swirly whirly doodles of madness I've drawn over and over again in those notebooks meant for pulitzer prize material. I've spent hours up at the house scribbling away. I haven't written a damn word.

Labyrinths within labyrinths within labyrinths.

"Oh, fine."

It's such an absurd little answer I almost choke on it.

Buddy's not convinced, but wisely lets it go. And I can see it in his eyes. He is really worried about me. But the house, she has her hooks in me again. And I'm bristling like a porcupine. Or maybe it's all me. Maybe I'm just blaming the house. Maybe, in the end, there is no fucking house. Yeah, that's it.

And I can see myself all of a sudden, lying on top of that hill where the house on Witcher Street should be. But it's just me and those drippy red tentacles have burst out of my chest and they're writhing-- glistening in the sunlight. And I start chuckling a little.

The truth can set you free. It can also, I fear, kill you.

"I am the House."

"What was that?"

"Nothing."

Buddy's presence is suddenly an intolerable intrusion into my mental, soul shattering revelation.

He just wants to laugh at me. I know it.

It's like that phone conversation I had with Alan-- only this time, it's Buddy that's the bad guy. Isn't he talking to me all sarcastic like? He's being condescending to me again-- same as always. Right? Why is he acting like this? Who does he think he is? I was his guest. He should have treated me better than this. Yeah, he's giving me a sanctimonious look, I'm sure of it. I oughta punch his lights out. They're all in this together, y'know-- the whole damned town.

"Dr. Crickshaw says your family's been calling. He asked me where he could find you, but I told him I don't know where in the world you've been staying. They've been trying to reach you. Seems they called the Sleepy Time, couldn't get ahold of you."

"I've been out."

"Estelle-- over at the Sleepy Time, told them she hasn't seen you since the night you dropped off your luggage."

"I'm mostly in my room writing."

"Kevin, where have you been staying? You know if something's wrong, you can talk to me. I may not be good for much, but I'm a pretty good listener."

It's true concern. There's a reason, after all, that everybody in town calls him *Buddy*. And for a moment, I can almost tell him, I can almost lay it all out. Something tells me, deep inside, if I do, I'll be saved. I want to tell him that the house is killing me-- that it's tearing me apart. But I don't. I can't. Humility flees in Her shadow and I lash out at Buddy Haygood-- my one true friend in this crazy fucking, spider infested, cannibal cat breeding town.

"I don't need to talk about anything. I don't need anyone to listen. I need people to get off my back."

"It's just-- I like you kid and I got a funny feeling like you're in some kind of trouble."

"Mind your own business," I snap.

He looks hurt. I feel ashamed, but I can't tell him-- not about Her. She wouldn't like it.

There's nothing I can do but turn and walk away.

God, Buddy, forgive me. Please.

As I'm walking down the street, I pass Dr. Crickshaw staggering shakily out of the door of his office. For a passing second, I entertain the brief hope that maybe the attack-- the attempted murder-- it was all a hallucination. Maybe I didn't almost try to dissect him with a scalpel. But-- no, one glance at his bandaged hands and I know the truth of the matter.

One look in his terrorized eyes and I know...

I tried to kill Afton's finest, whiskey guzzling doctor. That means I probably also tried to kill Scottie Allgood.

But Dr. Crickshaw...

... he'll never tell.

I have broken him.

One glance in his eyes and I know it for a fact.

He thinks I'm insane. A homicidal maniac, disguised as a Korean American nurse from Seattle.

Maybe I am.

Yeah, probably so.

It must have been a bad night for Bub Higgins, too, because when I walk down the street, I can hear him wailing somewhere behind me in the dark.

"The house! It got her!"

Willie Higgins sees me, stumbles after me, grabs hold of my arm. "Did you stay away, like I told you? No, you didn't, did you? I can tell. I can see-- She's got those veiny red hooks in you, too. You'll never get away now. I tried to find her, to get her back after the house took her-- my wife. I went down, down, down into the dark. Did you know there is a city under here. A whole city-- a maze-- a labyrinth, built by the dead, built by the ancients-- when there were still wooly mammoths tromping around. They built it for the Old Ones, you know. And deeper still, there's a gate and purple light-- and the land of the dead."

I jerk my arm back from Willie Higgins. I wish I could call him crazy, dismiss his talk as the ravings of a mad man. But I know, in my heart, I know, he's telling the truth.

Where do I go after that?

Back to Her, of course.

I don't really know why. There is nowhere else to go, I guess. Some people are just drawn inexorably to their doom. *It's in their stars*, like Margaret Dobbs says. And maybe, just maybe, I can't beat the House because I can't truly admit to myself that this monster is not just something that exists outside of myself. But within as well.

And like Willie told me, the House, it has it's hooks in me. I'm nearly reeling, myself, same as Willie, staggering drunken like, out of my mind, being drawn back, back, back to the Beast.

The house is a labyrinth of dark secrets and shadowy terrors. But I can never leave her.

Not now.

I am trapped by a dark obsession.

Even though I know about the spider. Even though I just heard Sean's story. But the pull is that powerful. I'm snared like a human fly in it's web. There's no one to cut me loose or smash me with a rock and put me out of my misery. I'm just along for the ride.

She's promising all the while to show me more dark mysteries and terrifying truths. Same as she promised Cranston, I imagine. Will it lead to the same end? God, why do I want to-- have to-- *need to see* these horrors unfold? Without a doubt, I know the dam is about to break on me. The floodwaters writhing with the undead are going to sweep me away. Soon. Soon. Soon. I know it beyond all certainty. Why can't I just--

--Leave?

Go ahead, give it a try.

She has no qualms about mocking me. Who has trouble mocking an ant, especially an ant you're about to incinerate with a magnifying glass turned towards the sun?

Yes, I'll leave.

It's a fool's threat.

Sure I will.

Easier said than done.

Kevin, love, we've been through this before.

Yes, I know.

Well, if I can't leave-- I will fight you. I will destroy you.

And Her?

She just laughs.

PART VI

DESCENT

*He who fights with monsters should look to it that he himself does not become a monster.
And when you gaze into the abyss, the abyss also gazes into you.
--Friedrich Nietzsche
Beyond Good and Evil*

WHEN I GET back to the house, I can see someone sitting on the front steps. I open the gate, start towards the house. I think maybe it's the gunslinging samurai, but no...

I am halfway up the walk when I recognized who it is.

"James?"

I stop, puzzled, shake my head, try and rub the illusion out of my eyes. He smiles up at me.

I am beyond flummoxed. Seeing someone from the outside world sends my head spinning-- especially if that person is James.

"How did you--"

"I called your cousin. He said you were here looking at old houses. I said, yup, that is just the sort of lame-a-zoid thing my boy, Kevin, would be doing." His tone is oddly flat, almost like he's reciting this from memory. More likely, I tell myself, he's just tired after his flight and the drive.

I take a few steps towards him, not sure what to expect. But why would he have come all this way... unless...

He stands up, walks down the steps and hugs me.

For a moment he is quiet. We just stand there, holding each other. He pulls me close, kisses me. But it's not the kiss I want, expect or need. There's something...

... something sour, briny, almost-- in the taste of his lips, like he's just swum up from the bottom of the ocean. I pull back, study his face. He still has the same James Dean good looks, but it's weird, not quite right-- like a photocopy of a photocopy. Slightly blurred, less glamourous than the original. A ghost photo, a desperate attempt at, but miserable failure to, capture the life of the original living, breathing subject.

He's wearing a ratty old *Star Wars* t-shirt-- same one he wore the day we rode the Ferris Wheel together. I thought he got rid of that shirt a while ago.

And James? He's looking hard at me, staring-- as if he's trying to convince me or him or both of us-- to will his dreams into reality and assure me that this is honest and true and right and not a shadow play illusion.

A spider's trick--

--with an eight legged horror lurking just under the surface, promising the moon to get what it wants.

My blood.

No, no. I shove the thought away. I've been alone too long. Living exclusively in my head. Nearly driving myself crazy. That's all. This is James. My James. I'm just being paranoid. This is the love of my life. I'm sure of it, despite the funny, earthy, basement smell wafting from his clothes. This is James in the flesh, come to save me-- and he'll succeed where Buddy and Alan and everybody else has failed.

There are a couple of spiders crawling on the front of his shirt.

"Hold on," I say. Reaching out, I flick them away.

He looks startled for a moment, almost a little upset.

"What'd you do that for?"

"You had spiders crawling all over you."

He forces a smile, dismissing what just happened with a wave of his hand. "We need to talk. I miss you." There's a note of urgency in his voice like he can't wait to get me inside.

"I miss you, too. But what makes you think I'm going to take you back?" Can I risk playing hard to get?

James clenches his jaw, then drops his head. "I was an idiot," he says.

Yes, the ball is in my court. But I can't help but get the feeling his pronounced sense of humility is a ruse-- a ploy to get me inside the house. James has never apologized-- not once in the nearly five years I've known him.

"Why are you here? You show up out of the blue-- so desperate to make amends. Why? It's a little weird. You said I ruined things. You said it was over."

"No, it wasn't your fault. It was mine."

I'm doing it again, same as always in his presence, folding like a house of cards.

"No, no-- I was awful."

"*I* was awful," he smiles at me.

God, suddenly, I'm ten beers drunk.

Her.

I know it.

And yet...

"None of that matters now. You're here. Come inside. Do you want anything? Beer? Wine? No, let me guess-- tea. Earl Grey."

"You know me too well." But the answer-- supposed to sound so self assured and nonchalant, is stilted and awkward as if James doesn't know that's what he wants to drink or not.

We go inside the house. I tell him to sit down while I make some tea. I am so excited, my heart is beating so crazily, that I don't even remember making the tea. I just remember standing at the door to the room with the big fireplace, tea tray in hand. There's a fire crackling, though I never lit one. And all the beheaded animals are staring down at me with glass eyes. The firelight casts stretched out shadows of horns and antlers and claws, snaring us both in a flickering net.

I set the tray down, pour James a cup of tea, hand it to him. My hand is trembling a little, I notice-- with fear or anticipation, I don't know.

I always thought when-- and if, I saw James again, I would really let him have it. But one look at him and I'm melting.

I am so happy. All I want to do is look at him-- even this poorly made double-photocopy image. This desert *trick-you-to-your-doom-by-thirst* mirage.

I can't believe it. I tell him so.

"You came all this way."

"For you."

He takes a sip of tea, puts the cup down. That's when I notice it. My stomach lurches. The hairs shoot up on the back of my neck like sewing needles. I'm in the room with the undead. It's sitting an arm's length away.

Faint bloody prints on the cup's handle.

"Are you okay?" he asks me.

I look up at his face, startled by his eyes. A bitter taste rises in my mouth, a surge of bile.

I kissed it-- I kissed *IT*; oh God, I put my mouth against that.

Against...

...Her mouth.

And his eyes. Soulless as a soul damned to the deepest pit of hell.

Black, shark's eyes, just like Cranston's. He smiles the same vulture smile. I can see blood like black tar seeping out from between his teeth, spilling over his lower lip, dribbling on his lap. He stands, reaches for me, grabs my wrist.

"All I want is you," it gurgles, spitting up blood bubbles. "You're all I've ever wanted. You're the only one."

It lurches towards me, pulls me closer with that rot blackened hand. I jerk back, knock the teatray over. It clatters to the floor. I clamp my hand on its wrist trying to pry myself loose, to shove it away. The wet skin sloughs off in my hand, discharging a rancid stench that causes me to gag. I am overwhelmed by a sickening reek of rot and decay as the thing leans in towards me, mouth agape, worms writhing in the back of its throat.

I gasp, stagger backwards, pulling myself free. I stumble away, overturning the chair and land with a thud on my back, a handful of rotted flesh clenched in my fist. I fling the shreds of skin away, jump up, fearing the ghoul is about to leap on top of me. But when I get to my feet, the thing-- the dripping, black-goo horror is gone.

There are only telltale dribbles of sticky, blackened gore spattered on the floor where it stood. And a half dozen bloody footprints leading across the main hall and stopping just outside the basement door.

She is playing games with me.

Teasing me.

Giving me what I want.

To the best of Her ability, that is.

Forget about spiders, she tells me.

Forget about lurking, nighttime horrors in this silly, little town.

These things do not concern you.

Not in the least, dearest... not in the least.

She is luring me in-- the ultimate angler with the surefire bait.

A lost love.

Luring me in, promising whatever I want if it will get me to stay. She knows I know her secrets now, am starting to put it all together-- and she'll do anything to stop me, to keep me quiet. She's pulling out all the stops. No holds barred. And me, I let myself believe. Why? Because, like Eunice Bailey said, it's easier to sleep, not to dream, not to face the horrors, to deceive yourself. Earlier, in town, my head had been clearing a little, but now I'm drowning again in delicious, dark waters.

"Can you make him real?" I ask aloud. "Can you bring him back? Please. I'll give anything. Anything. What do you want from me?"

It's foolish to expect she will answer with anything even remotely resembling mercy, but I give it a go.

"Can you bring him back?" I'm crumpled to the floor, sobbing now. "Goddammit, goddammit... "

A sensuous sigh drifts down from the attic. A melodious wind from the south seas. It wafts down the stairs from one landing to the next, swirling over the floor like a deadly, potent witch's brew-- a lethal fog, climbing up my shaky legs it goes, twining round and round, wisp upon wisp. Up to my desperate ears its tendril fingers stretch, down my ear canals until it snares my brain with its honeysuckle sweet breath.

There's the hint of death and rot and ultimate decay wafting underneath the sweetness-- it's a spider's breath, after all. But I don't hear the note of doom. And I tell myself I do not smell the graveyard stench. All I hear is Her willing and whispered promise...

Yes. All that and more. If you'll love me. If you'll give yourself to me-- and me alone. Will you do that?

"Yes," I promise her. "Just bring him back."

Soon, love. Soon.

It just doesn't matter what I do, I can't find my way out. I'm giving up. My spirit is slipping away. Kevin, you dolt, you're just not going to walk away from this one. I'm succumbing to Her will. Plain and simple.

It's too late.

Darkness overtakes me.

I wake that night in bed, sweating. I have had the dream again, the one where I'm clawing my way in the muddy darkness, trying to get away from It-- the hideous black heart beating in the basement. I lay in bed. The thudding sound is my own heart, beating in my ears. It slows, regains its normal rhythm. Even so, I hear another thudding coming from all around me in the darkness, muffled by the walls.

It sounds just like a huge heart, beating in the night.

I think this is the first time I truly understand that the house is a living, breathing thing-- a beast that has swallowed me whole.

I have a momentary impulse to throw off the covers, run down the stairs and out the front door and never look back.

Even as I have the thought, I feel the covers constrict around me, not warm and cozy like wool blankets, but cold and slippery like slices of deli meat. There is a pulsing in the layers holding me down. I can feel the heat rising and at the same time, the air being sucked out of the room. My bedroom is quickly becoming an airless vacuum, a ogre's oven. She means to kill me if I resist, to broil me alive. I gasp for breath, can just barely manage to raise my head and get a glimpse out the window. A shadow lurks just outside on the roof, hunkered down.

It takes a second for me to realize it is a figure, grotesque and rotten, hunched down, the knobs of its spine sticking up through thin stretched, green-grey flesh. It peers in through the glass. It doesn't have any eyes, just two black sockets where the eyes should have been.

It's the final transformation, the hideous ultimate incarnation of that imitation James I saw in the parlor. I know that now. This is the thing I kissed. This is the thing to which I professed my ever and undying love.

It stares at me with those black pits in its skull. I cannot mistake the look of longing in those abysmal depths. Then it reaches out its chicken bone fingers and scratches at the window, its nails *scrick* down the glass.

I try to leap out of bed, but the covers hold me tight, squeezing me to death. They are pulsing again, sickeningly alive like thick slabs of quivering meat constricting around me. The veins in the flesh throb and throb and throb, rattling my teeth.

I groan, trying to cry out, but there is no air in the furnace hot room.

Hush. I will make all the bad things go away. But you must do as I say. This is for your own good. Do you understand, my beloved?

I try to hold out. I'm having a sudden and unexpected attack of will power. But She can keep the air out far longer than I can ever hold my breath. Eyes closed, through gritted teeth, I pant out an answer, barely audible but heard well enough by her.

"I understand."

The thing at the window backs away. It crouches down, its bending bones go *crickle-crack*. It is no longer as intent about getting inside. It sinks down, kneeling almost out of sight, claws still clutched on the windowsill, black sockets still peering in at me.

The covers loosen and relinquish their rib crushing hold. A refreshing, life saving draught of cool air floods the room. I gasp in lungfuls of air.

You see, I can give you everything you need. Now, go to sleep, dearest. I will keep the monsters away. Do you know that I can give you everything you want? That I can give you your heart's desire?

"Yes."

And I will. But there is still something you must do, a task you must complete.

"What is it?"

Soon, dear boy. Soon.

I wake to a car horn honking outside. I sit up, shout when I see the spiders swarming over the covers.

"Damned hairy little bastards! *Charlotte's Web* mother fuckers!"

I fling back the blankets, kick the spiders out of my sheets-- more angry now than terrified. After smashing them to bits, I go to the window. The eyeless thing does not leap out at me. I didn't think it would, the graveyard ghoul does not seem like a daylight kind of horror.

I can see someone standing at the gate down below, next to a yellow taxi cab. It takes a second for the face to register.

It is James. He has seen me peering down at him. He stands there, smiling and waving.

I wave back weakly, uncertain if this is another trick of the house. But he is beyond the gate. And it is broad daylight. All the powers of the house I have witnessed so far have taken place on the grounds. Never beyond. The house has its limits, a range to its power.

But it must have known-- sensed that he was coming-- was on his way. To what?

To save me?

She won't like that... not at all.

I run downstairs in my pajamas, throw open the front door and hurry down the path.

I meet James at the gate.

"Long time no see," James says. He is smiling like it is no big deal, like I should be expecting him-- and grateful.

"What are you doing here?"

"No hug?"

I step forward, embrace him hesitantly.

"That's more like it. I've missed you."

I'm feeling suddenly unsettled, the exchange is eerily similar to the one I had the night before with the thing that looked and spoke like James, right before its flesh peeled off. I look hard at him, reach up, touch his face. But, no-- this is him-- the real James, in the flesh, the one that would never ask for me to forgive him. His handsome profile is sharp and clear and oh-so-painfully beautiful in the midmorning sun.

"Are you real?"

"What?" he asks with a little laugh, but another glance at my face and he knows I'm serious. He frowns. "Kev, you okay?"

I don't answer. I honestly don't know. Am I okay?

I doubt it.

His concern deepens. He wrinkles his nose. "Whoa, Kev, you're starting to smell a little ripe-- no offense. How long have you been in your pajamas?"

"Um, three days," I say absently. "I think, maybe. I'm not really sure."

"Uh-oh, good thing I'm here. Dr. James to the rescue."

"How did you find me?"

"I called your sister. She's worried sick. She said your cousin came up here to find you, came to this address, but all he saw was an abandoned house. He must have had the wrong place." He looks somberly at me. "Kevin, your stepfather passed away."

"I know."

"And I got your letter."

"My letter?"

"Yeah, silly. You mailed me a letter about two weeks ago. When I opened it up, I knew you were in trouble. I couldn't make out anything at all. Your writing was atrocious. It looked like crazy person scribble. It was all swirls and whirly squiggles like fingerprints. I knew something was wrong. Guess I was right, as usual."

"I don't remember sending you a letter."

"Well, you did."

Of course, I don't remember punching Scottie Allgood, either. So maybe I did send the letter.

For the first time, I notice James has a duffle bag in his hand.

"What's that?"

"What does it look like, goofball? It's my bag."

"Where are you staying?"

He looks up at the house as if the answer is self evident.

I feel suddenly frantic. "No. No, you can't stay here."

James misinterprets my meaning, says, "Relax, Kev, I'm sure this place has more than one bedroom." He's still shaking his head and laughing as he skips up the steps.

He pauses, looks up at the house, gives a low whistle.

"That is some house. A real monster."

"Don't call her that."

"Don't get defensive. I'm just joking," and then all of a sudden, "Holy shit!"

He has noticed the endless trail of spiders trickling into the house over the threshold.

"Um, Kev, you might have an infestation."

He kicks and stomps at them, shivering as he does so, shaking imaginary spiders out of his clothes and hair.

"Stop-- Don't!"

"Don't what?"

What can I say? Don't do it? She won't like it. Instead, I just shrug.

"Well, aren't you going to invite me in?" Looking again at the spiders, he adds, "Do I really want to go in?"

He doesn't give me a chance to answer, he has already passed through the front door.

From somewhere out of the woodwork, I hear a rumbling sound seeping out.

A faint but ominous growl.

"You don't look so good, Kev. I think it's time for you to come home. Honest to God."

"I am home."

"You know what I mean. Back to Seattle."

"What are you talking about?" My initial puzzlement and relief over seeing him evaporates and I'm flustered suddenly by his presumption. Who does he think he is, showing up like this, telling me how things are going to be? It's so like him. And it's so infuriating. He's the one that kicked me out. It's his fault. Everything was fine. He's the one who blew it. Not me.

"Jeez, what's her problem?" he says, looking up at the portrait of the woman in black.

His being flippant about the house only irritates me more. And I get that same acidic feeling again-- It's James-- he's the real villain here. he's the one who tricked me. He was cruel to me-- just like Alan and Buddy. I never did anything wrong.

"Why did you come here, James? You're the one that kicked me out, remember?"

"The phrase *'kicked out'* is a little harsh, don't you think?"

"You're the reason I moved here."

"No, *you're the reason* you moved here. I only wanted you to move out of the apartment, not across the damn country."

"You said you didn't love me anymore."

He cuts me off quick. "No, I said I wasn't *in love* with you anymore." He sighs, shakes his head, looks puppy dog sad. "But that was a mistake. I just needed some time. We both did. I should have tried to help you."

I feel guilty with him looking all sad eyed at me like this. Damn, I hate how he does this to me. But I let him win. I give up.

"Now what?" My voice comes out like a sigh.

James doesn't have an answer, is good, as usual, at avoiding the subject. Somehow, he has already drawn me close, is holding me in his arms.

"So, why don't you give me the grand tour. Normally, you'd already be rambling a million miles a minute about mullioned windows and gabled roofs and all that crap."

"And you'd be bored as hell."

"True. C'mon, let's have a look at your lady love, huh? Is this who you left me for? Should I be jealous?"

He's being playful. But the house, She doesn't like it. I can tell by the subtle shifting of the light to gloomy shadow. She's getting angry.

I start talking to shut him up, do my best to show him around a few of the rooms, tell him a little bit about the history of the house, but it's like a fog has swallowed my brain all of a sudden and I can hardly remember a thing.

I don't know who built the house or when. And when James asks me how I ended up here, I can't-- for the life of me, even remember Cranston's name. I try to play it off, act nonchalant, like I'm just a little fuzzy from waking up. But he can tell something is wrong. He frowns at me.

I go on with the act, trying like hell to shake off the descending fog, but I can tell it's just making James more worried. But I have to keep going. I'm doing it for Her-- trying to convince Her, I guess, that we can all live here together-- me and James and Her. We can all get along.

She is not convinced.

I show him around downstairs, anxiety growing heavier the whole time, weighing down on me like a lead weight. The air starts to grow heavy and hot to me, oppressive. The house doesn't want him here. I can feel it. My eyes keep darting off to one side then another, seeing monstrous, eight legged shadows he can't see. I'm tense, on edge, waiting for the attack that doesn't come. Every time James opens a door or turns a corner, my heart leaps up in my throat, clogging my windpipe. I keep expecting to see a thorny arachnid leg dart out of the shadows, snag him, drag him screaming into the dark. But nothing happens.

The House, I tell myself foolishly, maybe she is accepting James, accepting us, willing to have us both.

I'm sweating now, exhausted from the ocean of anxiety pounding down on me. I can feel my heart racing. My forehead is getting shiny, I can tell. And my mouth is stuffed with cotton.

"Okay-- that's enough," James says, genuinely worried. "I need to get you out of here for a little while. I think maybe we should get you out of those pajamas and go outside-- get some fresh air, huh? What do you say? Why don't we take a nice long walk down by the lake, yeah, Kev?" He's talking to me very straight forward like a doctor to a patient-- like he fears he might lose me.

I manage to swallow what little spit is left in my mouth, shake my head, say, "Yeah, sure-- uh, that sounds good."

He insists that I show him the sights of this 'podunk' town. And I want to get out. I do. If not for my sake then for James'.

But where can we go? Not back to town. I'm probably wanted for attempted murder. I wonder if maybe Dr. Crickshaw has had a change of heart and called the police.

I tell him, "Later, later; we'll go to town after while. But not now."

Instead, we walk down to the lake together, spend the morning in peace and quiet, hardly saying a word to one another. James just lets me lean against him and rest. We sit together for what seems like all day, just watching the wind make ripples on the lake.

I can't be certain, but at one point I think I see someone standing on the far side of the lake, near the bench where Sean and I sat a few days earlier. It looks like a man in a black trenchcoat. Maybe I'm imagining it, but I can almost swear he's staring at me across the waters. I raise my hand and wave.

"Who are you waving at?" James asks.

I look again. There's no one there.

"I don't know about you," he says after a long while, "but I'm starving. You hungry?"

"Yeah, I could eat something. Should we drive somewhere?"

He tells me I'm in no shape to go anywhere-- that I should stay put and rest. "I saw a grocery store on the way here. I'll go grab a few things. You gonna be okay?"

I tell him I'll be fine.

He leaves me for about half an hour, and I sit alone, breathing deeply, trying to clear my head.

The madness of the House, I don't want to be a part of it anymore-- the drinking, lingering in darkness and shadows. I want to be free of Her. I want to be in the daylight, beneath a clear, blue sky. I have told Her no before. But she doesn't listen. I always give in-- but not anymore. I'm done. This time, I mean it.

James returns with a bagful of groceries: fancy crackers, grapes, salami, pimento cheese, a couple of apples, a bottle of wine.

"I know how you hate to go out," he says, smiling at me.

I eat almost the whole box of crackers, and a whole tub of pimento cheese. I bite into the apple, so sweet and juicy. Delicious. Real food.

"Damn, you were hungry. Don't you have anything to eat in that house?"

It's been a mostly liquid diet, but I don't tell him that. And all the food has been provided for me by Her. No telling what she's actually been feeding me.

"This is just what the doctor ordered," I say, mouth crammed with sweet apple. "This is the best apple ever. I'm gonna get back on track now-- start exercising again, eating right."

I mean it, too. Today is the day for healing to begin. I'm worn out. I need this peaceful moment. It's like a bandaid for my soul. Seeing James smiling at me changes everything. And all those things I thought were important-- those things that have come to consume me over the past weeks-- counting light fixtures, cataloguing old, dusty furniture, delving into the house's wicked secrets-- none of that matters now.

I'm with James now and we're alive, like Holly said. I'm embracing life not feasting on shadows.

James brushes my bangs out of my eyes. "You look so tired, Kev. What happened to you?" He touches my cheek with the back of his hand.

"Just been really tired lately. Not sleeping well, I guess."

"I've missed you."

"I've missed you, too."

"Why did you come here, Kevin, really?"

"I came here to heal."

"Be honest, Kev. You came here to hide. And it's not working out. You can't keep running from life. You have to face it."

IT.

Does he mean the House? No, he means the metaphorical monster, not the four storey nightmare lurking behind us.

We talk dreamily for hours about familiar things from before…

Before Afton.

Before the House.

And I feel lighter, free, like the healing has begun. And all I want is to walk away from this place-- to leave it all behind-- to embrace days of peace, to live in a little house with a garden and to spend my life at James' side. But I know, with a sudden sinking feeling-- the House--

--She is right behind me.

And at some point, I will have to go back.

And I fear, in my heart of hearts-- I'm not going to get it, will I? --that little house with the garden and James at my side every evening, am I?

No, She says, reassuringly. *There are worse things in store for you, beautiful boy. Far worse.*

"You know, out here in the sunlight, you're a different person all of a sudden," James says. "Like the old Kevin, before the gloom." He pauses, looks out at the lake, then deeply into my eyes.

"Kevin, come back home."

That night, we make love. It starts with us just cuddling, then a few playful kisses-- then open mouthed sucking kisses. Then we're pulling off each others clothes and James is laying me down gently on the bed, careful of all my bruises and scrapes. I haven't been touched in so long, when he finally puts his hands on me it's like electricity is coursing through his fingertips into my body. He is gentle, careful, sensitive. He knows I'm hurting-- on the edge of breaking down completely. He tells me he wants to heal me. This is the real James-- warm and alive. This is real human touch, full of love and warmth-- not unsettling and bestial like that night that I woke with the eyeless thing on my chest.

He kisses all my wounds, telling me he will heal every single one-- exterior and interior with love. "Kevin, my poor Kevin, you're all banged up. But I'm gonna make it better. All better. I love you my sweet, sweet boy."

I'm completely under his spell. I've made my decision. In the morning, we'll leave together. Once and for all. I'll never look back. I make this promise to him before drifting off to sleep in his arms.

I wake once in the night to a thumping noise coming from the downstairs hall. It sounds like someone landing after jumping from a high place. It's followed by a rustling of heavy fabric-- like a thick curtain... or-- or a black dress.

The woman in the painting. The eyeless thing with meathook fingers.

It's coming.

I nudge James. He is sound asleep, snoring gently.

Heart pounding, I pull back the covers, slide out of bed. I can't let it get James. I will fight the thing if I have to to keep James safe. I open the bedroom door, creep out into the darkened hall. I hardly realize I'm holding my breath. I approach the stairs, peek down, trying to catch a glimpse of the painting on the wall.

There's a sudden hissing rush out of the blackness, like the thing in the black dress is slithering rapidly up the stairs towards me.

And I can see it without seeing it. The House-- She shows me--

--a pale wraith, cloaked in black, with eight corpse white arms. And at the end of each, a white hand, bloodless as alabaster with long, thin fingers tapering to needle points. And it is on these jagged fingerpoints that the black shrouded wraith is pulling itself up out of the shadows, rushing headlong towards me, twisting, turning, flipping madly in the dark.

I suck in air to shout, but the cry freezes in my throat. I turn and flee, rushing down the hall-- in my frantic flight, bolting past the safety of the bedroom, down a back staircase. All the while the hissing black shadow rushes after me, slithering here and there, first on the floor, then along the wall, then sliding serpentine fashion up onto the ceiling, closing in faster and faster, ready to drop down on me like...

...like a hideous spider.

I'm running up towards the front hall, trying to make it back around to the grand staircase before the thing catches me. If I can just round the corner, get back up the stairs and to the bedroom I'll be safe. James will be there to protect me.

I round the corner. I slip-- no, the oriental rug crumples up under my feet all of a sudden and I trip, dive forward, land on my chest. My face hits the floor. I cover the back of my head with my hands, ready to feel the pale, spider-like thing-- whatever it is-- pounce at any second and start tearing into my back, knifing me again and again with fingers like thorns. The hissing noise swoops over me. I tense up, ready for the attack, unable to escape. Death is here. I hear the whipping of fabric, followed by a brief smell of pungent incense.

And then?

Silence.

I raise my head slowly, look up at the portrait.

The woman in black has her back to me.

I stand and run, back up the stairs taking two and three at a time, expecting to hear the hiss of fabric again as the thing rushes out after me. But the phantom remains in the painting and I make it safely back to the bedroom, close the door, crawl back into bed, terrified, panting.

James lies unmoved, one arm draped over his head, eyes buried in the crook of his arm. The only sound, other than my heavy panting, is James' gentle snores.

...In the night, I dream that the thing in black has escaped the painting once more and it is in the bedroom, crouched upside down against the ceiling, in the far corner of the room, its numerous ivory pale fingers ticking and twitching. Some of the hands are weaving threads of gore. It reaches down with its forearms, grabs James out of the bed, clutches him, limp and unconscious, in it's long white fingers. It jerks him up, hanging him, stitching him against the wall with the gorey woven threads, crucifying him with his arms outspread. More black veins slither out of the wood, pulling him into the wall. I reach out for him, but it's too late. She has him, is dissolving him down to the bone right before my horrified eyes. He wakes suddenly, eyes bulging with terror, weeping tears of blood. His scream turns into a bloody gurgle as the house sucks him in.

I wake with a shout.

I'm lying in the bed alone. The spot next to me is cold.

I fling back the covers, shout, "James?"

No answer.

I run out into the hall, shouting his name. I hear a thudding sound coming from the washroom.

Oh God, the hideous heart.

I look in--

No... The dryer is on, rumbling away.

"James?"

"Kev, what is it?"

The voice startles me. I shout, spin around, see James, standing in a towel, toothbrush in his foamy mouth.

"Whoa, easy there. Why are you so jumpy?"

"You startled me, that's all."

"Man, I didn't think you were ever gonna get up, sleepy head. You were always the early riser."

"What time is it?"

"Almost one. You okay?

"Yeah, just a bad dream."

"You know, I think I could get used to this place." He gives me a playful wink.

And I dare to think, maybe this could be it, the change in my fortunes.

That's when the dryer stops with a heavy thunk and when I look back, the door swings open and five decomposed heads spill out onto the floor. I scream, staggering back and James is grabbing for me, trying to get a hold on me and calm me down.

"Kevin! Kevin, calm down, what the hell has gotten into you, huh?"

"Heads! Heads! Severed heads!"

"What the fuck are you talking about, man?"

I turn, pointing at the clump of bloody severed heads on the washroom floor.

"Kevin, it's just my shoes."

And he's right. Just his worn out Reeboks. Nothing more.

"They got muddy when I came up the path yesterday and I thought I would wash them, that's all."

I'm breathing heavy, leaning against James, almost sobbing. I walk over to the tennis shoes lying on the floor, lean over them, study them hard.

"I could have sworn…"

"What? That there was a dryer full of severed heads?"

I'm picking up on his sarcasm. I can tell he's already getting exasperated with me, just like he always has. I want this morning to be different, but I can already tell, nothing has changed. There is a disturbance beneath the seemingly still waters. We're about to head down the old familiar path to self destruction.

"Kevin, get dressed," he says a little too sternly. "I'll fix you some breakfast and then we're getting the hell out of here."

A few minutes later, we're sitting down together at the table for breakfast. James won't let me do a thing. He pours coffee for us. He picks up his cup, takes a sip, puts it down, never taking his eyes off me.

And for a minute, I see it-- faint, bloody fingerprints on the handle of his cup. And James, his eyes are black and dead like a Great White's.

"Oh God, no!"

"Kevin?"

I jump back, nearly fall out of my chair. I glance again at the cup. The white, porcelain handle is totally clean. Just to make sure, I pick up his mug, check the handle for bloody fingerprints.

James has that deeply worried look again. "What are you doing?"

"Nothing. Just checking."

"For what?"

"Nevermind."

"You sure you're okay?"

I look him in the face. His eyes are bright blue, not dead black like a shark's. It's the real James.

"Positive."

"Because, this is starting to remind me of-- "

He doesn't finish. He doesn't have to. I know what he wants to say.

It's reminding him of why he broke up with me in the first place.

C'mon, Kevin, keep it together. Keep it together. Just a little while longer and you'll be free of this place.

The House. This morning, she is pulling out all the stops. She's not going to let me out of here alive. She's going to crush me or James or both of us.

I look back down at my cereal. The milk is bloodied and full of worms and chunks of flesh. With a shout, I fling the bowl across the room. It hits the walls, shatters.

"What the hell, Kev?" James shouts more angry than concerned now. Perhaps the house has its hooks in him, too, tugging at his anger in subtle ways I can't see, showing him things he doesn't like and doesn't want to see.

"Worms-- worms."

"What?"

"There were..." I look at the floor. Milk and Cheerios are scattered everywhere. Not a single bloody chunk of meat.

"If you don't want cereal, I'll be glad to fix you some eggs," James says. I don't know if he's trying to make a joke or if he's serious. I don't think he knows, either. But one look at him and I do know one thing-- he thinks I've gone crazy. I feel shaky all over. The room is starting to spin a little. The fog is pouring in again.

He reaches over, takes hold of my trembling hand, but I shake it off.

"It's-- it's this house. Sometimes I think it's driving me crazy."

He snorts. "Here we go again."

"What's that supposed to mean?"

He has reached the tipping point, he's sliding over from concern to anger. Just like old times.

"It's always somebody else's fault. You know that? It's my fault. It's your step father's fault. Now it's the house's fault. You want to blame the house, huh? Truth is, Kevin, whatever it is that's driving you crazy-- you brought it with you. You were the one that ruined it, you know that, Kevin-- what we had. You're not the innocent little victim. You're a goddamned saboteur. I wasted two years on you, you miserable little head case."

Dammit, things were going so well. I can feel myself getting angry. Things are spinning out of control. The house is feeding my dark energy. I don't want to let it loose, but I'm going to. For a split second, I feel like I could kill him for talking to me like this.

"I didn't ask you to come here."

"I came back because I care for you, Kevin."

The house stretches out dark, invisible tendrils of hate. It seeps into me and I raise my arm, twirl my finger.

"Whoop-de-doo."

James looks at me bitterly, disgusted.

"You're not nice, Kevin; you're weak. It's all a charade with you. All these layers of subterfuge. All that niceness-- it's the inverted anger of a sullen malcontent."

I've been thinking the same thing lately, but being called out on it just makes me even angrier. "Oh, God, did Dr. Schwartz teach you that? Your psycho babble crap makes me want to puke. *I am a nice guy!*"

"Bullshit, Kevin. Bullshit."

Silence.

"God, I knew this was a mistake. Alan called, he was worried to death about you, said he wanted me to bring you back home. He said I was probably the only one that could make it happen. Why in the hell did I listen to him? I thought maybe I could help you. But you know what Kevin, the fact of the matter is-- you don't want to change. You love being miserable. You bring all this crap on yourself, you know that?"

"Get out."

"You're never gonna learn."

"Get out."

"Always gonna fall flat on your face."

"*GET OUT!*"

He's surprised by me shouting. I never shout. I can't even say *boo*, most of the time. But there must be something rabid in my face because he gives me a disgusted look, says, "With pleasure."

He gets up from the table, says coldly, "You're flippin' crazy, you know that? This place, this house-- you deserve each other."

He steps out into the hall and I follow after, spoiling for a fight. I fight hard but can't resist the demonic urge to grab a knife from the butcher block on the kitchen counter. I'll do it. I'll stab him in the back with it. The maelstrom of rage is whipping round and round like a cyclone inside me. The fight goes out of me, though, when I see the portrait hanging in the front hall by the stairs.

I drop the knife.

I've seen it dozens of times, and although for weeks I've tried to tell myself there's nothing to it-- it has filled me with dread since the first day I laid eyes on it. And after last night, I know it-- like the rest of the house is evil. The old oil painting, darkened with age-- was bad enough before-- the dour, middle aged woman in a black hoop skirt, standing with her long, white hands clasped in front of her. It has given me the creeps since day one. I've always felt like she is watching me and I have been convinced that there are subtle differences that show up in the portrait from day to day-- the way her hands are clasped, the tilt of her head. One thing has been constant, though, the stern-- no hateful, countenance and menacing air that surrounds the painting.

But now when I look at it, I nearly cry out in terror. Gone is the woman, replaced now by a shadowy fiend, a hideous distortion of the image that was just there moments before.

It is a similar figure, but the lines are blurred and indistinct as if someone has spilled turpentine on the canvas. The long fingered hands are gripping the sides of her blurred head, as she shakes her head, mouth hanging agape in a silent scream. She has no eyes, only smears of flesh where they should be. Her fingers are as long as chopsticks and dripping with gore. She has three sets of arms. And behind her lies a barren wasteland in which the forms of a monstrous squid, moth, rat, centipede and spider strive for dominance. And rising in their midst, a black tower lit with purple light.

James stops, sees the portrait, too, grimaces with disgust then tilts his head like he's listening.

"What was that?" he says all of a sudden.

"What?"

"That noise. It came from upstairs. It sounded like a little girl laughing."

"I didn't hear anything." A lie. I hear it. It's the house. She's setting a trap. I don't want to know what. Suddenly, I want to get James out of here-- out of Afton, right away. But he's intrigued, says, "C'mon, let's check it out."

Oh god, no. I've unleashed it. It heard my cry. I didn't mean it. I don't want anything to happen to James. I take it back. I take it back!

I realize I've shouted it out loud, because James shushes me.

"No, you're right, James. Let's go out. Let's get out of here for a while. I've been crazy. I'm sorry. I blew it. Forgive me. Forgive me. Take me back. Take me away." I grab his arm, try to hold him back, but he tugs away from me. "Let's go-- right now, back to Seattle. Give me one more chance. Please. I'm ready. Just don't go."

"Would you calm down. I think someone-- it sounds like there's somebody up there. Are they laughing or crying? It sounds like someone in trouble."

"I wanna go."

"Sure, sure, in sec. It sounded like it came from up there," he says nodding towards the attic stairs.

"Hello? Who's there?" he calls out. And the thought of something answering from the shadows above fills me with mind numbing terror.

"No, James."

But he's already started up. "Kev, did you move into a haunted house," he says in a mock scary voice. "How cool is that?"

Gone is his anger, his disgust. She is luring him, snaring his brain in a mind numbing fog.

I follow up after him. The house won't hurt him-- will it? Not with me around.

She wouldn't dare. Trying to kill Mr. Allgood is one thing, trying to kill the man of my dreams is another thing entirely.

"If you hurt him, I'll leave," I tell Her, "and never come back."

I hear something like a laugh. She's mocking me.

"There it is again," says James. "Yeah, it's a laugh-- I think."

I can't stop him. I can't drag him back. He's climbing higher and higher with me following desperately after him, trying to hold him back, to turn him around, to get him outside. But he won't listen.

The attic is dusty, filled with mounds of old junk, heaps of broken furniture-- chairs, tables, wardrobes, lamps and couches. A junkyard. Our footsteps stir up eye watering eddies of dust. The miniature snow storm swirls around us. Slivers of light seep in through a boarded up window.

"Whoa, this is pretty cool," says James snooping around, pausing here and there to pick up a dusty object and examine it. "Hey, check this out."

The heaps of junk, old furniture, portraits in gilt frames, all of it is shrouded in web.

"You have a spider problem, Kev." And then suddenly, James exclaims in disgust and amazement. "Is this a cat? Holy shit, it is."

I look over his shoulder. He takes a broken chair leg, pokes at a mummified lump, cocooned in dusty grey webbing. The dead cat is just a withered husk, a dirty fur coat wrapped around loose, dry bones.

"Kevin, you need to call an exterminator. Seriously."

He's in a far corner of the attic, looking up at a trapdoor in the ceiling that leads up to a crawl space beneath the roof. He stops, tilts his head listening intently.

"That scratching noise, you hear it? It's coming from in here. The laughter, too."

He grabs an old broom, starts jabbing at the hatch with the broom handle.

A sudden realization of terror floods my mind.

The spindle legged horror stalking back and forth behind the red litten glass. It was here-- in this room. I saw it, that night when I looked up from the yard.

"Oh God, no, James, don't do that! *NOOO!*"

But it's too late. The hatch swings open and the eight legged horror of the catacombs drops down from the darkness above. The spider is as large as a volkswagon and covered with red fur. It pokes two thorny legs out of the crawlspace, dislodging a half dozen skulls as it does so.

James never has a chance to scream. I see his face, frozen with terror as the spider lunges, pierces him with its glistening, dagger-sized fangs. James gags and flails, kicking his legs violently as the venom courses through his veins. The veins on his neck bulge out like cords of rope and turn black. His eyes roll back in his head, until only the whites are showing. He gives a sickening gurgle as yellow foam boils out of his mouth. Then the spider wraps two spindle legs around him and it pulls him up, kicking and flailing, back into the crawlspace. The violent flailing subsides as he is swallowed by the shadows.

The last thing I see are his fingers twitching weakly.

The thorny legs retract, slamming the hatch closed behind.

I stagger backwards, stumble down the top story flight of stairs. I hit the landing, stand up, out of my mind with terror. The wood goes soft beneath me. The stairs below me snap and crack and I see a dark slit, ever widening, opening in the stairs, revealing a gaping mouth with needle sharp teeth. Dozens of red, reptile eyes open in the walls. The landing tilts forward, pitching me down the living stairs and I tumble down like I'm being swallowed by a giant throat. I bounce on the stair above the mouth, shoot over the gaping maw and hit the bottom.

Above me, the stairs shudder and crack once more, collapsing back into place. The shark's mouth champs closed. The red eyes go back to sleep.

I try to lean up on my elbows, but terror floods over me. My senses flee.

My consciousness is devoured by blackness.

That night I dream I see my father. My real father. He looks sad and far away. He is in the garage, a freshly painted model car in his hand. He is calling for me.

"Daddy!" I shout.

"Kevin, where are you?"

"Daddy, please wait, I'm coming!"

I try to catch up with him.

But *She* stops me.

The palely lit glimpse of the garage fades away.

I cry out for my father. My voice echoes in the darkness.

The house looms up horrible, pulsing with life, writhing on a base of slippery pulsing veins like squid tentacles. It slithers after me, mouth yawning wide to swallow me whole and above my screams I can hear the pounding of that heart in the gorey darkness beyond the threshold.

And there is the vulture-like Arthur Cranston standing on the steps to greet me.

"You-- you're Cranston."

"I *was* Cranston," he says with that dagger smile. "Just like you *were* Kevin Yoo."

"I'm still Kevin."

"Not for long."

"What am I now?"

"You're hers, dear boy. I warned you, didn't I? Not to cross her."

I want to tell him he's wrong-- that he's a liar.

But I know that the Cranston shadow is telling me the hideous truth.

"I want-- I want James back," I cry, tears streaming down my face.

"Of course you do," he says in a comforting tone. "And you can have him. Look, he's right here-- just inside."

I glance past Cranston, catch a glimpse of James standing at the foot of the stairs. I start to rush inside, but Cranston stops me with one of his skeletal hands pressed against my chest.

"Not so fast, young man."

"Get out of my way!" I shout. "I want James!"

"You shall have him. But first, there is something you must do… for Her."

I don't trust him. But what choice do I have?

"You know now she's far more than a mere house, don't you?"

"Yes."

"You know what she is?"

"Yes. A gateway-- to another world."

"That's correct. You're a smart boy. You've done your homework. They've been keeping an eye on her for years-- trying to stop her."

"Who?"

"Harold Trout, for one," he says with a sneer. "Cecilia Jacobs, Buddy Haygood, Emery Marsh, Walter Reeves. The damned do gooders. I used to help them, you know-- until She showed me the way, promised me rewards beyond imagining for my faithful service. I saw that to stand against her was futile. I gave myself willingly-- body and soul-- just as you must do."

"No, I'll warn them-- tell them what I've seen."

"Go ahead. Tell them. It won't do any good. The old fools-- they've worked together for years, trying to keep people away, trying to stop that which cannot be stopped. They've been at it their whole lives; but the time is drawing near. For I have servants, too. And they have raised me from the dead, as you know. The last sands are falling from the hourglass. The end is near, dear boy. Doom is at the doorstep. They think they can stop her. But they can't. Shall I show you what she intends?"

He doesn't give me a chance to answer. He reaches out, grabs my wrist with his claw of a hand and I feel like all the breath has been sucked out of me. My flesh blisters, same as it did in the crypt. I'm being sucked back inside the house through the gaping front door-- which is no longer a door but a dripping, fang ringed mouth. The interior of the house collapses in on itself, sucked down into the earth. I can see the black earth opening below me, whirling round and round like a vortex and deep down at the center of the whirlpool shines a ghastly purple light. It gleams like a dead star from the shadows.

And I am falling, falling, sucked down towards oblivion, past tier upon tier of arches and labyrinthine, red litten passages. The city of the dead. I get sucked down into the whirling abyss with a silent scream. The purple light engulfs me and I shut my eyes against it.

When I open them again I see a desolate land, devoid of life, blasted, charred, a cursed realm straight out of *Dante's Inferno*. Shadow shapes wander mindlessly across the grey wastes. I shudder at sight of the countless living dead. Hundreds. Thousands. Millions.

And then I see--

Her. It. The House.

She rears up amidst the hordes of undead, glowing with a noxious greenish purple light-- like corrupted amethyst, all her walls pulsing with hideous life. As I watch, she changes, grows, molts, mutates, sheds her skin, thrusting up taller and taller like an evil tree, twisting skywards, transforming into a wicked tower of stone punctured by countless blackened windows. Babel like, she rises to the dead sky, casting her shadow over the ruined land.

And I am cowering naked and afraid before the Beast-- this living tower.

"Who-- who built you?" I ask, shivering in my fear.

"Why you did, Kevin," Cranston says. "You and others before you. Brick by brick and stone by stone. And we want to thank you. Truly. She's constructed of a million little fears and hatreds and desires. All freely given. Her cornerstone is despair." He gives a callous little laugh. "You didn't actually think that you could stand against her-- did you, my boy? It's so much easier if you don't fight. If you join with us, you will be made a prince of the earth when the time comes. Unleash the dark potential of your wretched soul. Sacrifice yourself to her willingly, or be dragged screaming to a miserable doom."

Below, at the base of the tower, crawling amongst the dead, crushing the damned in its wake, dragging its hideous hairy bulk up to the top of a massive stone altar is the red spider, with malice filled eyes. Scattered across the land is the collected withered husk of humanity. The spider has grown bloated on the blood sacrifice of mankind and it squats in an ocean of filth-- loathsome and vile-- larger than a battleship now in the midst of this ultimate desolation.

This is the god of the dead.

This is the spider's plan. It is ancient and wickedly wise beyond the ages.

This is Afton's ultimate horror.

This is what lies beneath the streets.

The end of the world.

I can hear Cranston chuckling now in my ear.

And standing amongst the dead, like a high priest looms a terrible lich in rotting robes, eyes glowing like fire akin to the spider's. An iron crown is set upon its withered brow. Even in such a state of decay, I recognize those vulture features, undead and rotted as they may be.

"Cranston. It was your bones I saw in the catacombs beneath the house. It was you they raised from the dead."

Cranston answers, dry, disinterested. "Very good, Kevin, you are a natural scholar."

"The spider killed you. And dragged your body back and hid it in the crypts."

"Yes," he says proudly. "My death was inconsequential. She forgave my presumption, promised to resurrect me, when the time came. And now-- the time has come. My death was a necessary part of the process of awakening the Old Ones. Who better to spread the plague of the dead than an undead necromancer?"

"Who better than Arthur Cranston, lover of spiders?"

"No," he says fiercely. "That was my name. But now I am reborn. Henceforth shall I be known as Agruun, greatest of all liches. I, too, shall be worshipped by the last of a trembling and wretched humanity after the dead have risen and eaten their fill. When the gate is open, my spirit will journey through-- to the other side, to the land of the dead. There I will receive the sacred vessel-- the chalice of unlife to bring back here to the very town of Afton-- the cup from which I will pour out the plague of the undead upon mankind. And I will be given eternal life by Unglit, last of the great gods before Atlantis. And with my eight brothers in living death, we shall rule the earth from indestructible towers."

As he says these things, I can see it clearly, Cranston, in some other plane of existence, approaching a stone pedestal, reaching out to claim a perverse blackened grail full of noxious green liquid overflowing with smoke. And the moment he claims it, he takes a sip and his human features wither to become that of a king of the dead.

And I hear myself shouting at the House-- at the Spider, "Why are you doing this? *WHY? WHY?!*"

It is the spider that answers. I hear its voice inside my head. The sound of it is black beyond the spaces between the stars and hearing it nearly drives me mad, even in dreams.

"Why do you sleep and eat? Why do you, selfish fool that you are, consume life merely to defecate? It's what you do, Kevin Yoo. It is merely what you do. It is your nature as a brute beast of the earth. Why do men wage war on one another? Why do they lie, cheat, murder and steal? Why do they destroy the planet? It is in their nature. Man has been a death dealer all his days, a bringer of doom, perpetrator of mass extinctions. But now-- it is his turn.

"Bringing the end of the world, the end of this age and the beginning of the rule of the dead-- that is what I do. To devour mankind and make and end of his foolishness is my nature. It is why I was called forth in the first place from the black spaces between the stars."

At the end, the spider's voice is starting to sound like Cranston's and I cannot tell which is which. They are melding together, human and arachnid like a hideous flow of supernatural wax.

"Yes, this is the way the world ends," Cranston says. "It won't be long now."

"No! I won't help you!"

I am screaming, determined for once in my life to make a stand.

But who am I to challenge the Old Gods?

"But you will," the unseen Cranston rasps. And at his voice, I crumple, crack down upon myself like splintered wood. And there is agony, pain beyond words for my insolence.

But then, in an instant, there is mercy-- as only She can show.

The scene of ultimate horror and despair shifts, changes, dissolves in a glimmering of sunlight and a blessed glimpse of green grass growing, a fresh breeze blowing takes the place of the stench of death. The house stands before me. She is beautiful again, just as she has always been-- sitting on a high green hill covered with wildflowers. I feel the pain seep away. I am able to lift my head and look up. And James is there, standing on the front porch, leaning against a wooden column. He sees me, smiles, raises one hand in a casual wave.

The House-- she speaks to me then, soothing my pain, allaying my fears, promising-- promising that everything will be allright.

Do you know that I can give you everything you want?

I believe her, of course. I have, without a doubt, since the day I first laid eyes on her.

I can give you your heart's desire?

"Yes. Give me-- give me James back. Please. I'll do it. I'll help you raise the dead. Just bring him back."

And I will. But first, in the morning, there is something you must do. A final task. There is someone still in this town who would harm us-- and you don't want that, do you, my love?

Mr. Allgood arrives at noon the next day. He sees me from the gate, looks like he might turn and run, but I wave to him real friendly, hurry down, apologize profusely for my behavior the other day. I even return his pork pie hat with a smile. I invite him up just like *She* wanted.

He snatches it out of my hand, looks it over, appears nearly convinced.

"I don't want any trouble, kid. I don't want to have to throw your ass in jail, understand?"

"I understand."

"That's good, 'cuz, in all honesty, you seem like a pretty likable guy-- and you got one hell of a upper cut, I'll give you that!"

I tell him there's something I want to show him inside. I pretend like it's all innocent enough, like I don't know what she has in mind.

But I do.

She's doing her part, too-- casting some sort of spell over him, snaring him with an illusion that will draw him closer.

"Well, I'll be damned," he says looking up at the house. "You've been a busy little bee."

I can still tell him to go. I know what the house intends. But I say nothing.

The house is projecting a hallucinatory vision of splendor at him and it's working. I can see it in his eyes.

"Why didn't you tell me you were staying here. Did you do all this work?"

The house is putting up a mirage for him. I can only guess what he sees. She looks many ways to many people, depending on Her moods and their desires.

For him, it's probably a grand estate, a gilded palace-- a chance to make a million bucks.

He shakes his head. "But how did you do it? How did you do all this work so fast?"

I just shrug. "Inspired, I guess."

"I'll say. Damn shame to turn this place into a parking lot. You know, this might make a great clubhouse. Don't know that anyone would want a membership after all that bloody stuff that's happened here. But it's worth a try, right, kid?"

"I think so, yeah. I mean, why not?"

"You know, when you asked me up here-- I thought you must be out of your damn mind-- after what you did-- busting my chops like that."

"I want to apologize about that." My voice sounds mechanical, almost lifeless, but Allgood doesn't seem to notice. He's already making plans, thinking of money-- how he'll make a million.

"You know what-- why not let bygones be bygones. Stick with me, kid. We'll make a million. Well, I'll make a million-- you can have a grand."

He guffaws, clutches my shoulder with one meaty hand, gives me a good shake. He takes out a cigar, lights it, takes a few moments to get it fuming.

"Would you like to come inside?"

"Does a bear shit in the woods?"

I open the door and we go inside.

He gives a low whistle when he sees the entrance hall, shining and splendid like a fairy tale castle.

"Hot damn," he says, voice breathless with wonder. "We're gonna make a fortune. Is that tiffany glass? Kid, how in the hell--"

The attack happens faster even than I imagined. Shark attack fast.

The door slams shut behind us, closes so hard it embeds itself in the frame. Cracks like veins spread up the walls, seeping red blood. The seam between door and lintel melts away, sealing us inside.

The fairy tale illusion vanishes as we step over the threshold. The shadows deepen in the front hall. Nighttime falls in an instant.

Mr. Allgood senses it, can see what is happening, the terrors that are about to leap out at him, though his brain doesn't fully comprehend it. The house is coming alive in an instant.

"Hey-- hey, what the hell, kid? What is this-- some kinda trick?"

His voice is trembling. He turns for the door, reaching for the knob, but the wall draws back, bulging. And the portrait of the woman in black looks down on him, opens her fanged mouth and hisses.

Allgood screams, mind reeling with terror.

The floor ripples grotesquely beneath his feet. He wobbles and falls. A fissure opens up at his feet, sucking him down to the knees. He screams in agony as the floorboards snap close on his legs like a pair of splintered jaws.

I stagger back, overwhelmed by the horror, too, fall to the floor and crab crawl away from him.

He reaches for me, cries out for help.

"Oh God, help me kid! Help! Help! *HEEELLLP!*"

His cry twists up into a scream.

The jaws open again, gaping wide, gulping him down. The teeth smash together again, crunching down on his chest, like a steel toothed bear trap. A geyser of blood squirts out of Mr. Allgood's mouth, painting his face bright red. His bald head glistens with gore. The jaws twist and shake violently like a dog with a rabbit in its mouth. The floor gapes wide again, sucking Mr. Allgood down, swallowing him whole.

The jaws snap close.

The world swims around me and everything starts to go black, but I this time, I fight it. And my fear is mixed with a red rage.

I can hear the heart beating now all around me. Pounding. Pounding. The walls shudder every time it contracts.

I feel violently sick.

What have I done?

I let it kill a man.

I tried to tell myself I didn't know that was going to happen.

But that was a lie.

I knew.

Sure I did.

"Why did you do that?" I shout.

I stagger to my feet.

It has no intention of giving James back. I know that now. James is dead, his bloodless corpse stuffed in the attic crawlspace. What it showed me was just an illusion, a trick to draw me deeper into the trap.

"I'll kill you!"

I grab the butcher knife off the floor where I dropped it the day James died. I head for the basement door, fling it open, rush down into the cobwebby darkness, brandishing the knife.

In the darkness, I see the black heart beating hideously in the shadows. Sight of that grotesquely pulsing mass makes me want to throw up. I can see a gurgling Mr. Allgood, being pulled into the twisted veins beneath the heart, sucked in, feet first into a forest of gorey spaghetti. He's clawing weakly at the slithering strands of gore, but it's too late. I see the top of his bald head swallowed up, then his hand, still reaching out for me. His fingertips vanish. I raise the butcher knife, rush towards the pulmonary monstrosity, hacking at the forest of veins spreading out from the beating heart.

I swing the blade, slicing veins. The heart shudders, starts pulsing more rapidly, veiny mass throbbing. The House roars with pain and rage. Blood spurts everywhere, spraying my hands, my chest, my face.

Before I can raise the blade again, I felt a slimy vein wrap around my wrist and twist the knife out of my hand. It falls to the ground. I try to retrieve it, intent on killing this evil once and for all, but more veins snake in around me, wrapping around my legs and arms. I am being lifted off my feet, hoisted up into the darkness.

I am dragged forward, feeling certain I am the next victim.

But no.

No yet, love. Not yet.

The veins thrust me up into the darkness and I feel soft and mouldy earth closing in around my head, cutting off my scream.

Stealing every ounce of oxygen.

And then the darkness is complete.

"Hey, Kevin, you okay?"

My eyes flutter open.

I am lying on the ground in the back yard.

The sun is shining overhead.

It is morning.

"Oh my gosh what are you doing out here? Come on, let me help you up."

Holly stands over me. She reaches down, tries to help me stand.

My left foot is embedded in the ground. I reach back and tug at my ankle. My foot pulls loose of the soft earth. It is dripping with red gore, thick and sludgy as ketchup. But I'm not hurt. It is the earth. It is full of blood. The veins and guts of the house must run everywhere beneath the yard.

"Is that blood? Kevin, are you hurt?"

I wobbled drunkenly.

"I don't think so."

"You're filthy. What have you been doing? Look, you've got scratches all over you."

"I'm okay, I think."

"Have you been out here all night?"

I nod. Nothing is making sense right now. I can't tell if I dreamed it all or did it...

... did the house eat Scottie Allgood?

"Holly, have you seen anything strange around here? This house? Has it ever-- attacked you?"

She looks puzzled, then worried. "Kevin, did you hit your head?"

"Did you see Mr. Allgood?"

"Who?"

"Allgood-- the head of Afton's board of developers."

"Never heard of him."

Now I'm even more confused. Doesn't she know anybody in town?

"They warned me about this place. Harold and Emery and Willie Higgins."

"You saw Willie? When? How is he?"

"The other night. But I didn't listen to him, because, well, he's the town drunk."

Holly looks suddenly very sad. "Willie... he doesn't drink."

I squint up at her. "Holly, he drinks like a fish. Emery Marsh said he hasn't been sober one day in the past thirty years-- not after-- "

I stop suddenly. It looks like Holly is about to start crying.

"Holly, what is it? What's wrong?"

She shakes her head, fights back her tears, changes the subject quickly.

"You poor thing," she says, swallowing her own grief, taking control of the situation in a motherly fashion, "let's get you inside, get you cleaned up."

I let her help me up. In the golden sunshine, everything is starting to seem more normal. It was all a bad dream. Maybe all I need is a drink. The house didn't eat Scottie Allgood. It all seems so ridiculous now in the morning light. The house didn't eat anybody. I stop suddenly. My blood freezes. In the weeds behind the house, I see it…

I jerk away from Holly, stagger over to the tangle of bushes and vines. There is something sticking out of the ground-- something metal, half buried but still discernable in the tangled growth-- the battered front bumper and hood of a late seventies station wagon. Allgood's car.

"Oh God," I shout. "It's true! It killed him. The House got him."

"What are you talking about?"

"That's Allgood's car. She-- the House-- It must have pulled it in-- to hide the evidence! Don't you see?"

I'm looking wild eyed and crazy. I sound, in fact, just like Willie Higgins. The irony makes me cackle. Holly reaches out, despite her fear, to steady me, to lead me back inside.

"C'mon, sweetheart, let's get you back inside. You'll feel better if you lay down for a minute. I'll fix you a glass of sweet tea, okay?"

"No!" I shout.

"Or coffee, then. It's okay, darling. You'll feel better once you've had some coffee."

"No! Don't go in there! Do you understand me?"

"Kevin, you're acting awfully funny. Are you drunk?"

I've never been more sobre in my whole life. I get it now. I see what the house is trying to do-- what Cranston was helping it do.

"They were working together-- Cranston and the House. If they feed it enough-- a portal will open-- a gateway to the land of the dead. I saw it. There'll be no stopping it!"

"Kevin, I don't want to sound judgmental, but this is crazy talk. You're scaring me. I'm going to call Dr. Crickshaw, love."

I grab her by the shoulders, shake her. "Listen to me, Holly. I want you to promise me you won't set foot inside that house, understand?"

"What's--"

"Just promise me, okay?"

She looks concerned, but she agrees. "I promise."

"I want you to go back to your house and stay there!"

I start running down the hill.

"Where are you going?" she calls after me.

"To town! I need to get some things. I'm going to end this!"

"Kevin!" she cries out, but I don't look back.

At the Oasis the other night, Emery told me that Willie Bub Higgins lived in a shack behind Tater's scrapyard and that's where I find him, not far from the fruit stand where Harold Trout gave me a cupful of steaming, boiled peanuts.

God, was that during this lifetime?

It is a small sagging clapboard structure made of grey wood scraps. It is dismal, rundown and ramshackle as the man himself. A broken hearted place.

I knock on the door. I can hear somebody stumbling around inside, feet scuffing, glass beer bottles clinking together as Bub stumbles to the door. He opens the door a crack and peers, bleary eyed, out at me.

I catch a sour whiff of his breath, mixed with worse smells from inside-- beer and urine.

"Sorry to bother you Mr. Higgins."

He takes one look at my wild, disheveled appearance, says, "Shit, boy, you look like I feel. What do you want?" He stands, leaning against the inner wall, head lolling forward.

"I need to talk to you."

"About what?"

"About... the house."

He shakes his head, disgusted like he has been tricked and tries to close the door.

"Wait, wait, please," I say, pushing back to keep him from closing the door in my face. "I believe you. I've seen things."

"What things."

"It's alive-- just like you said."

"Yes. You messing with me?"

"No sir. I understand now. I believe you. I'm so, so sorry. You tried to tell me, to warn me, and I didn't listen. I didn't believe you."

"It's okay. I wouldn't have believed me, either. What have you seen up there, kid?"

"A lot. Worms in the walls. Rooms stretching and shrinking. Things without eyes lurking at windows."

He's nodding as I say all this. "Yup, sounds about right."

"And-- a spider."

"Yeah, there's that, too. And the heart. You've heard it beating in the dark, ain't cha?"

"I have."

Looking him in the eye, I start to understand. I'm looking at myself. I get it now, too late maybe. I'm headed down the same dark path that Bub Higgins took thirty years earlier. I have never felt so much sympathy for another human being as I feel at that moment for this sad, drunken man with his corroded liver and nose crisscrossed with a forest of busted capillaries. The house, it has driven us both crazy. Who knows how many others, too?

"Can it be killed?"

He starts to shake, holding his head. I can't tell if he is going to laugh or cry.

"Burn it! Kill it. Burn it to the ground. You have to kill the heart. That's the only way to make sure it's dead. You have to kill the heart."

I leave him standing there at the door to the shack and head for Buddy Haygood's Feed and Seed. Behind me, I can still hear Bub wailing, "The heart! The heart! You have to kill the heart!"

I'm grateful Buddy is out of the store. I can't face him now. There's some kid helping out at the counter and I buy two gallons of gasoline and a box of matches.

"Making a bonfire?" the kid asks.

"Yes, something like that."

I hurry back across town, lugging the gasoline cans. I have to put an end to this.

Now.

I get to the gate and stop.

Panic fills my chest and all my hopes come crashing down.

At the top of the hill, I catch a glimpse of Holly slipping in through the side door. I shout for her to stop-- to come back, but it is too late. She is inside the house. The beast has her.

I drop the cans and start running. I fling open the side door and rush in.

"Holly! Holly!" I shout. There is no answer.

I run down the hall. The cellar door is open. Holly is standing just in front of it about to go down into the darkness.

"Holly, get away from there!"

At the sound of my voice she spins around, hand at her heart.

"Kevin! You scared the daylights out of me."

"I told you to stay out of here."

"I know but then I heard you calling for help," she says. "It sounded like it was coming from the basement. So I came back. I thought you were in trouble."

"I'm fine. I'm right here. We have to leave here. Right now."

She sees that I am serious. She does not understand, but she nods. There is a worried look on her face. A look of half remembered, dream veiled horror. She starts to step away from the door when the house attacks.

Thick red veins shoot out of the darkness behind her, snaring her with a satanic roar. The pulsing cords whip around her wrists and ankles. She screams. I reach forward, try to pull her back. Another artery shoots out of the darkness, slams me in the chest knocking me breathless across the room. The last glimpse I have of Holly is her terror stricken face, eyes bulging, as the red veins pull her down into the darkness. The door slams shut.

There is a moment of silence as deep and still as eternity.

And that's when it happens.

That's when the house comes fully to life.

It starts to shake violently. Down the hall in the kitchen, I hear water erupt from the sink and a moment later the hallway floor is flowing with black water. The walls split, shooting out nests of writhing veins. Blood streams down from the ceiling. A hundred red rimmed eyes open in the woodwork with slivered reptile pupils. The walls stretch like sheets of rubber as tormented faces push through gasping for enough air to scream.

One of the faces-- it looks just like James, only his face is grey and shrunken, withered as a raisin, drained of all its blood and his features are twisted in agony. He reaches out a clawing hand, beckoning me to join him in.

The sticky tendrils lash out, twirling around my ankles and my wrists.

A croaking belch explodes from the hallway above and a tidal wave of worms rushes down the stairs, spilling over the bannister, crashing to the floor with a sickening splatter. It's a slithering mess of monster worms, long as shoelaces, thick as kielbasas with red rimmed, toothless, sucker-mouths opening and closing. They mean to suck the flesh off my bones.

I tear myself loose from the veiny tangle, run screaming from the house.

The moment my feet hit the front porch, there is a sharp crack. The wood warps and bows like a wave under my feet. It buckles and snaps upwards, throwing me into the air.

I slam face first in the dirt, hit the ground so hard the force of the impact knocks me out of my shoes. Behind me, the house writhes and contorts, growls and snarls. I stagger to my feet and start running, gibbering like a madman, still trailing shreds of dripping veins as I run.

PART VII

FACING THE MONSTER

Monsters are real and ghosts are real too. They live inside us and sometimes, they win.
--Stephen King

I LOOK BACK AT Sheriff Sadler. He is looking at the house.

For a long time he does not say anything.

"You think I'm crazy," I say bitterly.

"No, I don't think that at all."

"What about Mr. Allgood? Has anyone reported him missing?"

"As far as I know, Scottie-- that little meatball, is down in Savannah at some south eastern regional developers' conference."

I don't tell Sheriff Sadler, but I doubt anyone will ever see Mr. Allgood again. He is not in Savannah, or anywhere else for that matter. He is in the house-- well, his bones anyway...

...and probably his spirit, too.

Sheriff Sadler reaches in his back pocket, pulls out his wallet. "This girl, Holly, you say she was in her early twenties?"

"Yes."

"Hair bobbed, old fashion like?"

"Yes."

"Does this look familiar?"

He hands me the picture. I shouldn't be surprised, I guess, not after everything I've seen there. But seeing the picture is still something of a shock.

"Holly was my sister. That's her senior picture. She went missing in the summer of 1963, not long after graduation. In that house. They never found her. Never found her body. Not a trace."

I know they never will. It's hidden somewhere deep in those catacombs and endless passages beneath the monster. The house will never give up its dead until it is finally killed and destroyed utterly.

"She was a newlywed. Just married to Bub Higgins. That's before he became a drunk."

I don't say anything. There is nothing to say. I grip the granite tabletop to keep myself from falling over. I squeeze so hard I scrape the skin off my fingertips.

"She didn't know," I whisper. "She didn't know that she was dead. She thought he left her."

"Come on, kid. I'll take you back to the motel. And in the morning, I'll take you to the airport. You can go back to Seattle be with your family and never think of this place again."

I let him lead me away. I look back at the house. The sunlight is shining like fire in those two fanlight windows in the high tower. As we drive away, I glance back, catch a glimpse of a young woman with bobbed hair standing by a tree in the front yard. She's looking after me sadly.

Holly Sadler-Higgins.

She doesn't know she died. She can't face the truth that the house got her, that it pulled her in with those slick, dripping, gore slathered veins. Willie Higgins didn't leave her like she told me-- like she believed. The House killed her, dragged her screaming into the dark, but she can't believe it. She doesn't know. Poor Holly. Like me, she is a victim of her own delusion. She's trapped there in the depths of that house-- between the unhappy land of the living and the unhappier land of the dead. A prisoner. For all eternity. I can't help her. Can I?

Goodbye Holly.

I think about grabbing Sheriff Sadler's arm, making him look back. But I know he won't see her. The House-- It won't let him.

And Sheriff Sadler? He's had a lifetime of dealing with unhappy illusions. I can't burden him anymore. It's too late anyway.

He drops me off at the Sleepy Time Motel.

Tomorrow I can leave Afton. I will board a plane, fly away, never look back. I will go back to my job.

But what about-- *Her*.
The House.
It.

If I leave it alive, if I pretend that none of this ever happened-- how many people will it snare in the future? It will be on my conscience. All that future blood will be on my hands.

And what about the plan-- The Spider's plan. What happens if that gateway to the dead is opened? What then?

I have to go back.

I have to destroy it.

It's evil.

I wasn't there for my father. It killed James. I failed Holly. It's killing me. Slowly. Draining my life away day by day. Feeding off my misery, sucking up my life force like a hideous parasite. Even if I go back to Seattle, I will have no peace. The House. It will murder me long distance. That's well within it's power.

I can picture myself victorious, house burned to the ground, me having stabbed the black heart, hacked it to quivering pieces. The house will collapse in fire and ash with a hideous, otherworldly groan. The gateway will be closed forever. Afton-- the whole world, will be safe. Holly will be at peace. I will climb back up to the light. It will be a new dawn, a new day. The curse of the House of Witcher Street will be at an end.

The people of Afton will cheer for me. All of the Demon House's trapped spirits will be put to rest.

I can see it behind my closed eyelids, clear as day-- all the people of Afton gathered around, giving me pats on the back.

I will get in a car and drive away and live a life of peace and contentment.

I will move into a modern apartment and never even think of old houses again. I will go out dancing. I will change...

My eyes snap open. I am lying on the bed in my room at the Sleepy Time Motel.

That happy ending-- right now it's just a fantasy. If I truly want to see that bright dawn there's something I have to do first.

I have to kill Her.

It.

Destroy the House on Witcher Street, once and for all.

I leave after midnight and walk across town. The moon is out. The stars are twinkling brightly over the sleeping town. I have my doubts as to whether I can kill this beast alone. I am debating about going back, but that's when I see it-- lights on in the library.

After midnight?

I stop, creep up the steps, peer in one of the big front windows. Buddy Haygood, Harold Trout, Cecilia Jacobs and Emery Marsh are seated around a table in the reading room. A late night meeting of the Afton Historical Society this late?

No.

I remember what Cranston said to me.

The Afton Historical Society is just a cover. They're here to guard the house-- to stop it.

I knock on the glass.

They look up in unison, seem a little startled until they realize it's just me. Mrs. Jacobs comes to the door, unlocks it.

"Kevin, what are you doing here? It's late-- you look awful."

"Is this an impromptu meeting of the Afton Historical Society?"

"Um, yes, that's right," she says unconvincingly.

"After midnight?"

"Well... "

"I know It's alive. It's trying to kill me-- to kill all of us."

She frowns, tries to look like she doesn't know what I'm talking about.

"Don't pretend you don't know. He showed me-- Cranston-- showed me what the house-- what *It* intends."

"Good Lord." Cecilia bites her lip, glances back at her companions at the table. Harold and Emery exchange a glance, then look back at her and nod. She opens the door, lets me in.

"What do you know?" Buddy says.

"Everything--"

Emery chuckles. "Well that's a damn sight more than we know."

"Well, maybe I don't know everything, but I know enough-- enough to know we're all in danger-- not just us. Not just Afton. The whole world. He showed me."

"Who?" says Harold.

"Cranston."

"That damned vulture. I knew he was at the bottom of this."

"If he's restless again, that means we don't have much time," Buddy says. "We've got to do something-- and fast. Before it's too late."

"Best not to rush into this," Cecilia says. "Let's hear what Kevin has to say, first."

Harold Trout pulls a chair out for me. "Have a seat kid."

I sit, exhausted and shuddering. I shake my head, run my fingers through my hair. "This town-- it just keeps getting weirder and weirder. But it's not just me. There's something strange going on here-- not just strange. Monumentally evil. This place, it's like an onion and I've been peeling back one weird layer after another. Now I've gotten to the core. And just like an onion-- it reeks. This whole town is one otherworldly nexus of the bizarre."

Harold just nods. "Didn't I tell you? Things-- they aren't always what they seem, kid."

"And all the weird things happening around here-- like what I read about in the paper-- the cats turning into cannibals-- the most haunted town south of the Mason Dixon-- all those things that Eunice Bailey has been writing about for years and years. It's not just gossip. It's not just tall tales or bullshit."

"Yes, it's true," says Cecilia. "And with the Old Ones waking up, writhing fitfully in their sleep, the strange and horrible things in this town keep increasing. Birth pangs you might call them-- signals of the end of the world."

"Old Ones?" I ask, though I've heard the term before from Cranston. I've also heard Vera Griswick scream it at me, too. Still, I have no idea what it means.

They look at me somberly, but say nothing.

Harold heaves a sigh, arms still crossed. He's thinking things over, deciding what to tell me and how.

"And-- what I saw-- that thing. The spider-- is that one of your Old Ones?"

Harold sits up straight all of a sudden.

"A spider?"

"Yes."

"You've seen it up there?"

"Yes. A huge red spider with eyes… eyes like fire."

Harold has a nearly stunned look on his face, like he's remembering something from a long time back. He and Emery, Buddy and Cecilia exchange dismayed looks.

"Have you seen it, too?" I ask.

"Not in a long time."

"What is it, Harold? What is that place? Dammit, tell me! It's not just a house. I know that now. What is It… really? Is it a gateway, like Cranston says?'"

"It's not a house. Not at all. Of course, that's what it looks like now. It's a gateway, like you say. A door to another world. A passage to the land of the dead."

He looks at me, a heavy hearted look. "I'm sorry kid, I should have told you earlier. It would have saved you an awful lot of heartache. I just didn't think you would believe it."

"Who would?" says Buddy.

"I saw it all. Beneath the house there was a city-- like an endless maze or a labyrinth and it went down and down into the earth and then there was a purple light and beyond it-- a wasteland."

"Yes, Afton sits on top of a-- what did you call it-- a nexus? There's a rift here in space and time. Different realities overlap, time washes back and forth over itself like waves lapping on a beach. Other dimensions share a temporal space here with our own. From time to time, you can catch glimpses of windows into other worlds, other times, other realities."

Time overlapping. Time washing back and forth over itself.

"Sounds crazy, right? But you've seen enough to know it's true."

"Can you tell us, Kevin?" Cecilia says. "From the beginning? We need to hear everything that's happened up there."

And I do. I don't know how I have the strength to tell it all, except that they know and they believe and they have had experiences with that house-- the horrors of which rival my own.

When I finish, I'm crying, Cecilia has her hand on my back.

"That thing you saw, what you call a spider-- is Unglit," says Buddy Haygood. "One of the last great gods before Atlantis."

"There were nine of them-- the Old Ones. Ancient gods of long ago. A spider, a squid, a serpent, a moth, a centipede, a rat and others. These were the forms they took. Well, they ruled the earth for ages and were worshipped by men with sacrifices of blood and fire and living flesh; but a time came when men no longer worshipped them and they rebelled. People fought back. And the Old Ones, weakened and despised, abandoned the world of light. They slithered down into dark places, a long, long time ago. But they've never forgotten it. And they want it back. The world above. They've spent millennia in the dark, sleeping fitfully and plotting their revenge, sending out troubled dreams to men above. And the closer they come to waking, the stranger and more dreadful are the things that happen here where we are-- in the land of the living."

"Like all the cats in Afton going rabid."

"Exactly. Strange happenings, rumblings, you might say, whenever the Old Gods stir in their sleep. The disasters that follow are gifts-- courtesy of the Old Ones waking."

"A moth? A centipede? A rat?" I say, "just like in those articles by Mrs. Bailey. They're not urban legends."

"That's right. Those are not random supernatural occurrences or tall tales or simple, pulp horror magazine rejections-- or the ravings of madmen. Those were deliberate, yet thankfully-- unsuccessful attempts by certain individuals in this town to wake the Old Gods from their sleep. But Cranston, he was successful. He managed to rouse the Unglit. And has very nearly opened this gate."

"*This* gate? There are more? More houses like the one here?"

"Yes. Nine," Buddy says. "One for each of them. Nine gates. Nine gods."

"In appearance they vary," says Harold. "They are scattered across the globe. But like I told you-- and as you well know-- they ain't houses at all. They're roads to the underworld. And when all nine gates are opened-- the dead will rise and it will be the end of the world as we know it. And then the nine gods will war-- one against the other, for control of the ruined earth, vying for the honor of bringing ultimate desolation upon the world, for being the destroyer of mankind."

"And the gates," I say, "they will rise up like black towers against a dead sky. I saw it... Cranston showed me. He came back to life. I saw them do it. They said words, poured blood on his bones. After it killed him back in 1984, the spider must have dragged Cranston's body back through one of its tunnels and hid him in the crypts beneath the house. She was there, too-- the woman that everyone says is crazy. The one with medusa eyes."

"Vera Griswick."

"Yes, that's why she attacked me in town that day. She knew I saw her. But who would believe me about such an insane thing? Why is she helping him?"

"Her maiden name is Cranston," Cecilia says. "Arthur was her brother."

"There were others down there with her in the crypts."

"Yes, Unglit has many willing servants."

"But I didn't see their faces."

"We know a few of them already," says Harold. "Jasper Dupree is one of them. Abel Crickshaw, another."

"And your pal," Cecilia says, "Eunice Bailey."

"But you told me she didn't know what was going on."

"I was trying to get you to leave well enough alone."

"She said she wanted to help me."

"Of course, she did. She's a liar. All Unglit's servants are. She was helping you to get yourself tangled in its web. As Unglit's servant, she's been weaving her own web of fear in this town for half a century. Unglit feeds not just on blood, young man, but on despair."

"Do they know what they're doing? Are they serving Unglit willingly?"

"Yes and no. Vera, yes. The others? Well… The spider has clouded their minds. I've known Eunice my whole life. We've played bridge together once a week for thirty years. Sometimes I think the spider takes over. Possesses her. How that originally happened, I haven't a clue. If you were to confront her about it, I honestly don't think she would know what you meant-- maybe deep down, but not consciously."

Emery snorts. "Don't see how they couldn't know."

"I do," I say. "I understand that much, at least. The spider has been controlling me, too. Playing on my secret fears and desires. My darkest fantasies. Spinning a web around me. I didn't know what was real and what wasn't."

It comes back to me now and I remember-- "--the gold rings. They all had the same gold ring, shaped like a spider, with rubies for eyes-- Vera Griswick and Crickshaw and Jasper Dupree and Eunice Bailey-- Cranston, too. I thought, at the time, I was imagining it."

"You weren't imagining it, unfortunately. They have the same ring because they are all lifelong members of the *NSA*."

It's baffling news to me. This conspiracy plot to end the world goes all the way to the highest branches of the government of the United States of America.

"The *NSA*-- the *National Security Agency*. I-- I can't believe it."

"No," says Buddy. "*The Necromancers' Society of America*. Our government don't know a damned thing about this. Vera, Eunice, Crickshaw-- they're all card carrying members of the same Necromancer's Society-- the oldest one in North America. It was founded in 1777-- one year after the split with the *NSE*."

"The-- um, *Necromancers' Society of England*?" I venture.

"Correct. For years they've been trying to wake the *Old Ones* and lately to raise Cranston from the dead."

"They've been working hard to get you trapped, pulling strings to draw you deeper into their plot."

I remember the package Jasper Dupree was going to mail that day at the postoffice-- the package covered with labyrinthine scribbles. Did they send the letter to James to lure him here to his death? And Crickshaw, he wasn't afraid to call the police-- not really. Unglit wouldn't let him. I was playing right into their trap. Bastards.

"And now they have brought him back to life. I saw it in the tunnels under the house. They killed that girl-- the one who went missing, the one whose picture I saw on a milk carton at Watson's grocery. Missy Harper."

Harry hangs his head. "The murderers. Yes, it must have been her."

I must look pretty hopeless, because Cecilia pats the air with one hand. "Yes, they raised Cranston and yes, they raised Unglit, but the fact of the matter is, *this gate*, at least, is still closed, thank heaven. And not to worry, Kevin, there are other powers at work besides the will of the Old Ones. There are powers of light, too. And some people are being drawn here to do battle-- perhaps, even if they don't understand why they have been brought to Afton-- or even if the circumstances of their arrivals have seemed mundane enough."

At her words, the face of the Japanese kid with the Pez dispenser and the skateboard flashes in my mind. Is he here to fight the spider and the house? Does he even know it-- that that's what he's been called here to do? Is that why he keeps showing up in my ruined life?

"Eight of the nine gates have been opened already," Cecilia says darkly. "We've been in contact with others, like us, who keep a watch on different gates around the world. We just got word last week-- the gateway in China has been breached."

"Cranston said he would go through when the gate opened and get-- get a cup-- a vessel, he said, to bring the plague back through to this world."

"A cup brought back from the land of the dead," says Harold. "A grey wasteland, where shadows roam. Lit by a purple-green sun."

"That's right," I say as he describes it just as I saw it in the nightmare vision Cranston showed me. "How do you know?"

"Because I've been there... Twice. It's a long story."

"So that's his plan, is it?" Buddy says with a sigh. "Not if I have anything to say about it."

"This is the last sealed gate," Cecilia says. "Cranston, that bastard, used to help us in protecting this town and making sure the gate stayed closed. But she tricked him-- seduced him, same as she did Crickshaw and the rest. Made him all kinds of promises the fool believed. In the end she only gets those who give themselves willingly. He knew all about the Old Gods, was really the most knowledgeable one among us. The most well versed in ancient lore. After all, he is the one who convinced me to join the *ANSA--* "

"The... *Anti Necromancers' Society of America?*"

"Correct. That was in 1963. I was supposed to replace the former head librarian who died fighting the servants of Unglit while trying to save Holly Sadler from Demon House. Shelby Verner."

"Andy's father?"

"Yes. I've been trying to train Andrew to take my place, but the stubborn jackass won't listen-- can't bring himself to believe in all this supernatural mayhem."

"And Cranston recruited me," Harold says, "one year later, after I saved Sheriff Sadler from one of the Old Ones down at Lake Afton."

"Cranston, you see-- he swore to help us defend against them-- the Old Gods. But what we didn't know-- "

"--He was serving Unglit, the whole time," I say.

"Yes, it was a terrible betrayal. We never saw it coming. Cost a few of our dear friends their lives."

"He had been serving the powers of darkness for years," I say. "He found Unglit's withered husk in a temple in South America. He brought the thing back here, kept it in the basement of the old high school. Some kids went missing. Cranston fed them to Unglit, revived the beast, started feeding victims to the house next, trying his damndest to open the gate."

They look vaguely surprised that I know so much about it.

"Did Cranston show you that, too?"

"No, I found out from Sean Neely. He was there the day the school burned down. He saw the Unglit kill Cranston in the basement. Sean saw it drag Cranston's body into a burrow and disappear."

"Yes, Sean was a brave boy," Emery says. "We tried, back then, to recruit him, get him to stay in town and help us keep a watch on the house. After all, we're getting too damned old for this sort of thing. But he wouldn't stay in Afton. And I don't blame him. Not long after the school burned down, he told us-- told us the same story he told you-- how the Unglit lived in the furnace room and how Cranston tried to control it with a medallion. The spider betrayed him, of course. Unglit will have no man as its master. That was Cranston's biggest flaw-- his pride. He thought he could turn the Old Gods into servants, get them to do his bidding. It killed him, like Sean said, and we thought that was that. But the spider-- if what you say is true, didn't die in the school fire like we, fools that we are, believed-- or hoped. It must have burrows among burrows-- a network of tunnels beneath the whole damn town. Now it's back up there at the house, trying to open that gate, luring people in-- like yourself-- to do its bidding."

"And I did it."

"Don't be so hard on yourself, kid. You didn't know."

"Yes... I knew. I let myself believe."

"That's how she tricks you. You're not the only one. She can throw out some powerful illusions. We've all seen it. The whole damned town is under the spell-- how else could that house still be there if it weren't so?"

"People died. Allgood and-- and James. Did they die, or did I imagine it?"

I hope to God, they tell me all that was a just a bad dream, a trick, an illusion thrown at me by the House. But--

"They're dead," Harold says. "I'm very sorry. But you need to hear the truth-- at least once while you're in this town."

I hang my head, shiver violently, on the brink of weeping. But tears won't come.

"And more victims will follow if we don't act fast. The house-- it needs just one more victim for the gate to open. The time has come. We have to destroy it-- once and for all."

"Then let's go-- right now," I say standing up, finding resolve in the fact that they are with me.

"Now hold on a second, kid, it's not that easy," says Buddy. "There's a certain way this has to be done. And if we don't do it right, it'll mean the death of us all, understand?"

"But you don't get it-- We can't just sit here and do nothing." I'm nearly frantic, almost shouting. "This is the end of the world we're talking about. You don't understand!"

"Now look here, in all fairness, Kevin," Buddy says, "you're the one that doesn't understand. You don't know a damned thing about it-- how this has to be accomplished. Will you go and face one of the Old Ones on your own? Will you kill a god by yourself, Kevin Yoo?"

A moment of silence hangs in the air. The answer is self evident. No, I can't kill anything, not even a fly.

"One slip, one misstep and it really will be the end-- for all of us. If you rush into this, you'll just make it worse."

"Irrevocably so," says Cecilia. "You must promise us, Kevin, that you won't set foot near that house again. Understand?"

I'm about to protest, but Harold holds up his hand. "They're right, kid. We're all grateful to you for your help, what you've told us, but preparations have got to be made. Certain words must be spoken. Certain weapons brought out of hidden places."

"The damned occult is complicated," says Emery.

"How long will it take?"

"Not long. We're waiting on the last member of our group. He has something that will kill that black heart and the spider. That medallion-- the one with the ruby Cranston used to control the Unglit-- it's turned up, under mysterious circumstances, not too far off. We'll need it to slay the monster. Our pal,

Walter-- he should be here any minute-- in the morning, at the latest. He's had a hell of a long journey getting back here. When he arrives, we go to the house and end this-- once and for all. Stop the dead. Save the world. Not bad for a day's work, huh?"

"Morning seems an awfully long way away to me."

Cecilia takes hold of my hand. "Don't lose hope. That's what It wants."

Buddy nods. "Now the best thing you can do is go back to the Sleepy Time and get some rest. This house-- we've been dealing with it for years. Our whole lives. We know how to handle it. We know its tricks."

"You'll just get yourself killed, kid, no offense," says Emery. "We're grateful beyond words for what you've told us. You letting us know in time might just be the thing that saves us-- saves the whole damned world."

"When it's all over," Buddy says, "I'll come for you, let you know that it's finished that Unglit is dead."

It's pointless to argue. They have a group. I'm not a part of it.

But I can't go back and do nothing. I have an ever mounting fear that the earth is about to split open and disgorge an ocean of undead to flood the world. I can't let that happen. I've been responsible for two deaths already. I won't be responsible for the end of the world. I can't wait on them. If they won't go with me-- I will go alone. I find the gas cans where I had dropped them the day before. I lug them up the hill, douse the foundations of the house. The boards are dry and rotten. They will burn like a match.

The windows are lit with a dead purplish glow. The time is near, like Cranston said. The House has had its fill of blood. The way of the dead will be open soon. I have to stop it. The last seconds are ticking by.

Pride goeth before a fall.

I should have thought of that, maybe.

But in this moment-- I can stop it-- I can kill a god, or, at least, tame it. We've all felt that way, from time to time, I imagine. Cranston certainly did.

The house growls at me like a rabid, slavering dog. And for the first time in my life, I feel sheer, ultimate, soul shattering terror.

The sky darkens ominously. Thunder rumbles. Supernatural clouds start whirling, cyclone like, around the jagged gables. The roiling mass is lit with flashes of greenish purple lightening.

This is it.

Above, beyond the darkened attic windows I see it--

IT.

--the black, many legged horror of horrors paces angrily, patience exhausted, back and forth, a killing light burning in its eyes.

That *Beast*-- it lingers all day in gloom, but it only comes out to show itself fully by night.

This is the black heart of Afton.

It is formed of my rage and repression, Eunice Bailey's gossip and fear mongering, Crickshaw's racism and blustering, Willie Higgin's desperate drunken depression and so on and so on…

And seeing it, I am filled with loathing and hatred for the spider. I want to smash it until its guts squirt out and all eight of its hell bright eyes burst and their fire is extinguished.

Will you kill me? Will you kill the thing you love?

You helped weave this web, after all, Kevin Yoo.

And I know she is telling the truth-- a twisted truth, a spider's truth, but a truth nonetheless.

I feel all of my gung ho bravery draining out of me. It's one thing to be a hero when your monster is far away, quite another when you're staring down its sharp toothed mouth, into its gullet. And the spider's mental poison is going to work inside me, numbing me, causing me to succumb to her terrible will. The house is pulsing with hideous life, its walls lichen green and red veined, throb and throb and throb. Red eyes snap open in the two front windows flanking the door, gigantic, bulging like cat's eyes with that weird jelly bubble capping each iris and pupil.

One eye opens fearsome wide, the other squints, irritable-- eyelid drooping with eons of restless sleep. She looks at me. For the first time we are seeing each other eye to eye.

The columns supporting the roof twist in the middle, splitting in half, forming two rows of needle like teeth. It almost looks like She is smiling at me, grinning, delighted to kill me. Her bulbous eyes roll in anticipation of a quivering, raw, bloody meal.

Hello, dear-- at last.

"Hello."

Tentacles writhe at the House's stone foundations. The eyeless thing-- the pseudo-James perches atop the roof, clawing for me with false love and desperation. The horror of *The House* revealed in Her true form is enough to send my mind reeling, strain my sanity to the breaking point. I have been living in its belly all this time. This is the thing I thought was so beautiful.

I can't do it. I can't save myself. I can't undo the past. I can't kill it. I have failed. This monster is too big. I cannot exorcise this demon.

Christ, how do I beat a creature like this? One-- partially, of my own making. It's as big-- as cruel as a mountain and as old as the black spaces between the stars. And pure evil.

I can't.

I can't win.

It's too late for me.

If I cannot defeat the monsters in me, how can I hope to conquer the ones that lie outside?

Who knows-- maybe if I had submitted, it would have spared me, like Cranston promised. Maybe it honestly loved me-- the House... the Spider. Perhaps it will still have mercy on me?

No. I know better-- surely, I know better by now.

It's a trick-- Her trick.

But her last one.

She means to kill me-- no matter what this time.

"You didn't love me. You never did. I trusted you. I loved you, even. And James-- you killed James. You murderer! I loved him. He loved me. And Buddy and Alan, they didn't try to hurt me-- they tried to help me. To save me. But you-- you twisted my brain. You fed me bullshit and I swallowed it! It was all a lie! You've made me afraid. You've made me hate the people I should have loved. You've taken everything from me. You've ruined my life!"

I'm sobbing now, feeling rage and confusion that I'm mistaking for bravery.

"All you wanted was my blood. But you can't have it, you bitch! I'm gonna kill you. I'm gonna burn you to the ground. Holly! Holly, where are you? I've come back to save you! You let her go-- do you hear me?!"

And the House? She just laughs at me-- a deep, roiling rotten belly laugh that is tinged with a sound like a tolling bell. Cranston's laugh.

I feel so torqued up, it's like I'm drunk.

I see a light come on at a house down the street.

"I'm not afraid of you anymore, do you hear me?! Not afraid! *NOT AFRAID! YOU EVIL FUCK!*"

I do not have to be afraid of the past-- the present-- the future.

And I hear Holly's words, plain as day--

--Kevin, you have to fight.

Is she standing in the shadows, watching? I can picture her sweet smile, that dreamy look she had on her face that morning her fingers tickled that beam of sunlight. And suddenly, I can do anything.

I feel a resurgence of hope. To be hopeless-- that's what It wants. If I lay down and die, It will win and then it will kill others. This House has hurt so many people. More people will suffer unless I stand up to It here and now.

I am not afraid... well, sorta not. The Old Ones, after all, they can be a little imposing. But I cannot fail myself... or Holly-- not now. If I'm going to die-- I will die trying to set things right.

The House must sense my resolve, because I see it shudder and catch a glimmer of doubt in its glaring red eyes. Its cavernous, black pupils narrow to hairline slits.

I have to do this fast before Sheriff Sadler shows up and hauls my ass to jail.

I light a match, drop it in the grass. The fire roars to life-- leaps up. It climbs higher and higher, devouring the dry wood, licking the warped eaves. I step back, smiling.

The house writhes, screams, lashes violently from side to side, contorting unnaturally, monstrously, shifting, showing many hideous faces. When it collapses, the basement will be exposed and when it is, I'll climb down and chop that heart to quivering bits.

I-- I can't believe it...

"I won! I beat you! I w--"

The storm cellar doors fly open with a demonic roar, revealing lashing veins like squid tentacles, twisting in the darkness below.

"Oh, shit!"

The ropey veins shoot out like the tongues of monstrous toads and snare me just as they snared Holly. It pulls me forward. I fall to my knees, clawing in the dirt with my hands. If It is going to die, I guess It means to take me with it. There is no beating it. I know that in an instant. My dream is coming true. The veins start to pull me down into the dark.

That's when I hear the shouts from the bottom of the hill as Harold and Buddy and the others come running up, ready to do battle-- to kill Her once and for all. I see another man with them-- who I guess is Walter-- the last member of their *anti-end-of-the-world* gang. Harold is holding the gold medallion with the ruby in its center. Walter is carrying what looks like a golden spear. I can see it flashing in the lightning. They have brought the weapons to slay Unglit. But they are too late.

Buddy rushes up to me, drops down on his knees, clutches my hand, tries to pull me back to safety. He has a machete in one hand.

"Kevin, why didn't you wait?" he shouts. "Don't let go! You hear me? You hold on tight!"

He raises the machete hacks one of the tentacles in half. It flops and writhes on the ground at my feet, spurting blood.

"Thanks," I pant.

I'm able to stand up again.

There's a sudden crack of thunder that causes Harold and the others to duck. A column of purple-green light shoots up from the house, penetrating the stormy sky. The black clouds swirl round and round this flaming beacon of doom. The red demon-- Unglit bursts through the attic window and drags itself up to the top of the house, thrashing its thorny legs.

At sight of it, Emery gives a horrified shout, looks away, unable to bear the sight of the beast. The earth rumbles beneath us and several fissures crack open in the yard and half a dozen grave rotted ghouls slither up out of the earth. They rise and and shamble with arms outstretched towards Cecilia Jacobs and Harold Trout and the others.

With a shout, Walter raises the golden spear, stabs one ghoul and then another, ramming the lethal point through the zombies' heads. Their skulls collapse as soft and easy as rotten pumpkins. The decapitated revenants stagger back. I see them wither to dust and ash and crumble back to the earth. But for every ghoul that Walter slays, it seems like two more rise from the earth. The dead are swarming down the hill after him like ants.

It looks like Walter and the others are going to be overwhelmed.

And that's when Cranston appears from a column of black smoke. He steps out of the swirling miasma and walks down the front steps, untroubled by the fury of the storm. He is fully resurrected, the flesh grown back on his bones. He strides down the path to meet them. As he passes by me, he smiles, gives me a wink.

I've walked right into his trap.

And for the first time since I came to Afton, I see birds around the house, swarming its turrets and gabled roofs, swirling round and round, flitting, darting, swooping-- darkening the sky like an ominous black whirlwind.

As Cranston walks, an invisible cloud of doom swirls up before him, a deadly miasma rises towards the sky and as it envelopes the birds, they fall by ones and twos. They rain down from the sky in little handfuls, falling like dark stones to litter the yard and barren hill. Everywhere Cranston steps, the grass withers with a hiss like his feet are veiled in invisible fire.

And I see Harold come at him-- this living necromancer ghost, trying to stop him, to get the cup, like I warned them he was planning on bringing back.

"Not another step, Cranston," Harold shouts, his voice rising over the fury of the maelstrom. "Hand it over-- the cup, the vessel."

Harold bars Cranston's path, the gold, ruby studded medallion clutched in his big hand.

But Cranston isn't carrying a cup. He grabs Harold, and squeezes his throat.

"Dear boy, whatever are you talking about? There is no cup, you fool. Don't you understand? *I am the vessel.*"

He lifts Harold up, leaves him clutching his throat, gasping for breath. Then he drops the big man like a ragdoll in the grass.

Cranston keeps walking, right past the others with the air of someone who knows they are victorious, head held high, chest thrust forward with imperiously regal strides. He chuckles, lifts up his hand, waves them aside. They fly back like ragdolls-- Cecilia, Walter and Emery. And after tossing them aside, Cranston, he just walks by them and when he passes through the gate at the bottom of the hill…

…he just vanishes, leaving only the ghost of his laughter hanging in the air.

Cecilia and Walter, Harold and Emery are getting overwhelmed by the dead.

"It's too late!" Emery shouts, helping Cecila to her feet. "We have to go. We can't stop them!"

Harold is brandishing the medallion once more, driving back the undead, trying to get to the top of the hill to help me. But there's too many of the zombies for him to get through.

"Harold, you'll never make it!" Emery shouts. "We have to go!"

And he's right. Harold and Walter are driven back down the hill by the undead. They have no choice but to run.

"Buddy, watch out!" I shout.

A zombie lurches out of the darkness, reaching out for him with its fingers like claws, but Buddy turns in time, swings the machete, decapitating the ghoul and sending its head flying through the air. The headless body takes a few staggering steps before collapsing in the dirt. Another zombie makes a grab for me. I kick its feet out from under it and it falls backwards. I grab a rock off the ground, clutch it tight in my fist. With a long pent up cry of agony and rage, I leap on top of the ghoul before it has a chance to rise and smash its skull in with the jagged edge of the stone.

Its skull splits, spilling its brains all over the dirt.

I sit back, panting, my hands and shirt spattered with brown cranial juices.

The ghoul's fingers twitch but it does not rise again.

"Not bad, kid," says Buddy. "Now let's get the hell outta here, huh?"

I nod. It's a plan.

We're about to run when a dozen dripping tentacles shoot out of the cellar.

The veins twist and twine around my ankles and give a vicious jerk. I fall back with a shout, land on my back. I'm being dragged towards the gaping hole. I'm clawing, screaming, reaching up for something to hold onto-- a jutting root, a stone-- something, anything to keep me from getting pulled into the darkness; but there's nothing to grab onto. Buddy gives a shout, drops to his knees, reaches out and grabs my hand. He's pulling as hard as he can. But I can't hold on.

Is this it? Is this how I die. I never thought it would end like this.

For a second, I can see my father standing in the garage, that freshly painted model car in his hands.

And now... I see the way it's got to end.

Hold on daddy, I'm coming.

Thank God, it's almost over. There's a little peace in that, I guess. Some small shred of consolation against the doom.

"Buddy-- Buddy, I'm sorry. I'm sorry."

Buddy is holding onto my hand and at the same time trying to shake off a ghoul that has crawled out of the ground and grabbed him by the ankle. He's going to get killed if he doesn't let go of me. Either the zombie will get him or the house will spit out more bloody veins and snare him, too. I can't let that happen. I won't be responsible for Buddy's death.

"Buddy, you have to let go! You have to run!"

"I'm not gonna let you go, kid! Just hang on! I got this!" he shouts over the storm.

But I can see he's going to get killed unless he runs. I stop struggling. I'll let the house have me if that's what it wants. There's no fight left in me.

Buddy shouts my name, "Kevin! No, don't-- *KEVIN! NOOO!*" He loses his grip on my sweat slickened hand and I go sliding away into the dark.

I catch sight of Buddy, helpless to save me, running away, tears streaming down his face.

It's a comfort to know he will live to fight another day.

As I am dragged down to my death I can hear it.

The pounding of the hideous heart.

The last thing I see is *IT* convulsing over me as it pulls me in, devouring me whole.

Come, love. Join me. At last. At last…

I scream with agony. I thrash and flail. But my strength is gone. My screams are useless. This is the end, Kevin Yoo. The blood drenched mass sucks me in, slowly, savoring this final meal of Korean American steak tartare. And the touch of that writhing mass dissolves me like acid.

With my death, the gateway to the land of the dead opens wide.

EPILOGUE

WAKING AND WRITHING

He knows when the Old Ones broke through of old and where
They shall break through again.
--H. P. Lovecraft
The Dunwich Horror

THAT'S MY STORY. Still not sure if you believe me, are you? You still think it's all crazy talk? Heh-heh, sure you do. That's what you want to believe anyway. After all, if the house burned down how can it still be standing there at the top of the hill behind me? You want to sleep, like Eunice Bailey said-- just like all the others.

The House--She's full of surprises. I didn't kill the heart. The house-- It grew back.

Sure, she looks great now. She has a lot of disguises.

And me?

I'm just an emanation from the house, a ghost, a wraith, a living shadow.

My bones are mouldering down there in the dark along with Holly's and Mr. Allgood's and James' and who knows how many others.

I'm just a shadow now.

Her familiar.

My life since then has been a grey and mist shrouded dream.

All Sheriff Sadler found of me were my glasses lying broken in the weeds. That's all they'll ever find.

And Cranston? Holly? The others?

I've seen shadows from time to time, the ghosts of other victims wandering lost in the halls. Sometimes I think I hear Holly crying in the dark. The House-- She holds on to all her victims. You can see them too, if you're brave enough to look into the darkness.

The gate? Well, it's open now, I guess. I, Kevin Yoo, have helped inadvertently to bring about the end of the world. I was her last victim.

And Cranston? I guess he's out there, even now, spreading the plague, raising the dead, making way for his master-- Unglit, last of the great gods before Atlantis.

Hmmm? The victim had to go willingly or else the gate wouldn't open?

You're right. But who are we kidding? I gave myself to her a long time ago-- the moment I laid eyes on her. I gave up, gave in, sacrificed myself long before the house ever physically devoured me.

At night, the House glows with a pale purple light. Soon, the dead will rise. Strange powers are waking. Strange things are coming up from the dark places under the earth. This is the beginning of the end. And the spider? Unglit. Yes, he's still being fed, growing large and abominable in the dark, just biding his time-- waiting for the plague of the dead before making his appearance on the world's stage. He's sleeping still, curled up in the dark somewhere beneath Afton.

But it's not over. The spider hasn't won-- well, maybe the battle, but not the war. There will be those who will stand against him, like Cecilia told me. People are being drawn here, unknowingly, to stand against the Unglit and the hordes of the undead. And do you know what I think? I think you're one of those that has been called to fight. And I hope to God I'm right, because it might be up to you to kill the spider and lay me and Holly to rest.

How do I know?

It's like this--

You see, time, like Harold said, runs in crazy ways here, washing back and forth over itself, swirling around and around. And I think I've figured something out.

And I've had the craziest thought.

It's-- it's like something out of a half remembered dream, this feeling I have that you have a part to play in what's happening. James, he tried to save me. I failed him. But I won't fail you, not if I can help it. It's like Holly told me, maybe it looked like I failed. But maybe I can succeed in ways I hadn't even imagined. I can still help you destroy it.

This is my chance at redemption. Maybe by helping you, I can finally save myself.

That Japanese man I saw that day in Watson's grocery store-- the one with the Pez dispenser just like yours-- with the scar over his left eye, just like yours...

What if...

What if that wasn't your dad or your brother or your cousin?

What if it was *you* I saw standing in line that day buying Pez? What if it was you from sometime in the future-- from after the end of the world? Because that man I saw, he was a wanderer, a hunter, grim and determined and I think he has spent years hunting that spider across the grey wasteland of the dead. And somehow he's come back in time to kill the Unglit.

Sounds crazy, right? But after everything I've been through, it doesn't sound so unbelievable anymore.

It's just a theory, but after what I've seen, it no longer sounds like an entirely impossible proposition. I really believe you have work to do. A task to complete. A spider to slay, whether you want to or not. What strange things, I wonder, has your future self seen? What dread horrors have you hunted and have also hunted you?

You're trying hard to doubt me. I can see that. But you can't. You saw it, too. You know. You've seen the spider. Has it been plaguing your dreams since you came to Afton? Yes, I thought so.

Don't worry, though. You won't be alone. I'm sure Buddy and Harold and the others will help you. And me too. I'll help... as much as any ghost can. Now it's time for you to get familiar with your enemy. You'll need to know how to find it-- where it sleeps-- in the dark. Because the house is just the tip of the iceberg. There are worlds beneath it. A labyrinth of the undead. Just like Willie Higgins told me. I've seen it. I can come and go as I please now, I'm just a shadow. The House. The spider. They can't hurt me anymore.

I'll be your guide, show you the way. And you'll have to remember, so when you do come back some day through that wormhole into the past, you'll know how to find the Unglit and kill it. We have to hurry-- while it's lurking in some other burrow in another part of town and while Cranston is away spreading the plague.

Hang on a 'sec, let me get the gate. Welcome, I guess.

The dog? No, she won't bite. That's just Goldie. Say 'hi,' girl.

Good dog.

Hey, what's your name, by the way?

Saito.

It's nice to meet you.

***

Article from the Afton Gazette
April 1st, 1994
Afton's Demon House Claims Yet Another Victim
by Eunice Bailey

*I*T IS APRIL fools, but sadly this is no joke. The only ones being made fools of are us-- the good people of Afton. There are other things, in this journalist's opinion, we'd rather be known for in Afton than demon haunted houses and things that go bump in the night.

What about sweet neighbors, beautiful old homes, a slower pace of life, an amazing Fourth of July fish fry on the lake-- to name a few.

But it seems that once again, a dark cloud has descended on our fair town. Yes, just last fall, a young man, a visitor to our own Afton, Kevin Yoo, of Seattle, went missing here like so many others. Six months have passed since his disappearance and so far there are no clues as to his whereabouts. Sources say he was last seen in the vicinity of a certain local blight known to everyone in Afton-- but for propriety's sake the name of which shall not be mentioned here. I, for one, have had enough and think the eyesore should be torn down immediately.

This is something that Mr. Scott Allgood had in the works, but when I reached out for comment, his secretary stated that he is long overdue to return from a developers' conference in Savannah. And so, we must wait in vain hope and expectation of his arrival. Our thoughts and prayers go out to the Yoo family. It is a sad thought that he *was not the first victim of that house and if something is not done quickly, he may not be the last, either.*

More strange happenings have been reported in the vicinity of Demon House lately. Strange shadows have been seen shambling-- zombie like, one might say, at night on the grounds. Red lights have been glimpsed shining in the windows. And a man-- whom some say bears a striking resemblance to old Arthur Cranston, has been seen stalking Witcher Street at night asking children if they've been nice to spiders.

At a town hall meeting last week, every citizen of Afton, it seems, attended to voice their growing concerns about the reputation our beloved hamlet is gaining-- this unwanted notoriety under which we are all suffering. Our local lawyers Mr. Salzburger and Mr. Goody voiced concerns, raising awareness for legal ramifications that could occur as a result of this latest disappearance. Vice Principal Norman Waters spoke of the safety of our children. Pastor Daniel Metcalf spoke of the need for spiritual unity during this dark time.

Even Vera Griswick made an appearance, barging through the doors, shouting and raving, telling us we were all going to burn in hell, that this was the judgment of the Lord-- that we would do well to repent. That worse things were on the way.

How many times through the years has she said the same thing? How many times have we dismissed her as a fringe lunatic?

But perhaps it is time to give Mrs. Griswick her due. This reporter, for one, is willing to consider the notion that Mrs. Vera is not as crazy as we have all hitherto believed. Perhaps we are truly, as she has said, "Sinners in the hands of an angry God."

And it is with growing concern that this reporter now turns her attention to another worrisome development-- that of the strange and virulent unseasonally late spring flu which seems to now be sweeping the nation and plaguing our fair town-- with a one hundred percent mortality rate. One has to wonder if things could possibly get any worse...